COTTONMOUTH

A JESSICA JAMES MYSTERY

KELLY OLIVER

A JESSICA JAMES MYSTERY

Book Six

By
Kelly Oliver

PART I

1

Witnesses were dropping like flies. Deputy U.S. Marshal Lexington Colt pounded the steering wheel with her palm. First that guy in Chicago, and now *her* guy in Montana.

Lexi left skid marks on the ice as she spun her Charger around to the McDonald's drive-up window. Without a word, she grabbed her Diet Mountain Dew and hash browns. Teeth chattering, she rolled up the window. *Damn blizzard.* The Charger squealed out of the freshly plowed parking lot and back onto the forlorn streets of Casper.

In five and a half years working for WITSEC, she'd never lost a witness. Not a single one. Now she had. And one was one too many.

Son of a—

She swerved to avoid smashing into a three-car pileup on the entrance ramp to I-25. White-knuckling the wheel, she skipped across the shoulder and grazed a signpost. *Great.* Her side mirror had ripped clean off. She cranked the steering wheel and bumped her way back onto the highway. There was a reason her army buddies called her "Grits," and it wasn't just because she was from Gleason "Tater Town" Tennessee.

She glanced at the clock on the dash. Just after six. Usually it took her exactly seven hours and nine minutes to drive from Casper to Jimmy's place in West Yellowstone, Montana. Yeah, it was a pain in the ass, especially in the winter. The Federal District of Wyoming covered all of Yellowstone Park, including the parts in Montana and Idaho. Even at top speeds, she wouldn't be there until early afternoon.

She slid onto the highway behind an 18-wheeler. *Just great.* After last night's blizzard, traffic was so slow it might as well be going in reverse. She opened her window, slapped the siren on the top of the car, and let it blast. *At this rate, I'll have to shave my legs again before I get there.*

With all the snowdrift, she couldn't see whether the centerline was yellow or white. *Who cares? I don't have all day.* She shoved the rest of a hash brown into her mouth and zipped out into oncoming traffic. If she was lucky, maybe she'd buy the farm and join the rest of her squad in heaven. *Where I should be too. That or the other direction.*

No such luck. Most regular folk knew better than to brave I-25 after "the storm of a decade." Only professionals on the road this morning. The Charger shimmied and skated on the black ice. *Like driving on air.*

With one hand on the wheel, she reached into her purse, fished for her pill bottle, opened it with her teeth, and shook a yellow capsule of courage onto her tongue. Her eyes watered as she chewed the bitter pill. "Survivor's guilt." That was another of her shrink's favorites. She ripped the lid off the diet soda and tipped the cup to her mouth in hopes of one last drop. *Lordy.* As dry as the Registan Desert.

She forced herself to swallow. Just like she used to do with her commanding officer, Captain Dirtbag Durbin.

By the time she pulled up in front of the plywood prairie house—favored in this part of Montana—her Mountain Dew was nothing but a distant memory, and all that was left of her greasy hash browns was a sorry sack crumpled on the passenger seat. *Caffeine.* She needed more. Especially to face a dead body. Sure, she'd seen lots of corpses in Afghanistan; that was the trouble. Her shrink called it "post-traumatic stress disorder," better known as "PTSD." Lexi called it "Puke Taliban Sucks Donkeydicks."

Two uniformed cops stood out front of the gray clapboard house. Both wore blue exam gloves and blue parkas. The one standing on the porch held a fat clipboard. The other stood legs apart, arms akimbo, watching from the snowed-in driveway. Yellow crime scene tape stretched taut across the length of a chain-link fence.

Lexi threw the Charger into park. She wished she'd stopped at Walmart to pick up a six-pack. When she opened the car door, a blast of frigid air almost knocked her back inside. Wyoming winters had a way of slapping you in the face. She reached into the back seat and grabbed her down jacket and slouched into it. She'd never even owned a winter coat until she moved to Casper a year ago. Heck, she hadn't seen real snow accumulation until she'd landed in Kabul in February, over five years ago. She was tempted to grab a handful of snow and suck on it.

"Cold as a witch's you-know-what in a brass bra," as her daddy would say. Of course, Lexington, Kentucky, was as far north as he'd ever gotten. She'd been born in Lexington, hence her name. *Good thing I wasn't born in Salt Lick or Tater Town.*

Even in her SOREL boots, she slipped and slid as she crossed the street to the crime scene. Snowflakes landed on her face and melted down her cheeks like tears.

"Good afternoon, fellas," she said, pulling her badge. "I'm Federal Marshal Lexington Colt." She licked her lips. "Jimmy Gordon was one of mine." Jimmy Gordon's real name was Jimmy Giordano, and until he'd screwed over his boss, Victor "Teeth" Marsiano—one of the biggest crime bosses in New York—Jimmy had been a drug kingpin pulling in six figures a year protecting Teeth's Las Vegas assets. After he gave Teeth the shaft and agreed to testify against him, Lexi was supposed to protect Jimmy's assets. A fine job she'd done.

"He's in the kitchen," the cop on the porch said, pointing inside. "We saved him for ya." He held the screen door open for her. She nodded in thanks as she passed.

When she stepped inside, the acrid smell of stale cigarettes cuffed her nose like a playful old friend. She'd smoked since she was fourteen. Every man, woman, and child in Gleason smoked. It was tobacco country, for God's sake. But she'd had to give it up during basic training. Running all those miles on half a lung had kicked her ass.

The culprit sat in the middle of the coffee table. One of those chunky glass ashtrays, overflowing with butts. Jimmy smoked Carltons, which always struck her as odd. The burly gangster seemed like more of a Marlboro or unfiltered Camel kind of guy.

You could learn a lot about a person from the brand of cigarette they smoked. Folks who ate deep-fried chicken feet smoked those gawd-awful mentholated numbers that taste like Vicks VapoRub—not that she had anything against fried chicken feet. Rednecks looking for a bar fight favored Copenhagen Straight dip . . . not that wintergreen-flavored shit—only wannabe dudes chewed that manure. (She should know. She'd kissed just about every boy in Northwest

Tennessee.) But only housewives too depressed to change out of their day dresses smoked Carltons.

Like most of the kids in Weakley County, Tennessee, Lexi was raised on good ole Marlboro Reds. Right now, she was half tempted to grab a Carlton butt out of Jimmy's ashtray and light up. If her hands weren't shaking so bad, she just might.

She followed the voices to the back of the house.

Holy Mother of God. Jimmy was tied to a kitchen chair. A cold plate of spaghetti with little orange islands of hardened grease sat on the table in front of him. He had a hole through his left temple, and his brains were splattered on the wall.

A guy in a white hazmat suit was taking pictures. *He must be the crime scene examiner.* Another plainclothes cop, wearing a tight black suit and a cowboy hat, was chewing on a toothpick and leaning against the kitchen counter, watching and smiling like he was at a Saturday matinee. *Probably a local homicide detective. One of those Wild West types.* A petite woman was groping at Jimmy's ankles. The coroner.

Bang! Lexi's heart nearly leapt out of her chest. Gun drawn, she dropped to her knees.

"Whoa. You okay there, sweetheart?" the cowboy asked. "It was just a car backfiring outside." He bent down to help her up.

She pulled out of his grasp, stood up, and holstered her weapon. After that stunt, she should paint the wall with her own brains.

"A little jumpy today, aren't we, darlin'?" He spit out his toothpick, and it landed next to her boot.

"Federal Marshal Lexington Colt." She held out her hand.

The cowboy smiled, took her hand, and held it for just a few seconds too long. "Dale Halifax, the new county sheriff."

In spite of her shakes, she squeezed as hard as she could. *A-hole.*

He rubbed his hand. She hoped it hurt.

"Quite a grip you've got there for such an itty-bitty thing."

Itty-bitty? She was five-seven for cripes' sake. Maybe she looked small to someone who had to be at least six-three. And she might be petite like her mama, but she had muscles like her daddy, and she wasn't afraid to use 'em. She clenched her fist. "What've we got here, then?"

"Well, honey, we've got a dead gangster tied to a chair." He took off his hat, ran his hands through his hair, and replaced the hat at an angle, like he thought he was John Wayne.

"Not *sweetheart*, not *darlin'*, not *honey*." She fingered her holster and stared straight into his shit-eating grin. "It's *Colt*. Marshal Colt."

"Marshal Colt," he repeated and tipped his hat. "You're quite a filly."

Horse jokes. Ha. Ha. Very funny. She glared at him. *Dickwad.*

"Right." His tone changed to all business. "We've got

what looks like a .44 at close range." He pointed to Jimmy's messed-up head. "Coroner puts the time of death between eight and ten last night."

"Who found him?"

"Seems he was cozy with the neighbor lady. She brought him coffee cake around seven this morning." The cowboy gestured toward the back door. "When he didn't answer, she peeked in the window, promptly dropped her cake, and called 911."

Lexi kept her distance but circled around the victim, taking in the scene. Her stomach churned. *No more McDonalds for breakfast before examining a stiff.*

"So this is one of your WITSEC guys?" the cowboy asked.

She nodded.

"Who'd want to kill him?"

"Jimmy has an enemy list as long as the Great Wall of China."

"Care to narrow it down some?" The cowboy slid another toothpick out of his shirt pocket.

"Well, for starters, Victor 'Teeth' Marsiano." She bent closer to Jimmy's bloody head. The bullet had gone in one temple and out the other. *Close range will do that. What's that brown smudge on his lip?* Her face just inches from Jimmy's parted lips, she sniffed. *Crap.* "Got a glove?"

"An exam glove?"

"Well, not a mitten." She squinted at the cowboy.

He reached into his back pocket and pulled out two purple latex gloves.

She grabbed them and tugged them on. Poking her finger into the hole in the wall made by the bullet, she felt around. "Did they find the bullet?"

"Nope."

"Figures." She retracted her finger, snapped off the gloves, and handed them back to the cowboy. "It was a professional." Jimmy's cold dead eyes were getting under her skin. She headed for the back door.

"Hey, where ya goin' sweet—" The cowboy followed her out back. "Marshal?"

"Getting some fresh air." She sucked in the frigid mist and shucked off her coat.

"Who's this *teeth* guy?" The cowboy chewed his toothpick.

"Mafia." She closed her eyes and let the frosty morning revive her. "Baddie outta New York."

"New York?"

"Jimmy overheard Teeth order his hitman to kill some Russian gangster. Saw him do it too." She exhaled a cloud of mist. "He was going to testify." Hands on her knees, she leaned over, panting. *Come on, Lexi. Get it together*. She stared down at her oversized boots. *Lordy*. She'd really messed up. Jimmy's testimony was a big deal. And she'd blown it. She straightened up and put her coat back on. "Without his testimony, both Teeth and his hitman will walk."

"Guess that's on you," the cowboy said with a smirk.

"Yeah. I guess so." *A-hole.* "If you don't have any more information for me, I'm gonna get back to work." She turned to go back inside.

"Say, wanna get breakfast or a coffee or something?"

She gave him some serious side-eye.

"I guess not."

Not on your life. Instead of going back into the house, she slipped past the annoying cowboy and tromped through the snow, taking the long way around to the front of the house. *Did the perp come in through the front or back door?* By the looks of it, no forced entry. So Jimmy knew the guy. Or gal. Yeah, lots of ladies were working their way up the ranks of organized crime. Equal opportunity killing.

Best go question the cake lady next door. As she made her way across the snow-covered lawn, Lexi looked for footprints. No luck. The blizzard had covered any tracks made yesterday evening. Only prints going directly from the neighbor's back door to Jimmy's were visible in the fresh snow. Cake Lady had small feet. Lexi tried to match her steps, then thought better of it. Maybe these prints were clues. She'd better not mess them up too.

She zipped up her coat and picked up her pace.

Cake Lady answered the door in a ratty pink bathrobe and slippers. Had she changed her clothes since discovering Jimmy's body? Or did she make house calls in her skivvies? Her puffy eyes and tearstained cheeks suggested she shared more than the occasional breakfast with Jimmy. *Crime of passion?*

"Federal Marshal Lexington Colt." She flashed her badge. "I hear you found Jimmy."

Cake Lady nodded and sniffled.

"I'd like to ask you a few questions, if you don't mind." Lexi peered over Cake Lady's shoulder to get a glimpse inside the house. Yellowed doilies, nicked furniture, and one of those inspirational embroidered wall hangings made her rethink Cake Lady as a suspect. The smell of cat pee and fried onions sealed the deal.

"Come inside," Cake Lady said, wiping her nose on a faded hanky.

"Thanks," Lexi said, shaking her head. "But this won't take long." No way she was stepping inside. "When was the last time you saw Jimmy? Alive."

"Last night." She troubled the corner of her hanky. "I took him to dinner."

"What time was that?"

"Maybe seven." She crumpled the snot-rag into a ball.

"You didn't eat dinner with him, then?"

"Jimmy said he was expecting company, so I didn't stay."

"Company? Did he say who?" Lexi hugged herself to keep warm.

Cake Lady shook her head.

"And you didn't see him again until this morning?"

She nodded. "That's right."

"Tell me about how you found him."

Cake Lady screwed the hanky around one finger. "I already told those policemen everything I know."

"Do you mind telling me?"

"It's so horrible." She wiped her cheeks with the backs of her hands. "That hole in his head." Her shoulders started shaking. "Tied to the chair. I mean, who would do that?"

You'd be surprised. Even weepy cake ladies could get violent when pushed far enough. And—like most men—Jimmy was a button-pusher.

Lexi listened for lies. She'd gotten pretty good at sorting out nuggets of truth from piles of slush. "Did you see anyone around Jimmy's place last night? Or any cars?"

"I don't spy on my neighbors, if that's what you're getting at." Cake Lady hugged herself and shivered.

"No. No. That's not what I mean at all." Lexi bit the bullet. "Maybe I will step inside after all, if you don't mind."

"Sure." Cake Lady pushed the storm door farther open. "It's raw out there this morning."

When Lexi stepped over the threshold, another pungent smell hit her nose. *Pot. So little ole Cake Lady was a pothead.* No wonder she liked Jimmy. Maybe Jimmy was dealing on the side and got into trouble. Or the mob offed him to get rid of the prime witness. She shuddered. Yup. She'd really messed up. She was dreading the call to Drake, her direct supervisor in the

Casper office. But it had to be made. She needed to find out if the Illinois killing was related to this one. *Too much of a coincidence not to be.*

"So you were going to tell me what you saw last night." Lexi glanced around the shabby living room, on the lookout for a cat. She didn't trust the sneaky little buggers. "And Jimmy's visitor?"

"Not that I was spying or anything." Cake Lady buttoned the top button of her robe. "Just that from my bedroom window, I can see Jimmy's front porch."

"Go on." Lexi nodded.

Cake Lady's mouth twitched. She glanced around the room, then lowered her voice. "Just after eight last night, a guy showed up. Had braces or something shining from his mouth. He wasn't dressed for the weather and was hopping from foot to foot like he had to pee. He was wearing one of them fedora hats."

For someone who wasn't spying, Cake Lady had gotten a darn good look.

"What else? How tall? Facial hair? Anything else?"

She shook her head. "A skinny fella. I didn't see no beard or anything like that."

"If you think of anything else"—Lexi reached into the pocket of her ski jacket and pulled out her card —"give me call. Okay?"

Cake Lady nodded.

Lexi couldn't wait to get out of the stinky cat-pot house. Once she was out on the stoop, she took in a big breath and held it.

Cake Lady waved from inside the glass storm door. Lexi waved back.

Cake Lady opened the door. "There was that delivery."

"What delivery?"

"Grocery delivery. A woman."

"Groceries? When was that?" Lexi hadn't seen any groceries in Jimmy's kitchen. Had Jimmy gotten groceries and put them away before he was killed? *He couldn't very well do it after.*

"I told him I could buy his groceries."

"When?" Lexi took a step closer. "When did the woman deliver the groceries? Before or after the skinny fella with the hat?"

"I don't rightly remember." Cake Lady screwed up her mouth like she might spit.

"Did he always have his groceries delivered?"

"He didn't like to go out. 'Aggerraphobic.' That's what he called it."

"Can you describe the delivery woman?"

Wrinkles formed on Cake Lady's forehead. "I told you: I ain't no snoop."

"I know. But if you saw something, it would help us find who did this."

Her head bobbled like she was making up her mind. "The woman was . . . well, I wouldn't say 'pretty' exactly. More like 'handsome.' Had on jeans and a leather jacket. Was all business."

"Why do you say that?"

"The look in her eyes."

Lexi couldn't believe it. *Cake Lady could describe "the look in her eyes" but didn't know what time the woman made the delivery.* Lexi's hands were turning to icicles, and she was losing patience with Cake Lady. No matter. She could have the office call around to the grocery stores. It would be easy enough to find out who delivered groceries. "Thanks. You've been very helpful."

Cake Lady flashed a sorry smile, closed her storm door, and waved again. More sad clown than princess.

Lexi waved back and then trudged through the snow and across the street. She sank into the driver's seat of her Charger, fired it up, and blasted the heat. Rubbing her hands together, she closed her eyes and steeled herself for the call. Knowing it was a lost cause, she looked for a last drop of Dew.

Here goes. Fingers stiff from the cold, she poked the familiar number and waited for her supervisor, Ben Drake, to hit the line yelling.

But he didn't yell.

"Get your ass to Chicago," he said softly, shuffling papers on the other end. *I must be on speakerphone.* "The Art Dealer was tied and shot through the temple, same as Jimmy Giordano. We can't risk the airports. Haul ass and go get our guy out."

Geez. She'd just driven over seven hours on icy roads, and now he wanted her to drive across the flipping country? Her stomach turned. Someone was killing witnesses. Not just killing—executing. Some sort of mob ritual? First The Art Dealer in Chicago, and now Jimmy Giordano. At least The Art Dealer wasn't one of hers. *Drake must suspect the killer will strike again. And soon.*

"How was Jimmy?" Drake asked. "Bet you didn't find the bullet."

"You'd win that bet."

"Odds are our killer is working for 'Teeth' Marsiano," Drake said. "One of his professional hitmen."

"Either Teeth or Sergei 'Sly' Yudkovich." She held one hand in front of the heat vent.

"The Russian mafia? Why would they hit a guy testifying against the head of the Italian mob? They want him gone as much as we do."

"An enemy of an enemy is a friend?" She switched the phone to her other hand and put her popsicle fingers against the vent. "Cake Lady said a guy with braces and a fedora visited Jimmy last night. Doesn't that sound like someone we know?"

"Who is Cake Lady?"

"The neighbor lady. She described a guy—sounds like the Butcher to me."

"Interesting. But why would Bratva want to kill Jimmy? It doesn't make sense. You sure the guy wasn't Teeth's hitman."

"I'm also following up on a grocery delivery."

"What?"

"Jimmy had groceries delivered last night. I'm going to find out who made the delivery."

"Maybe he delivered more than groceries," Drake said.

"Exactly. And it's a she. A lot of women are working for Bratva. Sly loves his tough women—"

"But why would Sly reneg on his WITSEC deal?" Drake interrupted. "He'll go to prison. And there are a lot of folks there who hold a grudge against Sly."

"He wouldn't be the first." Finally the vent was warming up. "The Italians or the Russians. Should I flip a coin?"

"Flip whatever you want." She could tell Drake was getting impatient. "If you lose another witness, you'll be flipping parking tickets in Timbuktu."

"I'm a federal marshal, not a meter maid." She wanted to pitch her phone out the window into a snowbank.

"If you lose another witness, don't count on it."

She wasn't about to lose another. *Not EVER.*

2

"Do you know the story of Abraham and Isaac?" Jessica James asked the class. It was a rhetorical question. The kind a preacher would ask their congregation. That's what she loved about teaching Kierkegaard. It made her feel like a preacher. It made her want to wave her Bible around and shout.

Instead, distracted by the snow, she stared out the window of the Victorian mansion that served as the philosophy department. The window was sealed shut by decades of various shades of paint. The latest was a rotting peach color peeling off the casement. The windows themselves were thick like Coke bottles with the greenish tint of old glass. From the second floor, she could see snowflakes floating through the barren tree-tops like confetti still wind-borne long after the parade had ended.

She'd grown up in Montana, notorious for some monumental blizzards. But she'd never seen a whiteout until she got to Chicago. The "lake effect" was real. At least she'd worn her parka and boots to campus. Still, she wasn't ready for a full-on blizzard.

She turned back to her students and took a deep breath. After her five years haunting the philosophy building, the musty antique books lined up in shelves around the seminar room smelled like family. *Eccentric mercurial uncles and batshit crazy cousins . . . but family nonetheless.*

"Yes, it's a story of faith: Abraham's faith that God will provide the sacrificial lamb." When she stepped away from the lectern, the old wooden floor creaked. "But it's also a story of belief. Belief in the impossible." She jabbed the air for emphasis.

Pacing back and forth in the front of the small seminar room, she held up her white King James Bible, the one her mom had given her on her tenth birthday. "Abraham believes both that he will sacrifice his son and that he won't have to." She stopped and stared out at the weary faces. None of them seemed excited about the mind-bending truth of Kierkegaard's *Fear and Trembling*. "But the true test is not giving up Isaac. It's accepting him back after having given up. Accepting him back with grace as if he was never at risk of being taken away." *As if he weren't really dead.* She thought of Nick.

She'd been trying not to think of Nick for the last six

months. *Nick. The not-quite-ex-boyfriend the detective told her had been found dead with an engagement ring in his pocket.*

Jessica stood there for a few seconds in a daze.

Nick. Not dead after all but in witness protection.

Outside, the snow was picking up. She needed to end class before it got worse. Returning to the lectern, she stacked her books with the Bible on top. "Any questions?"

Nick. The one that got away?

Blank stares. Cell phones surreptitiously held in laps. Books being stuffed into backpacks. Notebooks snapping shut. No one cared. No one but her.

"Any comments? Protests?" Nothing. Her heart shrunk. "Okay. Send your final papers to me through e-mail."

Shoulders slumped, she watched as they filed out of the classroom.

She'd just taught her last class at Northwestern. *Weird. Shouldn't I feel more . . excitement? Relief? Something?* She was numb, and her graduate career was ending with a fizzle.

On his way out the door, a pimple-faced kid named Yanis said, "Thank you, Professor." She forced a smile. She wasn't a professor, but she didn't bother to tell Yanis she was a lowly graduate student, one who had only just defended her dissertation a few months ago.

She stuffed her books in her bag and pulled on her parka. Before leaving Brentano Hall—maybe for the last time—she inhaled the heady scent of dusty books, stale bleach, and Donnette's overpowering perfume. Donnette was the office administrator, the only other woman in the philosophy department and Jessica's only ally in the whole of this stuffy old building. Five years she'd been swimming upstream, the only woman in the philosophy program.

As the heavy door closed behind her, a brisk gale hit her in the face. One thing was for certain: spring was gone and winter was here. The snow was coming at her sideways. Bracing herself, she put her head down and pushed against the bitter wind as she trotted across campus and turned onto Sherman Avenue, making her way to the Blind Faith Café. *Funny*. She'd just lectured about faith.

Jack would be waiting for her. He was taking her to lunch to celebrate her last class. Good old Jack Grove. He'd been one of her best friends since she'd arrived at Northwestern. She met him at a party her first week on campus. Jack loved to party. But he was also brilliant and witty and sharp... Sometimes too sharp.

Over the years, he'd made it clear he wanted to be more than just friends. After she'd lost Nick last spring, Jack had been a reliable shoulder to cry on. After a month, the crying had turned into kissing, which was a lot more fun. Like most things, Jack was good at it. And she'd discovered more than his shoulders for comfort. He'd helped her get over Nick. If she was just rebounding, she was rebounding hard.

By the time she arrived at the café, all her muscles were tight, her eyes were stinging, and her fingers were numb. The bright blue awning and the giant sunflower on the sign above it were welcome sights. As she pulled open the glass door, the heavenly smell of freshly baked bread greeted her. The comforting chunky tables, contrasting orange counter and blue bar stools, and shiny bakery cases made her feel at home. The warmth of the room and the din of chatting diners calmed her nerves, and finally her muscles began to relax.

Sure enough. There he was, his trusty shoulders leaning against the wall in a corner booth with his nose in a book and his feet up on the seat across from him. In his worn-out corduroy jacket and desert boots, with his too-cool-for-school slouch, he was just the kind of sexy nerd she couldn't resist (but usually wished she had). A smile bloomed on her lips as she snaked through the crowd and approached the booth.

The Blind Faith Café was always crowded at lunchtime, especially on Fridays. From ex-hippie professors who'd been vegetarians since the '60s and newly minted vegans trying to save the planet, to skeptical parents and reluctant boyfriends dragged there against their will, the place was hopping.

She slid into the booth across from him and pushed his feet off the seat with her book bag. "What are you reading?"

He held up the book. Nietzsche's *Beyond Good and Evil.*

"Just some light reading for fun, eh?"

He dropped the book onto the seat next to him and then held out his hand across the table. She put her hand in his. His hand was soft and warm.

"Your hand is freezing," he said, jerking his hand away.

She grabbed it with both of hers and held on tight. "You're not getting away so easily."

"Let me pay for my coffee, and then I have a surprise for you." Jack's eyes were bright and lively.

"What kind of surprise?" With Jack, you never knew.

"You'll see." He pulled his wallet out of his back pocket. "I hope you're wearing your long johns."

She gave him the side-eye. "Some guys go for Victoria's Secret, but long johns turn you on?"

He laughed that smooth aged-whiskey laugh of his. "You could be wearing a bearskin and bush hat for all I care." He slid out of the booth. "Back in a minute."

As she watched him snake his way through the crowded restaurant, she marveled at his perfect butt. With his wavy chestnut hair and crooked smile, he looked like a young James Franco. And like the notorious actor, he was unpredictable and kind of crazy but in a good way. Life was interesting with Jack. *What kind of surprise requires long underwear?*

She hoped it involved food. She was starved.

After nearly an hour heading north on the Dan Ryan Expressway, wipers waving frantically to keep the snow off the windshield, they passed a sign welcoming them to Wisconsin. If Illinois was the "Land of Lincoln," Wisconsin was the "Land of Cheese." Like Illinois, southern Wisconsin was flat as a board. Once they got away from the buildings and the burbs, the ground was so level that the horizon seemed a million miles away. Until she'd arrived in Chicago five years ago, she'd never imagined a landscape so monotonous. Coming from the Rocky Mountains, open spaces always made her feel vulnerable and exposed, like a bright dot on an empty graph. Most of all, the gaping nothingness made her miss home.

Once they left the expressway behind, the scenery became wintery and wild. The snow was reassuring like a liniment soothing the void. The further they drove, the deeper it got. Tree trunks disappeared under a white blanket. The barren brown sticks that passed for trees looked dead rather than dormant. Winter in the Midwest was depressing . . . unlike winter in Montana, which was a wonderland with mountains covered in Christmas trees.

"Where are we going?" Jessica hoped they weren't going all the way to Milwaukee just to have lunch. Her stomach grumbled.

"You'll see."

"I hope it involves food."

"Eventually." He glanced over at her with a mischievous smile. "If you're good."

She reached over and gently touched his hair. "I'm always good."

"Yes, you are." He smiled over at her. "That feels nice."

A few minutes later, Jack turned onto a side road called County Highway Q. "Be on the lookout for County Highway MB. If we hit Highway C, we've gone too far."

"Where are we going?" She sat up straighter to see out of the low-riding Honda Civic, which had seen better days. "Alphabet City?" Her stomach growled again, obviously hoping for alphabet soup.

The car fishtailed as it slid around the next corner. Most people in the Midwest had a four-wheel drive truck or SUV, but Jack refused to give up his old Civic. The nubs on its stained upholstery were almost as worn and bald as the elbows on Jack's corduroy jacket. And it reeked of cigarettes and weed from his old chain-smoking days, before he went to prison.

Jack parked in the lot at Bristol Woods Park, in front of a cute squat building that looked like it was wearing a pointy brown birthday hat on top of its little round head. There was only one other car in the parking lot. The place seemed deserted.

"What are—"

Jack cut her off. "Come on, cowgirl. It's going to be fun."

"But I'm hungry."

"After dark, we can still eat, but we can't snowshoe." He grinned as he opened the car door.

She followed in his footsteps in the deep snow until they reached the Nature Center. Inside, it was cozy warm. A young man who looked like a teenager asked her shoe size, then brought out a pair of metal snowshoes. As she grabbed hold of the cold metal bars of the equipment, she thought of the snowshoeing trips she'd made in the Flathead Mountains with her dad. Just her and her dad. He mom had preferred to stay home and smoke, drink coffee, and read celebrity magazines. Jessica preferred a brisk nipping wind to the stinky, smoke-filled double-wide she grew up in.

Her chest was buzzing with excitement as she sat on a bench in front of the Nature Center and clipped her booted feet into the snowshoes. "How'd you find this place? This is awesome."

"I knew you'd like it." He smiled.

Once they were both clipped, she took off on the self-guided interpretative trail. Stomping on top of the snow, she took long strides and eventually fell into an exhilarating rhythm. The only sound was the crunching of her snowshoes on the top crust of snow. Every step started with the tiniest pause while the snowshoe broke through the thin icy crust. She opened her mouth and turned her face toward the sky. Snowflakes gently landed and melted on her tongue and her face. She laughed from pure joy. She stopped and turned to face Jack.

Wait. Where is he? She was alone on the trail. No one in sight. She listened to hear him approach. Nothing. She strained to listen. Nope. Only the sound of a lone cardinal calling to its mate. She hightailed it back toward the Nature Center. Rounding the second corner, she saw him sprawled out on the trail.

"What are you doing down there?" She picked up her pace.

Jack propped himself up on his elbows. "Every time I try to stand up, I fall down."

She laughed. Maybe there *was* something Jack wasn't good at. Snowshoeing. She stopped next to him and extended her hand. He reached up, and she pulled. His feet slid out from under him and he landed back on his butt. *Yup. He sucks at snowshoeing.*

"Maybe we should call it a day and go get lunch . . . or should I say supper?" She stepped behind him and held on to his jacket with both hands. "Okay. Stand up." She held him steady while he got his legs underneath him. She put her arms around his waist and kissed the back of his neck.

As he took a step forward, he started to slip again. She caught him. "Hold still."

He obliged. "My hands are freezing."

"Yeah, because you have snow inside your gloves." She walked around to face him, taking wide sideways steps like Frankenstein's monster. Putting one fat snowshoe alongside his right foot, and the other between both his snowshoed feet, she moved closer until they were almost touching noses. She put her arms around him and kissed him.

"Umm," he said, still kissing her. "You taste good."

She pressed her body up against his. He dropped his ski poles and wrapped his arms around her. She could feel him pulling her down but couldn't stop the fall. He slipped backwards and she fell on top of him, her ski poles flapping like wings. She slipped her wrists out of the straps and plunged her hands into the snow, pulling up a big handful. She packed it into a ball.

"No you don't," he said, grabbing her hands and pulling closer.

A slight whiff of sandalwood soap put her entire body on high alert. She kicked off the snowshoes and kissed him as if her life depended on it.

"I love you, cowgirl," he whispered into her hair between kisses.

"Me too," she said. Even in the throes of passion, she hadn't been able to say it back. All she'd ever said was, "Me too."

She could feel Jack shivering. He was lying in the snow. And he wasn't properly dressed for outdoor activities. "Let's go get something to eat." She got to her knees, then stood up and snapped her boots back into the snowshoes.

"There's supposed to be a cedar grove up ahead," he

said, looking up at her. "I wanted you to see evergreens."

"You're the greatest." She smiled down at him. "Next time . . . after I've given you some snowshoeing lessons."

"Righto," he said, trying to stand up.

"Take off the snowshoes first, dummy, and then stand up."

By the time they made it back to the car, they were both soaked through.

Jack cranked the heat up. His cheeks were rosy from the frosty adventure. "Where to?"

"I'm starving. Aren't you?"

"I'll start with dessert." He leaned over the console and kissed her.

She returned his kiss. "For stamina, I need food."

"I may not be able to keep up with you snowshoeing, but you're going to need your stamina for the next activity I have in mind." He raised his eyebrows.

She laughed. She knew exactly what he had in mind. "Let's get dinner and go home."

He revved the car and headed for downtown.

Kenosha was a cute waterfront town on Lake Michigan. None of the buildings were over two stories. Most had colorful awnings. The street was decorated for Christmas with wreaths and lights. Jack cruised the main drag while she googled the best places to eat.

"There's one called 'Fireside' with a fireplace," she said, glancing up from her phone. She craved warmth as much as she craved food. She read off the directions.

Fireside Restaurant and Lounge lived up to its name. In the center of the cozy wood-paneled restaurant was a giant floor-to-ceiling brick fireplace that took up almost an entire wall. She requested a seat by the fire. They ordered a veggie pizza and a pitcher of beer.

After the exertion of snowshoeing in the cold park, anything warm would be welcome. *Even warmed over-cardboard would taste good right about now.* When the waitress sat the pizza in the center of the table, her mouth watered. The smell of onions and garlic mixed with roasted tomatoes was heavenly. She pulled out a slice and used her fingers to snap off the end of the stretchy cheese. *Yummy.*

They ate and drank and argued about Nietzsche until their clothes dried out. What a great way to celebrate her last class. As they left the restaurant, she took Jack's hand. She hadn't felt this content in a long time.

A pinkish twilight hung over the horizon, and a full moon was rising. It had stopped snowing, and the entire world looked fresh and new.

Since Jack drank most of the pitcher, she was the designated driver. She started the car and then held her hands to the heat vent, waiting for warm air. After the cold air turned warmish, she pulled out of the parking lot onto 30th Avenue per Jack's directions. The traffic light turned yellow, and she slowed to the stop. A bright blue Dodge Charger skidded to a stop next to them. She glanced over to see who was in such a hurry.

Oh. My. God. Her heart leapt into her throat. "It's him!"

"Who?" Jack said in alarm. "What's wrong?"

Jessica had a close-up view through the side window. He was right next to her. If they'd had their windows down, she could almost reach out and touch him.

I know it's him. In the passenger seat. *Look at me. Look over.* But he didn't. He turned toward the driver. *Wait. Who is that gorgeous woman driving?*

"Nick." She honked the horn. "Look at me."

The light changed, and the car took off. She drove after it, trying to make out the license plate. The Charger swerved left at the next corner and nearly ran the traffic light.

The stoplight turned red. Oncoming cars started whizzing past. Jessica was stuck. The Charger was gone. And so was Nick . . . again.

3

Jessica was squinting. Not that it helped her see any better. The fog was thick, the visibility was crap, and Jack's beater, with its bald tires, was threatening to slide out of its lane. Why had she offered to drive? Oh, right. Because Jacko drank three-quarters of the pitcher of beer. Lucky she was driving, or she might never have seen Nick.

What are the odds? She'd never been to Kenosha before. *Really.* What were the odds of Jack taking her to Wisconsin of all places . . . and then randomly picking the Fireside Restaurant . . . and then coming outside at the time when they did . . . and then her offering to drive . . . and then stopping at that light . . . at exactly the same time that the blue Charger pulled up next to her and she saw Nick sitting there. It was fate. It had to be.

"I thought we were going home." Jack's voice interrupted her thoughts. "I'll even brave your futon rat's nest tonight."

"It was him," Jessica said, concentrating on the road. The temperature was dropping, and patches of black ice had formed on the highway. "Nick. He's here." She glanced over at Jack. Her thoughts were as scrambled as a Western omelet.

"For the tenth time—it couldn't have been Nick. He's in witness protection." Jack's tone changed from pleading to peeved. "It was just someone who *looked like* Nick. It wasn't him. Why would witness protection place him so close to Chicago?"

"Maybe to prepare him for the trial?"

"They could do that from anywhere."

"I don't know. But it was him." She tightened her grip on the steering wheel. She slid her phone out of her pocket and laid it on her knee. "Siri, call Lolita."

"What are you doing?" Jack asked.

"Calling Lolita. What does it look like I'm doing?"

Lolita agreed to meet her at the Blind Faith Café in an hour for a nightcap.

"Siri, call Amber."

"Not Amber too," Jack grumbled.

Jessica didn't answer. She kept her lips tight, her fingers wrapped around the steering wheel, and her eyes glued to the road.

Forty minutes later, she pulled up in front of Blind Faith. "Go fetch Amber."

Jack just looked at her with his mouth hanging

open. She reached over and patted his hand. "Please? Pick up Amber, and then come back." She opened the driver's-side door and hopped out.

"Whatever you say, cowgirl." Jack slid over the console into the driver's seat.

She slammed the door shut and scurried inside the café. Second time in one day. It wasn't the first time. Blind Faith had been her home away from home for the last five years.

The lunch crowd had morphed into the late-night crowd. And the smell of baking bread had turned into the smell of greasy deep-fried veggies and undergrads pulling panicked all-nighters.

A sleek silhouette sitting at the counter, sipping from a demitasse, stood out from the crowd. Her best friend. Lolita Durchenko, the Poker Tsarina. They'd met at a poker game during Jessica's first week in Chicago five years ago—back when Jessica was still naive enough to think that just because she'd been a straight A student as an undergrad at the University of Montana, it would be easy to move across the county and spend another half decade getting a PhD.

Chicago. "Back East," as her mom called it. Thousands of miles from the high, wide lonesome of Montana. The big city. Who'd have thought she'd end up here? At least she wasn't living in a trailer park, cleaning dirty diapers and fetching some angry hayseed his six-pack of Budweiser like most of her friends from high school.

Lolita greeted her with air kisses to both cheeks and then patted the stool next to her. "Good to see you, *milaya*."

"The usual?" Sally, the waitress, asked from behind the counter as she set down a chai latte.

Jessica nodded. "The usual." The usual was Kamoosh—the Blind Faith version of nachos—and a chai latte. It was good to be a regular. Recognized in the crowd.

"So you think you saw Nick?"

"I know I did. It was him. I'm sure of it."

"Forget about him, *milaya*." Lolita shook her head. "How was class?" She changed the subject.

"I don't think my students get it." Jessica sipped her chai. Another advantage of being a regular—Sally had started the chai latte as soon as she'd cantered through the door, and it was ready almost before she sat down. She swiveled on the barstool to face her friend. "I guess I'll miss it."

"You'll be teaching art to refugees at the Center for Russian Art."

"At Nick's Center. *Nick*. It's fate."

Sally slid a plate of steaming Kamoosh onto the counter. *Yup.* She must have put in the order as soon as Jessica walked through the door.

"We make our own fate. And yours doesn't include that rotter, Nick."

Jessica scowled. *Nick isn't a rotter.* "Why else would I

have been up in Kenosha of all places? At that very stoplight? It's meant to be."

"Come on. You don't believe that *meant to be* crap." Lolita squinted at her. "Anyway, I thought you and Jackass were a thing now."

Jessica picked up a nacho and blew on it. "The only thing harder than losing what you love . . ." She took a bite. ". . . is getting it back."

"I wouldn't know." Lolita's sage-green eyes and long red claws reminded her of a cat's. "And if you're talking about Nick Schilling, you don't have him back." Lolita sipped her espresso. "He's in witness protection, remember?"

Jessica cringed. She shouldn't have told Lolita . . . or Jack. Detective Cormier had made her swear not to tell anyone. Heck, even *she* wasn't supposed to know her ex-boyfriend Nick was alive and in witness protection. But with her seductive charms and kick-ass karate, Lolita had saved Jessica's bacon more times than she could count. Her dad had always told her, "Never take a knife to a gun fight." But Lolita was one sharp blade.

Since Jessica had gotten her degree and moved downtown, she hadn't seen as much of Lolita, who was in the MBA program at Northwestern. Sure, her friend came by the Center for Russian Art and Culture to visit her dad, Dmitry Durchenko, who was the director now that Nick was gone. The Center for Russian Art and Culture had been Nick's brainchild. After he disappeared, Jessica went to work directing the education program at the museum. Working with refugee girls had given her life new purpose.

"But I just saw him with a . . . a woman."

"*Milaya*, please forget about Nick." Lolita shook her head. "He's not for you."

"For two months, I freaking thought he was freaking dead." Jessica's lip trembled just remembering that terrible morning. Even though it was months ago, the pain was still fresh and raw.

She and Nick had been planning a romantic stay-cation at the swanky Parker Hotel. Shortly after checking in, Nick had left her in the suite, saying he'd be gone for one hour. But he never came back. Detective Cormier had said that when they found Nick's body, they also found an engagement ring in his pocket. It had nearly destroyed her. But finding out two months later that he'd faked his death to hide from the mob—and hadn't even told *her* the truth—had been worse.

Jessica moved her fork around her plate. "You know what it's like to lose someone forever."

"Can't you get past that and just be happy he's alive?" Lolita stirred her coffee with a tiny spoon.

"When I saw him, everything came flooding back. I can't just undo six months of mourning and grief." She stared down at her half-eaten Kamoosh. "If only the detective hadn't told me about the ring . . ." Her voice trailed off, and she dropped her fork on the table. "But knowing he's alive somehow makes it worse. Like there's no closure." She glanced over at her friend. "Now that I've seen him, I need to see him again."

"Move on, my Montana friend." Lolita flipped her jet-black hair over one shoulder. "Anyway, there are plenty of other billionaire playboys in the sea—which, if you ask me, is where they belong."

"Nick isn't a playboy." She used her fork to pick a black fleck off her Kamoosh.

Lolita smirked.

"Okay, maybe he was once. Past tense." *But who was that woman driving the muscle car?* Thoughts of the pretty driver gnawed at the corners of her brain.

"Whatever." Lolita sighed. "Nick is probably recruiting nude models for a painting class—"

"He teaches art history, not painting." Jessica frowned. "Your dad's the painter."

"If there are any nudes in my dad's paintings, I can't see them. An elephant could draw more realistic figures."

"It's called abstract art." Jessica pushed her plate away. "Speaking of Dmitry . . ." She glanced around the café as if the janitor-cum-curator might be sitting in the next booth. Like the ex-mobster would ever frequent a vegetarian hippie café. If they were at Pavlov's Banquet, maybe he'd show up. But the Blind Faith Café? Never. "How'd he get Bratva off your tail?"

"Who said he did?" Lolita winked.

If anyone knew the dangers of the Russian Mafia, it was Lolita. Her dad had escaped Russia when she was still in her mother's womb to get away from her granddad—Anton Yudkovich, the biggest Russian crime boss in the world. Heck, with her bloodline, Lolita was practically Bratva royalty. For all Jessica knew, Lolita *was* Bratva, or at least still undercover as Bratva. She'd gone undercover as a big-time mafia operator last spring. Either way, she was better at keeping secrets than Jessica.

Jessica tapped her finger on the orange Formica counter. "I have a crazy idea." She stared at her friend. "Do you think Bratva could help us find Nick?"

"You want the Russian brotherhood to help you locate your ex-boyfriend in WITSEC?" Lolita arched her perfect eyebrows. With the tiny cup handle between her thumb and forefinger, she raised the espresso to her lips but didn't take a sip. "Actually, 90 percent of the asswipes in WITSEC are Mafia. Bratva is probably already looking for your boyfriend. Along with the entire East Coast Italian mob."

"That's why we have to find him first." *Nick's in danger, and there's absolutely nothing I can do about it.* She put her elbows on the counter and her head in her hands.

"Like I said, the whole purpose of WITSEC is to put witnesses where no one will find them. Not their girlfriends, not their families, and especially not the mob." Lolita signaled the waitress for another cup of espresso.

It was a wonder she didn't disappear when she turned sideways. She didn't eat . . . at least not in public.

But underestimate her at your peril. She was as flexible and strong as a tiger.

"Isn't that your third?" Jessica asked.

"And your point is?"

"Aren't you wired enough already? Isn't it too late for all that caffeine?"

"You're sounding like Amber again. Anyway, I have a long night ahead."

True. Their friend Amber was always harping on Lolita for drinking too much caffeine, telling Jessica to drink those disgusting herbal teas she made. Jessica shuddered. She never did trust them, especially not since they were suspected of containing poison. Of course, they weren't poison. But still. It was a good excuse not to touch the foul-smelling stuff.

The waitress delivered another tiny cup. Lolita downed it in one slug. "And there's no such thing as 'wired enough,'" she said as she handed the empty cup to the waitress. "One more."

Her friend was edgy enough without four double shots of espresso coursing through her high-strung veins.

"Can't we ask your cousin Vanya?" Jessica opened her palms as if asking for a handout.

"Ask him what?"

"About Bratva." She blew at her bangs. "Isn't he, like, the Miss Congeniality of the Russian mob?"

Lolita laughed. "Speak of the devil." She tilted her head in the direction of the entrance.

Is Vanya here? Jessica swiveled around. Through the flock of customers in front of the bakery case, she could make out a purple paisley muumuu and well-worn Uggs. That was enough. She didn't need to see the curly red hair to know it was Amber.

"I'll go get her." Jessica slid off her stool.

"I'll find us a booth." Lolita picked up her tiny saucer and cup and surveyed the café.

Sucking in her gut, Jessica squeezed between chairs and tables to make her way to the bakery case. *Too bad she couldn't suck in her butt.*

In spite of the late hour, the café was bustling. What a bunch of misfits. Students strung out on NoDoz, pulling all-nighters and studying for exams; professors wearing threadbare jackets and mismatched socks, drinking too much caffeine while reviewing yellowing decades-old lecture notes; and the occasional staff member looking far too normal to haunt the same halls as the rest. If she ever got nostalgic about grad school, she only had to come to the Blind Faith and watch the motley crowd to realize how lucky she was to be leaving academia.

As she approached the bakery case, she got a glimpse of wavy brown hair and a crumpled corduroy blazer.

"I brought the hacker as ordered." Jack pulled Jessica in for a hug. "I missed you, cowgirl."

"It's only been half an hour."

"Half an hour too long."

She had to admit, his earthy smell still stirred something deep inside her . . . enough to make her jerk away.

"What? Aren't you glad to see me?" Jack tightened his lips.

"It's just . . ." She didn't know what to say. Now that she'd seen Nick, everything felt awkward and weird, like she was betraying Nick.

"Nick," he said under his breath and stared down at his desert boots.

For a few seconds they stood there, not looking at each other.

Luckily, Amber's little squeals interrupted the awkward silence. "We were just talking about you." She kissed Jessica on the cheek.

Jessica's eyes watered from the piquant scent of patchouli. Amber was born a couple decades too late. With her snaky hair, flowing curves, and high-on-life attitude, she was the quintessential flower child.

"Lolita's here. Come join us." Jessica pointed across the crowded café.

"I just got these chocolate black bean brownies." Amber held up an oil-stained white sack.

"You'll definitely need something to wash down those turds." Jessica pulled at her friend's arm.

Amber scowled. "They're yummy and healthy."

"One out of two, maybe. Come on." Jessica led them to the booth where Lolita was stretched out, cooling her heels. Jessica pushed her friend's Harley-Davidson boots off the seat and scooted to the far end of the bench to make room for Amber.

But it was Jack who slid in next to her. The warmth emanating from his body made her shiver. She fiddled with a packet of raw sugar until it broke open and spilled all over the table. Sweeping the granules with her hand, she wiped the sugar onto the floor, then wiped her hand on the thigh of her jeans. *Weird.* Just a couple of hours ago, they were happily kissing and rolling around in the snow. Now every touch between them was uncomfortable and strange.

"So what have you two ladies been plotting?" Jack asked, waving off a hunk of black bean brownie on offer from Amber.

"The cowgirl wants to take on the feds." Lolita leaned into the corner of the booth and zipped up her black motorcycle jacket. "And go after Nick Schilling."

"'Take on the feds?'" Amber said with her mouth full of brownie.

"Nick's in WITSEC." Lolita raised her eyebrows.

"Shhh." Jessica put her finger to her lips and glared at her friend from across the booth. "No one is supposed to know that."

"What's WITSEC?" A chocolate crumb stuck to Amber's plump upper lip.

"Witness protection, baby." Lolita reached over and wiped the crumb from Amber's face. "Nick's going to testify against Victor 'Teeth' Marsiano about how Teeth and his dad were running dirty money through the

Center for Russian Art. He'll be taking on the whole East Coast Italian mob." She closed her eyes and shook her head. "For a spoiled playboy, he's got guts; I'll give him that."

"He's *not* a playboy." Maybe it was just wishful thinking. He had been with that pretty woman in the car. Still, there was the engagement ring. But had it been for her? Unless she found him, she'd never know. It must be fate. Why else would she be in Kenosha Wisconsin at that very minute? Nick was the reason. She had to find him.

If she could find him, so could the mob. They could be watching her in case all this time she went looking for him. She could lead them right to him. If only he'd call. *Why didn't he call?* How could he let her think he was dead? Was he just trying to protect her? Is that why he hadn't called? *He would want me to find him, wouldn't he?* Her thoughts swirled into a downward spiral.

"Wanker, more like." Jack's voice brought her back from her troubled thoughts. "With his designer jackets, fancy cologne, and pocket pistol. Or don't you remember when he pointed that thing at me?" He poked Jessica in the ribs. "Oh, I guess you wouldn't, would you. A few too many Jack & Cokes."

"A few too many *drugged* Jack & Cokes." Jessica scooted further toward the wall. "Nick was just trying to protect me."

"Oh, like you need a knight in shining armor to protect you." Jack scoffed. "You've watched too many

Disney princesses. Your boy Nick's a paternalistic prick."

"Don't lecture me about feminism." Jessica picked up another packet of raw sugar but thought better of it and dropped it back into its container. "And what do you know about Nick? You're just jealous."

"No. I'm trying to protect you."

"What, now you're my knight in shining armor?" She shook her head.

He turned to face her, his brown eyes fierce. "I just don't want you to get hurt . . . again."

"I can take care of myself."

"Yes, you can." He took her by the elbow. "But can you take care of Schilling and his double life too? I'm telling you, cowgirl, he's bad news."

She narrowed her brows. "You barely even knew—know him."

"I know he let you think he was dead." Jack sighed. "I'll bet he still hasn't contacted you, has he?"

"He's in WITSEC. How can he?"

Jack scoffed again. "Witness protection isn't prison. He could leave at any time. He could find a way to contact you. I would if it were me."

"But you don't play by the rules."

"Neither do you . . . and neither does Schilling. He's used to making his own rules, and therein lies the problem. He makes them and expects everyone else to follow them."

Lolita tapped her tiny spoon against her tiny cup.

"Kids, while I appreciate that the sexual tension between you is overpowering, could you just cool it? Either that or get a room?"

"Jack's right," Amber said, munching on a second brownie. "Nick's nice, but he shouldn't have let you suffer, thinking he was dead. That's like torture." She put her hand over her heart. "I know what it's like to lose someone you love."

"One of my former patients was in WITSEC, and he called his sisters all the time." Jack reached into the sack and broke off a piece of brownie. Before going to prison, Jack had been in med school studying criminal psychiatry and interning in Illinois prisons. He'd gotten out on parole on the condition that he'd continue working with prisoners as his community service. "The guy had a rap sheet as long as my leg—hell, as long as Lolita's leg—and he told me how he lived in luxury on the federal dime." He chuckled. "The cheeky bloke even got the feds to pay for his wife's breast enhancement, claiming it would 'keep him calmer' while he waited to testify."

Jessica rolled her mind's eye. Even after two years in prison, Jack liked to think he was British just because he'd spent a year on a fellowship at Oxford. Still, whatever his quirks, he was devoted to her. Maybe she could persuade *him* to help her find Nick. *And reunite her with his rival? Fat chance.* Then again, he'd committed crimes for her before. She cringed. It was her fault he'd landed in prison for freeing lab animals. "Do you think your former patient would know how to find Nick?" she asked, trying to sound nonchalant.

"I haven't seen him in years. I've been in prison, remember?" He smirked. "Anyway, that shite's as secret as it gets. Only a couple federal marshals know the whereabouts of any one witness. Talk about a needle in a manure pile. You'll never find your boy." He turned and gazed into her face. "Unless, of course, he wants you to."

Rub it in. Maybe Jack was right. Maybe Nick didn't want her to find him. Had he even *tried* to contact her? Her heart sank. She knew the answer. "There must be some central database." She looked across the table at Amber. "Right?"

"Don't look at me," Amber said, crumpling the empty brownie bag. "My hacking days are over." Seeming airhead Amber Bush had turned out to be a first-class computer wizard and expert hacker. She could compete with the best hackers in the world. And she'd hack for chocolate.

"As my dad would say," Lolita winked, "I'd like to drink honey with your lips."

"What?" Amber looked confused.

"Let's just say you shouldn't give up hacking." Lolita shrugged. "You can't just turn away from your superpower."

"You've got to play to your strength." Jessica smiled. "And yours, sweetie, is hacking."

"Wasn't sending Jack to prison enough?" Amber wrapped the end of a snaky lock around her finger.

"That's a bit harsh," Jack said. "I knew what I was doing. And as I recall, you wanted me to free those poor lab rats too. You even helped—"

"I don't want to go to jail." Amber flipped the hair into her mouth.

Amber had a point. Jessica really shouldn't drag her friends into her preoccupation. She'd given up trying to find Nick months ago. Now that she'd seen him, she was as desperate to find him as ever. But to find him, she needed help. If anyone could hack the federal system, it was Amber.

"Quit sucking on your hair." Lolita gently pushed the lock behind Amber's ear. "Jessica doesn't want us to do anything illegal." She winked. "Does she?"

"They don't call her 'Jesse James' for nothing," Jack said, helping himself to the rest of her Kamoosh.

"If you guys don't want to help me, I understand. I am asking a lot. But I've got to do what I've got to do."

"You have to let him go," Amber said. "Come over later—we can do a guided meditation and cleaning ritual. I know just the herbs to purge him from your system."

"I don't want to purge him." Jessica blew at her bangs. "I want to find him."

"Your obsession with Nick is getting boring." For some unknown reason, Lolita never had liked Nick. She sat up, dug in her pocket, and pulled out a twenty-dollar bill. "I've got to get to the clinic. My night shift starts in a half hour." Lolita volunteered at the Rape Crisis Center.

"What happened to Ready, Willing, and Able?" Jack pointed around the table: first to Jessica, then to Amber, and finally to Lolita. "We can't let the cowgirl philosopher go it alone."

"I would think you're the last person who would want her to find Nick," Lolita said.

"How will I know if she's over him unless she confronts him?" Jack's tone became serious. "That's why we have to help her. For my sake as well as hers."

"Speak for yourself," Amber said. "I'm with Lolo on this one."

"A heart full of courage and cheerfulness needs a little danger from time to time." Jack tipped an imaginary hat. "Or the world gets unbearable."

"It takes courage to indulge in wickedness," Jessica responded. "The 'good' are too cowardly." Quoting Nietzsche was a sexy game they liked to play. Well, they were the only ones who thought it was fun. Everyone around them found it annoying.

"And if you can't be good, be careful," Lolita said, waving Amber out of the booth so she could make her exit. She flipped her silky hair over her shoulder, pulled on her Harley helmet, and stood up to her full five feet, ten inches. "Why don't you ask your friend Detective Harvey Cormier for help?"

"Maybe you could ask him for me?" Jessica grinned. "I think he likes you best."

"I like him too," Lolita purred. "Keep your friends close and your enemies closer." When she smiled, a mischievous glint danced in her eyes.

4

The next evening, Jessica reluctantly accompanied her friend on a Saturday dinner "date" with Detective Cormier. Lolita had chosen the restaurant. For someone who never ate in public, she knew all the coolest spots in town. Clearly, she'd chosen Cicco's because of its seductive ambiance and fabulous view of Lake Michigan.

Jessica had to admit, the fancy restaurant was romantic, with its smooth jazz, twinkling lights, expensive table linens, crystal stemware, and floor-to-ceiling picture windows. Too bad she was the third wheel, turning this Harley into a tricycle. She tugged at the hem of her little black dress, trying to pull it down over her knees. She should have worn one of her great-grandmother's long vintage dresses. At least it would have covered her legs.

Who was she trying to impress anyway? Detective

Cormier? With his amber eyes, smooth brown skin, and muscular build, he was pretty darned attractive. And he was only about five years older than she was. Maybe in his early thirties . . . about the same age as Nick.

She shivered, but not from the chilly breeze coming off Lake Michigan, which she could feel even through the window. Wrapping her beaded black sweater tighter around her torso, she hugged herself and gazed outside into the blackness of endless water. *Why hasn't Nick called me?* Her thoughts were darker than the moonless night. What if Teeth found him before she did? And what about Bratva? He may be testifying against Teeth for money laundering, but he'd also seen Sergei "Sly" Yudkovich stealing paintings and shooting guards. For all she knew, the Russian mafia was after Nick too. She shuddered.

A pointy fingernail poked through the arm of her sweater. The sound of her name made her turn back to the table.

"Right, *milaya*?" Lolita asked, a stern look on her face. "You look a million miles away."

"Sorry." Jessica sat on her hands to keep them warm.

"I was just telling Detective Cormier—"

"Harvey," the detective said with a broad smile.

The vibrations of his deep baritone made Jessica think of a panther. The Poker Tsarina and Detective Cormier: two cats sizing each other up. No man was immune to Lolita's charms. Not even a homicide cop.

When her friend laid it on, the Russian beauty could slay a Siberian tiger with one breathy *"milaya"* whispered close to its ear. And if that didn't work, she could administer a wicked *Kin Geri* . . . kick to the bro-varies.

"—that we might have a lead on where to find Nick." Lolita flashed a fake smile.

"What?" Jessica's hands flew out from under her thighs, and she sat at attention like a cadet at a State Department dinner. "Did I miss something?" *Dang. I should have been paying more attention.* And she'd thought Lolita and Cormier were just playing verbal footsie.

"We've heard a rumor that WITSEC uses a chain of motels in the bay area." Lolita sipped her cosmopolitan and flashed a fake smile.

Jessica squinted at her friend. Was Lolita holding out on her? This is the first she'd heard of motels. "Ouch!" Lolita had kicked her under the table. Now Jessica glared. In addition to ratting her out to the detective, she'd just made a bruise on Jessica's leg. She kicked her friend back. She shouldn't have told Lolita about WITSEC. She'd thought she could trust her. She'd always known Lolita as someone who could keep a secret. But turns out Lolita wasn't trying very hard to keep this one.

"Hollywood Motel is the name." Lolita nodded, gesturing for Jessica to play along.

Did Lolita know something, or was she playing the detective for information? This couldn't possibly be right. She'd just seen Nick the day before yesterday. Unless he and the pretty woman were on their way to the airport and off to live happily ever after in California. Jessica nodded and repeated, "Hollywood Motel in California."

The detective's smile disappeared. "I'm Chicago homicide, not federal." He shook his finger. "Anyway, that information is sealed for a reason." He glared at Jessica. "The whole point of WITSEC is to keep witnesses safe from organized crime." The detective's intense eyes bore into her soul. "I never should have told you. But I felt sorry for you, thinking he was dead. I told you not to tell anyone. I told you it was a matter of life and death." He furrowed his brows. "But it's my fault. I endangered his life . . . not to mention my job." He grunted. "You really need to take this more seriously. Otherwise, Nick Schilling could get hurt or killed. And so could you."

"The engagement ring—"

The detective cut her off. "You've got to stay out of it. You hear? Nothing good will come of you looking for the Professor." He shook his shorn head. "Nothing good. Promise me, for your sake and his, you'll quit trying to find him."

Jessica nodded. "Okay." He was right. She was being stupid and careless even talking about Nick. She had to give up her obsession with that stupid ring. She had to give up Nick and move on. She was straining her friendships and her relationship with Jack, not to mention making herself a nervous wreck. Maybe she should take Amber up on the offer to purge her chakras or whatever.

"See?" Lolita smiled seductively. "Even Harvey doesn't approve of your obsession."

"Since I've known you, you young women have tangled with drug dealers, murderers, and thieves." He stabbed the air. "But you don't want to get mixed up in this."

"You have to admit, every time, we've come out smelling like roses," Lolita said.

"Even roses have thorns." The detective sipped his neat whiskey. "Sheer luck, that's all. And eventually, luck runs out. Even yours."

It was true. Up until now, they had been lucky. Lucky to be alive after all they'd been through. Jessica pulled her sweater tighter around her torso and changed the subject. "Remind me: why are we sitting next to the window at the end of November?"

"It's downright balmy." Lolita peeled off her motorcycle jacket to reveal a slinky red strappy number. "I'm hot. How about you, Harvey?" she purred. "Are you hot?"

The detective's full-toothed smile said it all.

At least the menu had several vegetarian pasta options, which made Jessica happy. She ordered *pesche e rucula*, peaches and arugula, to start and a four-cheese ravioli with pine nuts, butter, and marsala glaze. *Whatever that is.*

Lolita, as usual, ordered the meatiest beast on the menu—in this case, wild boar—which she would move around her plate for the rest of the evening without eating a single bite.

Jessica gaped as the detective ordered his dinner in Italian. *How many languages does he speak?* The man was full of surprises.

Lolita said something in Russian, and the detective laughed.

"*Vous aussi,*" the detective said.

Geez. He speaks French too?

"I like a man with an agile tongue." Lolita turned to Jessica and winked. "Don't you?"

Jessica's cheeks burned. "To be licked by lightning," she said, paraphrasing Nietzsche, "is to be cleansed by madness . . . or shock therapy."

The detective gave her a strange look as if she was speaking in tongues.

"Sorry," she said. "I've been contaminated by too much philosophy."

The waiter delivered the appetizers. Lolita had a glass of prosecco as her appetizer. And the detective had some disgusting thinly sliced raw animal with shaved cheese.

Jessica scarfed down the sweet-and-bitter salad and waited for her friend to make the next move. She'd played poker with her enough times to know Lolita was bluffing. She didn't know Nick's whereabouts. She didn't know Nick had been moved to Hollywood. She was just trying to get information out of Cormier.

Lolita may be a wicked seductress, but she sucked at poker. She wasn't called the "Poker Tsarina" for her poker prowess but for her aptitude for setting up high-stakes games catering to rich men, and fleecing them for big tips. That's how she'd paid her tuition at the posh midwestern university.

When the waiter set the plate of steaming pasta on the table, Jessica's stomach growled, reminding her that she'd been so busy at the Center for Russian Art and Culture she hadn't eaten anything all day except that tiny salad. She politely waited until everyone had their food in front of them and then dug in. Marsala glaze turned out to be a rich, creamy wine sauce. *Heavenly.* She closed her eyes to enjoy the burst of flavors on her tongue. Sometimes she forgot how much she loved eating.

Lolita had once asked her, "Which would you rather have? Good food or good sex?" And she'd answered, "For me, it's not an either-or proposition."

The lively spark in the detective's eyes indicated he thought he might be getting both. Jessica, on the other hand, had better enjoy this meal. 'Cause after that nasty fight with Jack last night over Nick, she surely wasn't getting any tonight.

Jessica felt sorry for the detective. *Little does he know, Lolita's the world's greatest heartbreaker. Funny thing . . .*

they always come back for more. She smiled, watching her friend reel in her prey.

Over dessert, Lolita made her next move. Pushing a piece of tiramisu around her plate with a fork, she nonchalantly dropped a tidbit about Nick being out west. "In my Montana friend's neck of the woods."

Jessica almost choked on a spoonful of *amaretto panna cotta.* She narrowed her eyes. Was her friend bluffing? She looked for the tell. Whenever Lolita bluffed, her cheek muscles flexed into a fake smile. Lolita wasn't smiling.

Had Lolita gotten some information from her mobster cousin Vanya? Then why hadn't she said anything before? Jessica wiped her palms on her napkin.

A gust of wind came through the window seal and blew out the candle centerpiece. Jessica rubbed her thighs. *Is freezing our butts off a test of endurance for these two tough guys?*

"Truly, I don't know anything about the location of witnesses." Detective Cormier stared down at the table. "Is that why you invited me to dinner? To pump me for information?"

"Who, me?" Not one to flinch, Lolita slid into her Harley jacket and zipped it up. "Would I pump you?"

Geez. She's laying it on thick. Do lines like that really work? Maybe if you look like a Russian goddess. Watching her friend flirt was making Jessica lose her appetite—which was saying a lot.

They finished their dessert in silence.

"Would you like to move to the bar and have a nightcap?" the detective asked with a smile. "We could sit by the fireplace."

"You're darn tootin'," Jessica said without missing a beat.

On the way to the bar, Lolita took the detective's arm as if they were sweethearts. Jessica felt like a spare tire as she followed the couple past the long oak bar to the other end of the restaurant.

Her friend and the detective, their heads together, whispering, sauntered to the sitting area in front of the fireplace. Jessica scooted past them and plopped into a sunken leather chair. She rubbed her hands together. *Ahhh. Warmth. Finally.* She waved to the bartender. Too cold for her usual Jack & Coke, she ordered Gentleman Jack straight up.

Given how friendly Lolita and Cormier were getting, she should probably just go home. But she couldn't resist finding out what the Poker Tsarina was up to.

Although the detective certainly had his charms, was Lolita seriously pursuing him? For Lolita, men were like plastic forks . . . disposable. Jessica hated to think where Detective Cormier would end up. Wrapped around her friend's bloodred fingernail, most likely.

They were on their second round and Jessica was finally starting to thaw out when the detective's phone buzzed.

He pulled his phone from his pocket and glanced at it. "I have to take this." He stood up with his back to them. "Cormier." After a second, he said, "What? Why not call WITSEC?"

Jessica strained to hear what he was saying.

"Winnetka? Okay. On my way." He stashed his phone back in his pocket. "Sorry. I've got to go."

"What is it?" Jessica asked. "What happened?"

"A witness was murdered." He sighed.

No. No. No. Her stomach flipped. "Is it Nick?"

"I'm sorry."

Jessica bit her lip. "Sorry you can't tell me, or sorry it's Nick?"

The detective turned to go. "I'm sorry," he repeated. And he was gone.

5

Lexi guzzled her Diet Mountain Dew. The freeway was plowed, and the road was bare. And it was pretty much a straight shot on I-80 from Chicago to Cheyenne. And now that she was out of the snarled city traffic, it should be smooth sailing. As long as the weather held out. At least the snow had stopped for now.

She wished Motormouth would follow suit. The dude was talking nonstop about his stupid art collection, slinging ten-dollar words around like a cook dumping salt into rotten collards to hide their stink. Who was he fooling? Snobby dude talked like his art collection was more important than his life. *Good thing he's easy on the eyes.*

She was tempted to gag him with her Chick-fil-A napkins and stuff him in the trunk. *It's going to be a long drive back to Wyoming.* She glanced over at him. Looking all hip and cool in his black turtleneck and tweed jacket. He was a pretty boy. No doubt about it. The kind that always got her in trouble.

After spending two nights in some run-down motel on the outskirts of Kenosha, she'd finally gotten through the red tape. Following the hit in Chicago on Friday and then the one in Winnetka yesterday, no way the Marshals Service would leave this witness only a few miles away in Kenosha. At least those last two poor slobs hadn't been her guys. Not like Jimmy. She cringed thinking of him tied to that chair, his brains splattered across the wall. What could she have done to prevent it?

Her therapist would say, "Lexi, you did everything you could. You can't save everybody." But it was her job. It was her job to save witnesses. She should have saved her platoon. She should have saved Jimmy. Dammit. She wasn't letting anyone else die on her watch.

Three hours ago, she'd gotten the green light and picked up the witness from his unsafe house in the Kenosha suburbs. Now he was one of hers. And it was up to her to keep him alive.

If he'd only shut up, being his cover wife might not be so bad. She squirmed in her seat, trying not to think about wrapping her legs around his six-pack.

This Nicholas dude was the only big witness left in the case against Teeth Marsiano, one of his daddy's old business partners. She was supposed to protect his cute butt and make sure he lived to testify—after what happened to Jimmy Giordano, she'd better keep him safe.

Weird. She didn't get many "civilians" in WITSEC. Most of the guys she babysat were midlevel lackeys in some crime organization who'd screwed up bad and then wanted the law to protect them. Criminals being housed and fed. Who was she to complain? WITSEC paid her salary and had put away some of the biggest crime bosses in history.

Drake kept her on a need-to-know-basis. So for all she knew, this dude *was* a midlevel lackey—or maybe even some high-level criminal. Sure didn't look like it though. Something about him was just too soft.

She swerved onto I-80. When Mr. Fancy Pants grabbed the chicken handle, she almost laughed out loud. *What a wuss.* Even if he wasn't a criminal, he probably hadn't done an honest day's work in his life.

"Blue is the color of the soul." The dude was going on and on about colors and brushstrokes and shit. "The deeper the blue, the more it awakens the desire for eternity."

She glared at him. "Your blathering is awakening a desire for silence."

"Sorry." He smiled sheepishly. "I guess I'm nervous."

Me too. But I'm not taking a dive off the deep end. "Russian mob and the Italians, eh?" She drained the last of her pop.

"Unfortunately, my late father's connections to organized crime are part of my inheritance."

She had to admit, it took guts to stand up to the mafia. One eye on the road, she reached around and tore another warm pop out of the six-pack. "Want one?" She held up the can.

He wrinkled his nose. "Not unless it's mixed with alcohol."

"Suit yourself." She flipped the tab and inhaled, reassured by the hissing sound of the can opening. She took a sip and grimaced. At first, warm Dew was always a bit rough. "How'd you get into WITSEC?" she asked. She'd read his file, but something didn't add up.

"I was having a martini with my father's widow. Next thing I know, I'm under guard in a hospital bed."

"Must have been some martini."

"Poisoned, as it turns out."

"Your daddy's widow is a mob queen?"

"Chrissy?" He laughed.

"Italian or Russian mob?"

"Chrissy?" he repeated.

For a professor, this guy was kind of dense. "If Chrissy is the one trying to kill you, then yes."

"It's a long story."

"It's a long drive." She glanced at the GPS on the dash. A straight shot on I-80. Google Maps put it at fifteen hours and twenty-four minutes, which meant it was at least eighteen—over twenty-four if they stopped to sleep. That would be interesting. Registering as Mr. and Mrs. Smith in some roadside motel. By the looks of him, she'd be the one sleeping on the floor.

"I collect Russian art, and my dad used my museum to launder mob money."

"So your daddy was connected to the Russian mafia?"

"No." He shook his head. "He used Russian art to launder money for the Italian mafia."

She squinted. *This guy made more sense when he was taking about souls and eternity and other horse manure.* "So the Russians and Italians are working together now?"

"Not exactly. But Dmitry, my associate director, is former Bratva. From long ago, before he left Moscow."

It was beginning to make sense. *Mr. Fancy Pants is testifying against his Bratva associate.* "Why do they call you 'the Professor'? Is 'Professor' your Bratva nickname or something?"

"I'm not a member of Bratva." He chuckled. "I'm an art history professor. And I collect Russian art." He gazed over at her.

Lordy, his eyes are blue.

"I like beautiful things." He smiled. "That's why I collect art."

"What other beautiful things do you collect besides art?"

"Why, Marshal Colt, if I didn't know better, I'd think you were flirting with me."

Good Lord, that dimple in his chin. She squirmed in her seat and took another gulp of warm Dew. "Just making conversation."

"What about you?" He reclined his seat and leaned back. "What do you collect?"

"Lives. New ones. Like yours."

He sat up. "I was quite satisfied with my old life."

"Then you shouldn't have gotten tangled up with the mob . . . Russian or Italian or Polish or whatever."

"You've got it in reverse." He put his hands behind his head and leaned back again. "The mob got tangled up with me. I had no choice—"

"You always have a choice," she snapped. She'd learned that the hard way in the mountains of Afghanistan. A choice to stand up or lie down. Had she made the wrong choice? Her friends had died and she'd lived. She wouldn't let that happen again. Even if her witnesses were spoiled rich boys like this douchebag or criminal scumbags like the rest, no one else would die . . . not on her watch.

"Why did you choose to become a federal marshal? Was your dad a cop?"

"My daddy was a miner. He worked his fingers to the bone and breathed so much flipping clay dust that his lungs collapsed." She glanced over at the smug professor. "But you wouldn't know anything about hard labor, being an art dealer and all."

"Collector, not dealer." He smirked. "You make it sound like I deal heroin on the playground or sell AK-47s to insurgents."

"Well, if you did, you wouldn't be the first dickwad dealer I've had to protect." She drained her pop, crushed the can with one hand, and tossed it in the back.

"You're going to protect me from the dickwads." He flashed a crooked smiled. "But who's going to protect me from you?"

"I'm sure you have a few tricks under your belt."

"Don't you mean up my sleeve?"

"Where you keep your tricks ain't my business as long as you don't pull anything on me."

"You're safe with me." He closed his eyes. "Anyway, I'm pretty sure you can protect yourself."

Pretty Boy slept all the way through Iowa and into Nebraska. Dead fields plowed into spirals, dusted with snow, gave way to barren plains interrupted by monstrous windmills that looked like propellor-headed robots marching in lockstep. The sky turned from an icy blue to an angry orange. A sinister anvil-shaped cloud on the horizon signaled storms ahead. As day succumbed to night, the lack of sleep weighed on Lexi.

She'd driven from Casper to Chicago nonstop to pick up her passenger, without a change of clothes or her toothbrush. Her shirt stuck to her back, and her mouth tasted like cat litter. She needed a shower and a good night's sleep. She glanced over at Nick.

He may not be a criminal. But with that lock of hair falling across his forehead, those lips looking as sweet as wild strawberries, not to mention the way he filled out those jeans, he was capable of stealing something more valuable than her worldly possessions. Just the way he slept—long lashes resting on his cheekbones, lips barely parted, a hint of wrist peeking out from the sleeve of his wool jacket—told her he was trouble. And it had been a long time since she'd been in that kind of trouble.

Just past Omaha, the sky opened up and sheets of water drowned out her headlights. Even 18-wheelers were pulling off onto the shoulder to wait out the storm. White-knuckled, she was determined to keep going. She reached in the back for another Mountain Dew. Adrenaline and caffeine got her as far as Lincoln.

After that, her eyelids were heavy and she was too weary to even take a deep breath. When vibrations from crossing the rumble strip jolted her awake, she knew it was time to find a motel.

"Are we stopping?" Nick asked.

"I need sleep."

"Would you like me to drive?" He stretched his long limbs. "I'm good with geography."

"No one drives this car but me."

"Okay. You're the law. I'm just along for the ride."

She pulled off at the next exit, and after a quick detour to the Arby's drive-through, she followed the signs to a Motel 6 and slid the Charger into a spot near the front door.

Lexi got out of the car, then leaned her head inside. "Wait here. I'll get us a room."

"Us?" He raised one brow.

"I'm not taking my eyes off you."

He grinned. "Fair enough."

LEXI THREW her purse on the bed closest to the bathroom. No overnight bag. No toothbrush. Heck, no hairbrush. After inhaling her curly fries, she collapsed on top of the bed in her clothes.

The bed was too hard. The room was too hot. And it smelled like stale cigarettes. But it was the only room they had with two beds. "I'm going to get some shut-eye, and I suggest you do the same." She glanced over at Nick.

He was sitting on the edge of the other bed, staring at her.

"What?"

"I feel like Clark Gable in *It Happened One Night*." He stood up and yanked the bedspread off his bed. "Maybe I should hang a blanket between our beds."

"Who is Clark Gable?"

"You've never heard of Clark Gable?" His voice was full of excitement. "He played Rhett Butler in *Gone with the Wind*. With that accent of yours, you must know *Gone with the Wind*."

"Frankly, my dear, I don't give a darn." She rolled over and put her arm over her eyes.

"Where are you from, anyway?"

She ignored him.

"Let me guess . . . Alabama."

"Don't insult me." *Alabama. Give me a break.*

"Mississippi?"

She scoffed and pulled at the side of the bedspread and rolled herself up like a taco.

"Arkansas?"

"I may have a *twang* . . ." She stretched the word as far as she could. "But I ain't no hillbilly," she said in her best Deep South accent. "I thought you were good with geography."

"Geography, not accents. Twang, not hillbilly. Got it."

She heard him rustling around but was too tired to care.

"Kentucky."

"My name gave me away." She tugged the pillow out from under the bedspread and stuffed it under her head.

"Lexington, Kentucky."

"Very good, Yank." She could barely get the words out. "Born in Kentucky, raised in Tennessee. Now shut up and let me sleep."

"Sweet dreams, Marshal."

NICK SCHILLING PACED the tiny hotel room. *Am I a prisoner?* The marshal was so dead to the world he could probably slide her car keys out of her purse and take off. But that wasn't his style. Anyway, if the feds were right, his father's former business partner, "Teeth," would find him and kill him without their help. He ran his hand through his hair. *I just want my life back.*

He patted his pocket. He'd carried the jade engagement ring around in his breast pocket for the last six months. Just his luck. The night he'd gotten up the nerve to propose, he was drugged, left for dead, and whisked away to witness protection. Did Jessica even know he was alive? *Dolce, sweet Dolce. What are you doing now?*

Ouch! He'd stubbed his toe on the bed frame. He dropped onto the bed and stretched out. He had to find a way to forget about Jessica and his life as an art professor. He'd been living a double life for so long; how hard could it be? He'd been born into wealth and art and culture—not to mention corruption, tax evasion, and white-collar crime. But he'd left that behind to get a PhD and teach and do what he loved: talk about beautiful things with smart people.

The Center for Russian Art and Culture had been his brainchild, his baby, his dream. He closed his eyes. *What a nightmare!* He was stuck in the middle of nowhere in a shabby motel with a hot hillbilly marshal. *Could be worse.* He smiled to himself. At least the marshal wasn't some thick-necked jock who took pride in his own body odor and made fun of other men's cologne. *Speaking of . . . I wonder if the hot hillbilly would mind if I took a shower.*

He slid off the bed, tiptoed into the bathroom, and

shut the door very slowly. He turned the lock on the doorknob. *Sigh.* Finally. He was alone. Sitting on the edge of the chipped bathtub, he cranked the hot water all the way on, waited for it to get warm, and then adjusted the knob back to cold. Back and forth . . . a little more hot, a little less cold, trying to get the temperature just right. God, he wished he was home in his own walk-in sauna shower that was already adjusted to the perfect temperature. He'd never take a good shower for granted again.

He stripped off his shoes, socks, jacket, shirt, pants, and boxers, folded them and stacked them on the closed toilet lid, and then stepped into the tub. He pulled the shower lever and took a step backward, waiting for the cascade of water. The water pressure wasn't great, but it was good enough. Good enough to wash away his rushed departure from Winnetka and the long drive to this dump. If only he could wash away his memories of Jessica and his dreams of the life they could have had together. He closed his eyes and tilted his face into the stream of hot water. *Ahhh . . .*

A scream jolted him out of his trance. *What the—?* He turned off the water and listened. The marshal was shouting at someone. *Merde.* He tugged on his jeans, reached into the side pocket of his jacket, palmed his P32 pocket pistol, unlocked the door, and flew into the musty room. He jerked his head from side to side, looking for the enemy in the dark.

A ray of light from the bathroom hit the marshal.

She was thrashing around on the bed, fighting with the bedspread. Nick set the gun on the nightstand and sat on the edge of her bed. "Marshal," he whispered.

She yelled something about a land mine.

"Marshal Colt." He put his hand on her shoulder.

She kicked at the blankets wrapped around her feet.

"Lexington." He shook her gently. "Wake up. You're having a nightmare."

She shot up in bed and wailed.

"Lexi, wake up!" He raised his voice and shook her harder.

She whirled around and socked him in the face. He toppled backward, banging into the wall.

"What the—" He held the back of his head. A bitter taste filled his mouth. He wiped his hand across his lip. His hand was wet. Blood. The hot hillbilly marshal had split his lip.

6

———

Monday morning, Jessica arrived at the Center for Russian Art and Culture—Nick's baby—an hour before it opened. She was the only one there. Usually, the dim lights in the temperature-controlled galleries calmed her down. Not today. Everything reminded her of Nick . . . and her desperate need to see him. Today, the sleek steel and glass and wood, all so perfectly clean and new, irritated her. She wanted to rip paintings off the wall and scatter art supplies.

She trotted through the galleries straight back to the classroom. Before she flipped on the lights, the sharp smell of paint greeted her. Kids loved to paint. The education room didn't have any windows, but it was sunny nonetheless. Instead of desks, the room had long tables where the kids could spread out their art projects. Along one side of the room, the wall was a giant corkboard where she displayed the children's paintings. When she was feeling blue, this was her favorite room in the Center.

The Center had opened last spring, two months after she'd been told that Nick had died and right after she'd defended her dissertation. She'd never intended to work there. She'd been planning a career in academia when Nick had waltzed back into her life, said he wanted her back, and offered her a job as assistant director. At first, she'd declined his offer. Eventually, she'd given in and accepted a position as director of education. Unfortunately, that's not all she gave in to.

She channeled her aggravation into setting out paints, brushes, and paper for the kids. They would show up shy and reticent, and leave buoyed up by the power of art. Refugee kids. Art gave them a chance to pour their pain onto the page.

Working with these kids made everything Jessica had put up with at the university, from her snobby professors to the stuck-up Ivy League wannabes, worth it. Hard to believe she'd actually done it. She'd gotten her PhD. She was Doctor Jessica James. She smiled to herself. Success was the best revenge.

Wandering from the education center back into the galleries, Jessica stopped in the Kandinsky room. Standing in front of *Autumn in Murnau*, she thought of Nick. She'd first seen the stunning landscape, with its thick smears of red, green, and blue, in Nick's apartment. That's when she'd realized he came from a world so far from Alpine Vista Trailer Park, where she'd grown up, that he might as well have come from the moon.

She stared at the streaky violet sky and the pastel hint of a village at the bottom of a yellowing meadow. *Where are you Nick? Have you been in Wisconsin all this time?* She hoped to heaven he wasn't the witness murdered in Winnetka on Saturday. *Why haven't you called me? Who is that pretty woman?* Maybe Jack was right. Nick didn't want to be found. Maybe he already had a new life . . . a life too big for her. His life had always been too big for her—maybe he already had a new girlfriend too.

She glanced at her watch. Thirty minutes until the doors opened. Her cowboy boots clicking across the marble floor, she hurried through the galleries, especially her least favorite—the gallery of Soviet art, with its tanks and guns and dead soldiers.

She headed upstairs to her office. The one right next to Nick's old office, now occupied by Lolita's dad, Dmitry Durchenko. He'd taken over as director after Nick died—after they were *told* Nick died. But he wasn't dead.

Unless . . . *I'm sorry*, Detective Cormier had said. So was Nick dead or not?

When she reached her office, she ducked inside, closed the door, and dropped into the chair behind her desk. She pulled her cell phone from her jacket pocket and scrolled through her contacts until she got to *C.* She tapped his number and waited.

"Harvey Cormier." She was about to hang up when his deep voice surprised her.

"It's Jessica James."

"What can I do for you, Miss James?"

"Why did you tell me Nick had an engagement ring in his pocket when you found him if he wasn't really dead and he was heading to WITSEC?"

"Engagement ring? Did I say that?"

"Yes. When you told me you'd found him dead in Chrissy Schilling's hotel room." At that moment, Jessica had thought Nick dropped her for Chrissy. In hindsight, that idea seemed completely absurd, born out of her own insecurity. Still, she couldn't be sure the ring had been for her. Nick had never mentioned marriage or even a permanent relationship.

When it came to men, she didn't know what to believe. She could read dense philosophy books with the best of them, but she never had been good at reading men. Ever since her first love, Michael, cheated on her in college, she'd never completely trust anyone, especially herself. Obviously, she was a crappy judge of character.

"I've already told you more than I should—"

"Was it Nick?"

"What?"

"The witness killed in Winnetka." She held her breath.

"I'm afraid I've already said too much." He sighed. "I'm sorry. I really am. I've got to go. I'm sorry." He hung up.

I'm sorry. That's all she was going to get after he'd told her the man she loved was murdered with an engagement ring in his pocket. And then he'd told her Nick was alive. And now Nick might really be dead. It was all too much. Talk about a rollercoaster of emotions.

She paced around her office. *Click. Click. Click.* The sound of her boots on the floor was reassuring. She was about to open her computer and search the internet to find out more about WITSEC when a shadow darkened the opaque window of her office. She glanced at her watch. *Crapulence.* She was late for the kids art class.

When she opened the door, she recognized Dmitry fiddling with the keys to Nick's—his office. "Hey, Dmitry."

Still holding his keys, he turned to face her. "Good morning, Miss Jessica." He smiled.

Unlike his reed of a daughter, Dmitry was more like a tree trunk. With his wavy hair and deep-set eyes, he reminded her of Omar Sharif in *Dr. Zhivago* . . . which didn't make any sense since Omar Sharif was Egyptian and just played a Russian in the movie.

She took a few steps closer. "Do you know anything about WITSEC?" Given his experience with the Russian mob, he probably had better information than the internet.

His smile faded, and he stood there staring at her.

"You know, the witness protection program?"

"Yes. I know WITSEC." He shook his head. "Only desperate men go into WITSEC."

Ex-Bratva, Dmitry would know. She was afraid to ask. "Why desperate?"

"Desperate to get out." He jammed the key into the lock. "Or desperate to save their necks."

"Does it work?" She bit her lip. "Does WITSEC get them out and save them?"

"No one can hide from their past forever." He opened the door and disappeared inside.

Was Nick hiding from his past? Was she part of that past?

She went through the motions in the kids art therapy class, but her heart wasn't in it. While the kids were painting their dreams from the night before, she checked her phone. She had a text message from Jack. "Lunch?"

"Not today," she texted back.

"I have info," he replied.

She glanced around at the kids and then took her phone into the hallway. She called Jack. No answer. She texted back, "What info?"

"Come to lunch and find out."

"Where?"

He texted back. "Fred's Garage ASAP. Lake Shore a mess. Take Dan Ryan." The Dan Ryan Expressway, what locals called I-94, went north from Chicago to

Milwaukee . . . by way of Winnetka and Kenosha. *Did Jack find Nick?* Or was he just playing with her?

She hurried back into the classroom and clapped her hands. "Okay, that's it for today."

The kids groaned.

"Pick up your paints, wash your brushes, and gather up your stuff." She clapped her hands again. She'd never clapped at the kids before. *Yikes.* Was she turning into her mother?

FRED'S GARAGE WAS A HIP, brightly lit hip service station converted into a restaurant with big glass-paneled garage doors that opened onto a huge outdoor patio. When she thought of food in a garage, the image of her dad hanging a freshly shot deer or elk upside down from the rafters came to mind. He would butcher it himself, and the smell of blood would linger in the garage until the next year's hunting season.

As soon as she stepped inside Fred's, she was hit by a wall of sound. The high ceilings looked cool but made for a terrible echo chamber. She could tell already, there would be nothing on this menu she could eat. Silver lining —the thought of seeing Jack killed her appetite. Only one kiss and the exchange of three little words, two years ago, and it was impossible to go back to being just friends.

She scanned the crowd. Fred's was a popular place.

A hand waved at her from a barstool. She made a beeline for the bar. Even if they didn't have any vegetarian food, they'd have Jack Daniels. As her mom would say, "It's five o'clock somewhere."

"Hey, cowgirl." Jack greeted her with a hug and a kiss on the cheek.

She inhaled the comforting smell of peat and sage. *Good old Jack.*

"You got here quick." Jack gestured to the barstool next to his. "I didn't think your ancient junker would make it this far, let alone go that fast."

"Just because it's the only Chevy Vega left in existence . . ."

"Because most of them died as infants." He sipped his coffee. "Yours should be in the Guinness Book of World Records." Even though he'd quit smoking while in prison, his voice still had a sexy rasp. "That car is older than you."

"It was my mom's. Back then, she was the only woman in Montana who didn't drive a Subaru wagon or a pickup truck."

"And now?"

"Crappy old rat-infested Subaru." Not that she was a big driver. Her mom was probably sitting in the ratty recliner in her trailer back in Whitefish, curtains drawn, chain-smoking, drinking Vodka Collins and watching soap operas.

"When in Rome . . ." Jack handed her a menu.

"Sorry. Probably not a lot of veggie options, but Winnetka isn't known for its progressive politics."

She took the menu. "When in Rome, eat animals?" *Turkey. Chicken. Cow. Salmon. Maybe not. Shrimp?* Even at the bottom of the food chain, she didn't want to risk eating something that could feel pain. She ordered a brownie sundae and a caramel macchiato. Can't go wrong with chocolate, ice cream, and sweet coffee.

Might as well get right to it. "Did you find out something about Nick?" she asked in a whisper. Her face burned. It was weird talking to Jack about Nick. Somehow it felt like a betrayal . . . *But of who?*

"Your lover boy billionaire?" Jack didn't make eye contact.

"He's not my—"

The waitress delivered her brownie sundae: a giant brownie topped with a cookie, toasted marshmallows, and chocolate chip ice cream. She liked chocolate as much as the next girl, but this was overkill.

"Can we not talk about Nick? Maybe at least for five minutes?" Jack played with his coffee cup. "Seriously, cowgirl. I don't think it's good for your mental health." He tipped his empty cup to his lips. "Lolita is right. It's become an obsession with you. An unhealthy obsession." When Jack gazed at her with those magnetic muddy eyes, a shiver ran up her spine. "I invited you up here for lunch to take your mind off . . . all that stuff."

She nodded. What could she say? She didn't appreciate her best friend turning on her like that. She pushed a blob of ice cream around the bowl with her spoon. Maybe it was hormones or that her current boyfriend wouldn't help her find her ex-boyfriend, but she wanted to cry.

It had been two days since Jessica had seen him. It had been Nick. She was sure of it. Maybe her friends were right. Maybe finding him had become an obsession now that she'd seen him. She knew she should forget about him. For his own protection, she should not try to find him. But she felt like she would go mad if she didn't find him. Just to talk to him once more. Just to get some closure. It was selfish. But she couldn't help it.

Where had he been going? And who was he with? Was the pretty woman driving the muscle car his new girlfriend? Her chest tightened. Nausea roiled her gut. She had to forget about him. She wiped her eyes with the backs of her hands.

"Hey." Jack reached over and touched her arm. "It'll be okay."

Forget about Nick. It was never going to work out anyway. He was rich and cultured, and she was a hick from Montana. *But that ring.* Why had Nick been carrying an engagement ring in his pocket the night Detective Cormier found him in the Parker Hotel? Had it been for her? Or someone else?

Sniffle. What did it matter now? Her friends told her to forget about Nick. The detective told her to stay away or someone might get killed. Jack was losing his patience with her, and she didn't blame him. She had to put on her big-girl pants and get on with her life. Instead, she felt like melting into a puddle of tears right there in the middle of Fred's Garage.

"Here." Jack held out a paper napkin. "Wipe your snotty nose."

She took a deep breath and held it. "You said you had info," she said in a small voice.

"Yes, I have info." He sighed and then leaned closer. "Remember I told you about my former client who used to be in WITSEC? He lives up here."

"Okay." She perked up. "Does he know something?"

Jack's pager buzzed. "Shit. I'm on call." He stood up and set his backpack on his chair. "I've got to call in. I'll be right back." He touched her shoulder. "Sorry." He headed outside to make his call.

Jessica wanted to scream. Instead, she snapped the plastic lid off her caramel macchiato and stirred. So much for giving up caffeine . . . and sugar. *Strong and sweet*. An antidote to the bitterness in her soul. She wrapped her fingers around the warm cup. Nick had died and was resurrected. Simply thinking about him hurt. Sitting alone in this noisy hipster garage/restaurant wasn't helping.

Paralyzed in a daze of purposelessness, she just sat there, sipping her coffee and poking at her ice cream, absentmindedly watching the battery of plugged-in hipsters Zooming with friends, swiping right, or laughing at TikTok videos. At once too old and too young for this world, she craved the thickness of flesh, with its pheromones and warmth. Flat screens simply didn't do it for her. But every time she got entangled with other bodies, she got burned.

"The flattening of psychic space," she'd called it in her dissertation. The opposite of the thick, juicy brush-strokes in paintings by Kandinsky or Picasso or Varo. Their work had a substance that couldn't be contained by any frame, with the paint practically alive, trying to escape from the world of representation into the world of beings. Nick would understand. He might be the only one who could.

That's why she had to find him . . . even if the ring was for someone else. She had to find a way to find him without tipping off the mob. If she could find him, then so could they. *Crapulence.* She wished he'd just call her.

Her phone vibrated in her jacket pocket. Her heart leapt into her throat. She pulled her phone out.

"I'm really sorry," Jack said. "I've just got to go check on a patient. It shouldn't take long. Can you wait for me? I do have something to tell you. I promise. Just wait. Okay." He was speed talking.

"Okay." She stabbed the ice cream with her spoon.

He hung up.

Great. Now she had no choice but to stay here alone, on the edge of tears. Her nostrils stung from the stench of burnt coffee. The smell would hang on her clothes for the rest of the day. Worse, her depressive funk would hang on her soul until she found Nick.

No one could understand what it was like—losing

someone, then finding out they were alive but not being able to see them or talk to them . . . and then seeing them again. Her friends didn't get it. They didn't know how she felt. No one did. She really didn't have anyone to talk to. Her best friend had called her "obsessed." Her current boyfriend agreed. Anyway, how could she explain her feelings to Jack? She couldn't even explain them to herself.

She closed her eyes and thought of Nick in that blue Charger with that pretty woman driving. The Charger had pulled out ahead. She'd tried to see the license plate. It was a Wyoming plate. She'd recognized the bucking bronco. But Wyoming was a big state . . . a big state with not many people. Was the driver from Wyoming? Was she taking Nick back with her? That made sense, actually. If a witness had been murdered in Winnetka and Nick was hiding just north of there, the feds would have to move him. Right? Maybe he and his girlfriend were leaving town. Going back west. Out to Wyoming. No one would find him there.

She googled "Wyoming license plate numbers." The first number on Wyoming license plates indicated the county. Same as in Montana.

On road trips with her dad when she was a kid, they used to play a game naming counties by license plates. She still knew by heart all the county codes for Montana. Lucky seven was the code for Flathead County, where she grew up.

She'd been in such shock when the Charger pulled

up to the light and she saw him sitting there . . . She'd seen the Wyoming plate but couldn't remember the numbers. She racked her brain. *What was the plate number?* Even the first number could tell her a lot.

A couple of times, her dad had taken her on horseback riding trips in the Tetons. She'd learned some of the Wyoming county codes back then. Teton was twenty-two. She remembered that one. *What was the first number on that plate? Think. Jessica. Think.*

First. Yes! It was number one. *The number one.* She'd seen the plate, and it started with one. Her heart sped up. She googled the counties in Wyoming to see which started with the number one. *Got it.* Natrona, county seat Casper. *Okay.* So, the pretty woman was driving a car from Casper, or someplace around there. *Is that where she lives?* Was it a rental? Did she live here but hadn't changed her plates yet? Casper, Wyoming. She tried to remember if she'd ever been there as a kid.

She sensed his arrival before she saw him. The door swung open, heads turned, and Jack stepped inside. Certain people had a head-turning intensity that went beyond their looks or clothes or hair. In fact, based on his scruffy good looks, wrinkled corduroy jacket, and unkempt hair, Jack looked more like a down-on-his-luck med school dropout than a board-certified criminal psychiatrist. In Jack's case, best not judge a book by its cover.

She'd known him for five years, been his girlfriend for five months, and still didn't really know him. Did you ever really know another person? It was hard enough figuring out yourself.

Jack made a beeline to the table. "Hey, cowgirl." He was breathless. "Sorry that took so long. But wait until you hear what I found out."

"What?"

"Let me get another coffee first." He pointed to the cup that had been sitting on the table, waiting for him for the last hour. "This one's cold."

"I'm dying here . . ." *What does he know?* "I've been waiting—"

Jack just grinned and took off. He stood at the back of the coffee line, moving from foot to foot like he had to pee. Watching him made her more nervous. She broke her stir stick in half, then in half again, and kept breaking it until there was a little pile of wood in front of her on the table. *Hurry up, dang it.*

A few minutes later, the barista called out, "Wolfgang."

She could always count on Jack to be a smart-ass.

Jack picked up two large cups and weaved his way through the tables to the corner, where she was bursting at the seams.

"Wolfgang?" She rolled her eyes.

"I considered Nietzsche, but I didn't want to torture the poor barista."

"So?"

Jack handed her a cup. He'd gotten her another macchiato with extra whipped cream and one for himself too. "So." He moved his backpack off the chair and sat down. "Remember my former patient up in Winnetka?"

"The one in WITSEC?" she mouthed.

He nodded and took a long sip of his macchiato.

"Don't keep me in suspense," she whispered.

He leaned back in his chair. He was loving this.

"Tell me," she raised her voice. *Arrr*. She wanted to slap the coffee cup out of his hand.

He took another sip of coffee. "I don't know how you drink this sweet shit." He wrinkled his nose. "Might as well snort sugar packets."

She ignored his complaints. "Well?" She threw her hands up.

A conspiratorial look on his face, he leaned forward and whispered, "Three years ago, when he was in WITSEC, my former patient got a visit from a federal marshal. A very pretty one, apparently. The Eva Mendes of federal marshals." He took the lid off his cup. "This is undrinkable. Don't go anywhere. I'll be right back."

Sometimes Jack was so annoying. *Hurry up, man.* Her knee was bouncing up and down so fast she thought she might fly out of her seat.

He returned with four packets of sugar, tore them open all at once, dumped them into his cup, and stirred . . . and stirred . . . and stirred.

"I thought you said it was too sweet?"

"Fight fire with fire." He shrugged.

"So this beautiful marshal?" She wanted to reach across the table and rip the information out of him.

"Guess what kind of car she drove." He raised his eyebrows.

"A blue Dodge Charger?"

"Bingo." He leaned back until the front legs of his chair came up off the floor.

"The gorgeous woman is a federal marshal," she said, more to herself than to him. *So she's not Nick's girlfriend.* "Do you know where she took him?"

"How would I know?" He let the chair drop with a thud. "It was unethical to call my former patient and pump him for information. I only did it because I love you and I want—"

"I know." She held her hand out across the table. "I'm sorry."

He took another drink and made a sour face. "My hypothesis is the Eva Mendes of federal marshals is assigned to your dickhead lover. Question is, did Eva Mendes take lover boy back to Wyoming or drop him off someplace else?"

"He could be anywhere between Chicago and Cheyenne." She bit her lip, picked up her phone from the table, and started tapping. "There are federal courts in three cities: Cheyenne, Casper, and Mammoth." *But what about federal offices? Casper, Jackson, Lander, Mammoth, and District Headquarters in Cheyenne.* "Siri what's the distance between Cheyenne and Casper?"

Waiting. Waiting. Waiting. "178.2 miles or two and a half hours driving."

"If I were a betting man—"

"Which you are . . ."

"I'd say your boy is in Wyoming."

"There's only one way to find out."

"Have Amber hack into the WITSEC website again?" He smiled.

"Go to Wyoming and look for him." She downed the rest of her coffee and slammed the cup on the table. "I'm going."

"Where?"

"To Wyoming."

"You're just going to go wander around the entire state of Wyoming?"

"I'm betting Marshal Mendes is from Casper."

"How do you know?"

"The license plate. It starts with 'one' for Natrona County. County seat, Casper." She poked the air with her finger. "In fact, Casper is really the only city in Natrona County."

"She can't be the only federal marshal that drives a blue Charger."

"How many federal marshals look like Eva Mendes?"

"What about work?"

"I'll take time off." She wasn't going to let Jack talk her out of it.

"How will you get there? Your crappy Chevy won't make it across town, let alone across the country."

He had a point. Her car was notoriously unreliable.

"I'll fly. Maybe rent a car."

"I thought you were broke."

"I am. Flat broke. Since Nick left, the Center is running on empty. I'm working for free until we can raise some money." She slouched back into her chair. *Dang. How am I going to get to Wyoming?*

She could always ask Lolita to take her to a poker game. Her stomach flipped at the thought. She was good at poker, but she hated playing. Too nerve-racking. And what if she lost? Then again, what choice did she have? Her mom was broke too. Anyway, she didn't want to borrow money from her mom. That would be admitting defeat. She blew at her bangs. "I'll hitchhike."

"No you won't." He reached across the table and grabbed her hand. "Do you know how many deranged men out there would like to assault a lovely lady like you?" He shook his head. "Unfortunately, I do. I treat them in the prison every day."

She pulled her hand away. "I don't have any other choice—"

"You always have a choice. Even deciding not to choose is a choice."

"I won't have any closure until I see Nick." Her lip trembled. "I can't get over him without . . ." She put her head in her hands. She had to find a way to get him out of her mind. If only she could talk to him . . .

Jack laid his head on the table and looked up into her face. "It will be okay." He sat up. "I know I'll regret this." He pulled his wallet out of his back pocket and opened it. "Here. Use this to buy a plane ticket and get a hotel or whatever." He slid a credit card across the table. "I'm gainfully employed. You aren't. I'll loan you the money until you get paid."

She lifted her head. "Really? You'll loan me the money?" Sometimes Jack was the best. She did a happy dance in her chair.

"Yup." He snapped his wallet shut. "On one condition."

She knew it was too good to be true.

Like a basketball player trying a three-point shot from across the court, Jack aimed for the trash can and tossed his cup. "I'm coming with you."

7

How *ow in Hades did I end up here?* A hunting lodge in the Wyoming mountains was about as far from Nick's former life as you could get. He paced the length of the barn. Again. He couldn't believe he'd only been here a week. It felt like a lifetime.

He stopped at one end of the barn and gazed out the barn door, across the snow-covered field at the mountains in the distance. He had to admit, the natural beauty of this place rivaled even Constable's romantic landscapes.

When he inhaled, the frosty air stung his throat. He pulled the borrowed sheepskin coat up around his neck and buttoned the top button. He'd take a city block over an expansive meadow any day. He shivered from his head down to his toes. The wide open spaces made him feel exposed and vulnerable.

Still, there was something about the light on the

high plains. The colors were more vivid. Crisp, even. He could understand why artists like Georgia O'Keeffe moved to Santa Fe for the light. The contrast between the deep blue of the sky, the sparkling white of the meadow, and the dusty violet of the mountains had an intensity verging on violence.

One bright, billowy cloud danced on the horizon. The only time he'd seen a cloud shaped like that in New York or Chicago, it was angry and gray.

But Ford's Cutthroat Lodge was a far cry from downtown Chicago. *What kind of name is 'Cutthroat'?* He'd been told it was a type of trout found in streams in the West. A trout with what looked like a bloody gash on its gills. Why would nature paint a target on a poor little fish?

When he was a boy, his father would say, "If you can't compete with the big fish, it's better to choose a small pond." His father had never appreciated his choices. From getting a doctorate in art history to becoming a lowly professor, his father had made it clear he didn't approve.

Nick headed back inside, picked up a pitchfork, levered it into a giant bale of hay, and lifted. How could dried grass be so heavy? He pitched the hay into the stall with the black gelding nursing a cut leg. Well, he tried to pitch it into the stall. Most of it landed on the dirt floor in front of the stall. He bent down, raked it up with his hands, and threw it at the horse. The black beauty shook his head around, creating a cloud of hay.

There was no doubt about it: Nick was not cut out to be a cowboy. *Brrr.* He rubbed his hands together. Blisters were forming on his palms, and he had a splinter in the pad of his index finger. *Hot Marshal Colt better get her fine ass back here and spring me from this dirty, stinking redneck paradise.* Either that, or he'd better get some work gloves. He refused to join in the hunting. So he was supposed to be here on vacation to get the "real ranch hand" kind of experience for fun. Yeah. Hard to believe people actually played ranch hand for fun. *Ranch hand, my ass. More like ranch pinkie finger.*

He decided to call it a day and head back to the lodge bunkhouse before he got frostbite. The snow-capped mountains in the background and the sprawling lodge in the foreground put him in mind of the romantic landscape paintings of Albert Bierstadt.

Twenty years ago, Ford's hunting lodge must have looked like something out of *Outdoor Life* magazine, what with its wraparound porch, once polished logs, and massive wooden beams. It was the kind of place his father had booked, along with hunting guides, to kill the local animals for trophies. The kind of place his father thought would make a man out of his son.

Nick's stomach churned just thinking about those hunting trips. The first time his father made him shoot a deer, his hands were shaking so bad he had to take five shots to put it down. He was sixteen. When he looked down at the dying animal, he promptly threw up. Eventually, his father gave up on making a man out of him.

Crunching through the snow in his Santoni ankle boots, he thought of all those spring vacations when his father took him skiing in Switzerland. One trip in particular came to mind: the time his father left him on the mountain because he couldn't keep up. Only thirteen and he had to hitch a ride back to the hotel.

He stepped in another man's tracks—someone with bigger boots than his—trying not to get snow in his Santonis, which were probably ruined by now anyway. Time to go shopping. Work gloves and proper snow boots. *Sigh.*

As he approached the bunkhouse, his new friend, Danny "Tiny" Quarrels, waved to him from the front porch. Tiny Quarrels had arrived two days after Nick. Tiny had a Long Island accent so thick you could spread it on toast. Nick wondered if that was his real name or if he was in witness protection too. Obviously, 'Tiny' was a nickname—the kind meant as a joke, given the guy was as big as a bull.

At least WITSEC had let Nick keep his first name. Now he was Nick Simmons. They'd said keeping the same initials made it easier. "A rose by any other name..."

The lovestruck tragedy of *Romeo and Juliet* wasn't the only Shakespeare apropos of his situation. *Julius Caesar* came to mind: "The evil men do lives on. The good is interred with their bones." He thought of his father.

There must be some good buried with him in that Brooklyn cemetery.

"Hey, man," Quarrels said. "You really need to get a hat and gloves and shit. It's so cold out I'm farting snowflakes."

He smiled. For a guy from Chicago, Nick should have been better prepared for the brutality of winter. But he hadn't exactly been allowed to pack for this trip. Now, how to explain that without blowing his cover? He'd rehearsed his new backstory with the marshal back in Chicago, but it still didn't come easy. Turns out, lying wasn't his forte.

"In Tarpon Springs, Florida, not much call for wool and sheepskin." His cover story was that he was on vacation in Wyoming while scouting for Western art for a small gallery back home in Tarpon Springs. The Marshals Service figured he couldn't hide his education or his interest in art no matter how hard he tried. It was in his blood. He pulled at the oversized coat. "Thanks for this, by the way."

"Sure, man. Don't want you to freeze your balls off." Tiny yanked his thumb back like a hitchhiker. "Come on in to lunch. One thing's for sure: chow's pretty good around here."

"Indeed." It was true. Nick had never eaten such wholesome and hearty food in his life. The cooks he'd grown up with prepared the Continental cuisine favored by his father. After a day's work on the ranch, a cheeseburger tasted like *boeuf bourguignon*. Out here, the phrase "I'm so hungry I could eat a horse" wasn't just hyperbole. *No offense, Black Beauty.*

"Venison chili and biscuits," Tiny said, leading the way inside. "I never ate deer before."

"Me neither." Nick smiled. His father had killed plenty of deer, but Nick had never eaten them. Haunted by the memories of the one and only he'd killed, Nick never ordered venison—not even at The Musket Room in SoHo, and they supposedly had the best wild meat in Manhattan.

In the foyer, Nick sat on a bench and removed his ruined boots. He peeled off his wet socks and rubbed his frozen toes. Maybe he should take his chances with the mob. His chances of survival might be higher than at this godforsaken ranch.

"Dude, your toes are purple." Tiny laughed. "You really are a city slicker." He pointed. "Get frostbite and you could lose your toes. I knew a guy once lost both little toes to frostbite. You don't know how important a little toe can be until you lose one . . . or two."

"Noted." Nick resigned himself to tiptoeing barefoot to his room. "See you in the dining hall. I'm going to get some dry socks."

"Okay, man." Tiny nodded. "I'll save you a seat." He lumbered off toward the dining hall.

~

WITH DRY SOCKS AND SHOES, Nick descended the

wooden stairs, stopping on the landing to admire the view. The lodge had high ceilings and crisscrossing wood like a rollercoaster's scaffolding. A three-story stone fireplace—the centerpiece of the lobby—strained to warm the cavernous space. Decades worth of woodsmoke was baked into the log walls and floor planks, which made the whole place smell of damp soot.

Bunkhouse Lodge might as well be in another universe from his gold coast penthouse. What had the feds done with his condo? Was some marshal living there? Cleaning out his wine cellar and smoking his imported cigars? Would he ever get to go home?

His stomach growled. Maybe he'd feel better after a hearty lunch. He took the stairs two at a time and headed around the corner into the dining room. Tiny waved from the end of a long plank table. The heavenly scent of fresh-baked biscuits encouraged him to pick up his pace.

No sooner had he sat down than a waiter—who looked more like a lumberjack in an apron—delivered a steaming bowl of chili and a basket of warm biscuits. The morning's work and fresh air had given him a hearty appetite. He dug in while Tiny kept up both ends of the conversation just fine. If Tiny was a witness, he had his backstory down pat. He said he was a real estate speculator who'd moved from New Jersey to Wyoming to get in on the fracking boom. He had already bought several properties in western Wyoming and was looking to expand into the eastern part of the state.

"I love it out here," Tiny said, his mouth full of biscuit. "I don't think I'll ever go back. How about you? Who needs the big city when you can have all this fresh air and space. Am I right?"

Nick stopped mid-bite. He hadn't told Tiny he was from a big city. In fact, he'd tried to avoid talking about his past life for fear he'd screw up and tell the truth. Tarpon Springs, Florida. That was his story. He was sure that's what he'd told Tiny. Then again, his nerves were shot. Constantly looking over his shoulder was exhausting. He wiped his mouth on a napkin. "Considering it." As if he had a choice.

"There's a lot of money in fracking." Tiny's craggy face broke into a smile. "Black gold. You should get in on it, man."

Nick bristled. Living undercover as a fake ranch hand was one thing. No way he was going to rape the earth and exploit the locals just to make more money. "Maybe I will." *Not.*

The lumberjack waiter reappeared wheeling a cart. "Fresh apple pie with homemade vanilla ice cream. Who wants some?"

To a man, everyone raised his hand . . . and so did the teenage girl with the pink rifle, who was hunting with her father, along with the three women hunters who were obviously bucking tradition in their matching camouflage. Only one person in the dining hall refused pie: a lone woman sitting in a corner, watching the rest like an eagle perched in a treetop.

"This pie is awesome." Tiny smacked his lips.

He was right. Warm apple pie with homemade ice cream. Pretty darn good. Better than any of those fancy desserts his father's private chefs used to conjure up, with their swirls of raspberry glacé or burnt-sugar figurines.

"I just might move in here for good." Tiny scraped the last crumbs of pie and drips of ice cream from his plate. In his tight gray suit, Tiny didn't look like a hunter ... except maybe a fortune hunter.

"Are you a hunter?" Nick asked, savoring the aftertaste of cinnamon.

"In a manner of speaking." Tiny licked his spoon. "This is the land of opportunity if you know where to look." He took another swipe at his plate. "And I know where to look." He licked his spoon again, glanced at his watch, and then stood up. "Excuse me. I've got to make a call."

DANNY QUARRELS SQUEEZED into the phone booth at the end of the hall. *Damn boonies.* No cell service. Even the disposable cell he'd bought locally didn't work. He hadn't used a pay phone in ages. Lifting the receiver, he wondered, *What next?* He patted his pockets for change. Was he going to have to go ask the owner for quarters?

Who had calling cards anymore? He tapped his cell phone to find the number. He'd have to call collect and reverse the charges. No problem. He knew the boss wanted whatever information he got, which wasn't much.

Patience. It would take time. And he had all the time in the world. Especially if it meant hanging out at this lodge, eating pie. Hell, it was practically a vacation.

"Hey, boss." The line clicked, and the familiar voice came on the other end. "Just checking in."

"What have you got?"

"Not much, I'm afraid." He opened his palms as if the boss could see him crammed into the phone booth. "Dude's tight-lipped . . . and scared."

His boss laughed. "Damn right he's scared."

"Want me to pull the trigger?" Danny asked. Usually he'd be itching to get it over with and get on to the next job. But this was a pretty sweet gig. "Or should I wait, see if I can get anything out of him?" He tried to turn around, but the phone booth was too damned tight. *There once was a lady from Wainwright . . . whose Tutu was twisted and too tight . . .*

"Wait until I give you the word, and then let him have it."

Danny freed his wrist from the phone cord. "Okay, Teeth. You're the boss."

Click. Nothing but dial tone.

8

Pacing around her efficiency apartment was no easy feat with all of the books and clothes piled everywhere. She really should straighten the place up before going on a road trip. She did throw out some moldy cheese from her mini-refrigerator. One advantage of not keeping much food on hand was she didn't have to worry about coming back to a stinky fridge full of furry green leftovers.

Jessica's one-room digs had become her cozy little nest. Lolita called it the "Eighth Wonder of the World" because it was a miracle Jessica could find anything in the "horrid mess." *Lolita. What's up with her anyway?* Her best friend had read her the riot act about going after Nick. She'd been kind of mean, even. Calling the trip a "narcissistic joyride" just to find out if some *"billionaire playboy"* had meant to propose or not. Usually, Jessica's best friend would be the first one in line for a big adventure. But this time, Lolita made her disapproval painfully clear.

Jessica chewed on her already jagged fingernail. *Why did Lolita hate Nick so much? Was she jealous?* Lolita wasn't the jealous type. Anyway, she usually took whatever she wanted.

Jessica walked back and forth across the length of her kitchenette, which was about five steps. Every few minutes, she stopped and peered out the little window over the sink at the street below.

From her ninth-floor apartment, she had a good view into the front courtyard and out to the curb. Where was he? She pulled her phone from the pocket of her fringe jacket and tapped it: 9:37. It wasn't like Jack to be seven minutes late. Maybe he'd changed his mind. She wouldn't blame him. It did seem kinda weird asking one boyfriend to help her find the other.

She shook her head. Neither one of them was really a serious boyfriend. Last spring, Nick had just sauntered back into her life and right back out again a week later. And about the time Nick had disappeared—presumed dead—Jack had gotten out of prison. *Crapulence.* She'd been living like a nun for two years. And then Nick comes back into her life. And then Jack. No, neither one of them was a serious boyfriend.

Maybe if she hadn't seen Nick in that blue Charger with that pretty woman . . . That was over a week ago now. A week from last Friday. But she couldn't get the image out of her head.

A high-pitched honk got her attention. Was that Jack in the green sports car? Where'd he get that? She stuffed her phone into her pocket, grabbed her keys, slouched into her ski jacket, and then slung her stuffed duffel bag over her shoulder. Who knew how long she'd be gone? She wasn't coming back until she found Nick . . . and found out if that engagement ring was for her.

She switched off the lights, glancing around the tiny apartment to see if she'd forgotten anything—not counting making her bed, which she never did anyway. Since it's a futon on the floor, it didn't really count. *Goodbye, little nest.* She shut the door, locked it, and galloped down the stairs. The elevator hadn't worked for months now. Anyway, she could use the exercise.

Jack was waiting with the trunk open. He looked cool with his aviator sunglasses and puffy bomber jacket.

"New car?" Jessica threw her duffel bag into the trunk of the sports car.

"New to me." Jack slammed the trunk shut. "Actually, I rented it for the trip. Cool, huh?"

"Nice ride." She admired the two-seater convertible. "What is it?" She hopped into the passenger seat.

"Classic MG, the best of British design." He settled into the driver's seat and caressed the steering wheel.

"Figures."

Since spending that year at Oxford, Jack loved everything British. Even after two years in prison, he still talked with a hint of a British accent . . . a fake British accent.

"Is this why we're not flying?" She fiddled with the buttons on the console. "You wanted to speed across the country in a sports car?"

"I've got to *try* to compete with your billionaire beau." Jack forced a smile.

"I didn't mean it like that." She blew at her bangs.

"Unlike some people . . ." He revved the engine and pulled away from the curb. ". . . I'm gainfully employed, but I don't have a rich daddy. Instead, I have a buttload of student loans."

ONCE THEY GOT out of the Chicago traffic, it was easy-going on the interstate. Jack cranked up the tunes, and she was enjoying the ride. If only it wasn't so dang cold, they could put the top down and really cruise.

After three and a half hours in the cramped road-ster, she was ready to stretch her legs. Anyway, her growling stomach said it was lunchtime. "Next exit, downtown Iowa City."

"Yup." Jack turned to her and smiled. "I know just the place. The Hamburg Inn."

"German food?" She wrinkled her nose at the thought of brats and sauerkraut.

"Nope." He grinned. "World-famous pie shakes."

"Pie shakes?"

"You'll see." He swerved onto the exit ramp.

Iowa City was a cute university town. And in its heart stood Hamburg Inn, with its aging black-and-gold awning and lineup of newspaper boxes out front.

Inside, it was as all-American as an apple pie shake, with American flags and pictures of presidents hanging from the wainscoting. The crowded diner sported black pleather booths, thick aluminum-legged chairs, and dark wood-grain Formica counters. Lots of vegetarian options if you liked deep-fried stuff or Carb City. Why eat fries or mac 'n' cheese when you could have the famous pie shake?

Jessica decided to double-dip and order pie for lunch and a pie shake to go with it. Cherry pie and a chocolate bourbon pecan pie shake.

Jack ordered a burger, fries, and a chocolate shake.

"How'd you know about this place?" Jessica asked, eager to taste a milkshake made out of pie and ice cream.

"When I got tired of reading, I watched a lot of TV in prison." Jack opened his expressive hands. "Greta Thunberg stopped here on her US tour."

"Greta Thunberg the Swedish climate activist?" Jessica narrowed her brows. "She ate here?" *Did they have any vegan pie shakes?*

"I don't know where she ate. But she spoke on the U of I campus."

The waitress delivered their lunch. A slice of pie

and shake for Jessica and a mound of ground cow between mammoth buns for Jack.

"Greta Thunberg went on a hunger strike until her parents became vegans." Jessica filled her fork with cherry pie and popped it into her mouth. *Yummy.* She washed it down with chocolate milkshake. The effect was bourbon-soaked chocolate-covered cherries with ice cream on top. *Delicious.*

"Another reason I don't want kids," Jack said with his mouth full of burger.

"So you won't have to give up eating animals?"

"So I won't have to give up anything."

"My grandpa says if I meet the right man, I'll want to get married and have kids." She scooped up another big forkful of pie. "But I can barely take care of myself." She set the fork back on the plate. "I don't know how I could take care of a kid." She wondered. Was Nick the right man? Did she want to marry Nick and have a family? She didn't know if it was the thought of having kids or the double helping of pie and ice cream, but her stomach didn't feel so good.

"Not having kids is the best way to cut down on your carbon footprint." Jack wagged his head back and forth as he chewed, like he was eating to some music inside his head. "All those generations of unborn polluters."

He waved a fry around in a puddle of ketchup. "Anyway, why is our obligation to the future any greater than our obligation to the past? The past is just as vulnerable to our actions as the future. Maybe more so."

"So you're a philosopher now." She laughed.

"An amateur." He grinned. "Not a professional like you."

She scraped the last of the pie off her plate and then licked her fork. At least if she had a bellyache, it would be for a good reason.

Jack waved a spoon in the air. "Human exceptionalism is the root of all evil."

"I thought that was money." Jessica vacuumed up the rest of her milkshake with her straw. "Money is the root of all evil."

"You only say that because you don't have any." He chuckled as he pulled his wallet from his pants pocket. "I guess lunch is on me."

Within an hour back on the highway, the sugar high wore off and Jessica crashed hard. It didn't help that the scenery was one brown field of dead nothingness after another. Wadding her jacket into a pillow and stuffing it under her head, she leaned against the doorframe and dozed off.

When she woke up, it was twilight. Jack had been driving for four hours straight. Had she been asleep that long? "I can drive if you want."

"I could use a break."

Jack pulled off at the next rest stop. She stretched her legs and used the facilities and took over driving.

Three hours later, it was pitch black and sleep was tugging at her eyes. She exited onto an access road for a nap. Jack was sound asleep. He could sleep through a train wreck.

She didn't know how long she'd been asleep when a kiss on the cheek woke her.

"Let's trade places," Jack said. "I can take over now. Unless you want to cuddle up."

"What time is it?"

Jack tapped his phone and it lit up. "Almost eleven."

"We should be to the border in a couple hours."

When Jack opened the passenger door, a blast of cold air hit her full-on. She shivered.

He walked to the front of the car and took a pee. She dreaded the cold air on her undercarriage but had no choice. She couldn't hold it for another two hours.

As soon as they were back on the highway, she conked out.

What the heck? She jolted awake. *No wonder.* Jack had pulled off the interstate, and the car's tight suspension was bumping over a cattle guard. The steel slats, spaced far enough apart that a cow wouldn't dare step onto it, reminded her of home.

"Where are we?" Must be getting close to Wyoming. The endless cornfields of Iowa and Nebraska didn't require cattle guards. "What time is it?"

It was still pitch black. But the stars. . . Holy crap. So many stars. She'd forgotten what it was like to see the Milky Way and thousands of dots of light in a black sky.

"I have to take a piss." Jack didn't sound happy. He didn't look happy either. Even his five o'clock shadow looked tired. He pulled over onto a side road and skidded to a stop.

"What about me?" she asked.

"What about you?" He opened his door and hopped out. "You're the one raised by wolves in the mountains of Montana. I'm sure you'll figure it out." He slammed the door, stomped a few steps away from the car, and stood with his back to her, legs apart. The classic "man peeing" stance.

She stretched and then crossed the gravel shoulder and wandered into the trees. Evergreens. They must be close. She could tell by the dryness of the air and the smell of the pine forest. The West. The mountains. Home. She was getting closer. Her mom would kill her if she knew she was this close and didn't visit, especially for the holidays. *What Mom doesn't know won't hurt her.* Somehow her mom always had a way of finding out.

Jack was leaning against the car, smoking a cigarette. "Now what?" He dropped the smoke and ground out the butt under his desert boot.

She shrugged. "We drive to Wyoming?"

"Then what?" He raised his eyebrows. "We go door-to-door until we find lover boy?"

Geez. He was grumpy.

"It's flipping freezing out here." Jack jogged around to the passenger side and opened the door. "I'm taking a nap. Wake me up when you have a plan." He slipped into the passenger seat, shut the door, and leaned his head on the window.

She trotted around to the other side of the car and jumped in the driver's seat. She wriggled out of her jacket and held it out to Jack as a peace offering. "Here. Use this as a pillow. It's not that soft, but it's better than the glass."

Without opening his eyes, he grabbed it and stuffed it under his head.

The reek of cigarette engulfed the tiny car. She frowned. Her mom smoked like a chimney, and Jessica had always hated the acrid smell of cigarette smoke, especially when trapped inside a car. As a kid, her mom's nasty smoke had always made her motion sick. "I thought you gave up smoking."

He didn't answer. Either he was already asleep, or he wasn't speaking to her.

Her plan? Her plan was to find coffee and then wait for Amber to get up and answer her phone and tell her what she'd found out.

A box of fancy chocolates had persuaded Amber to help. Amber had said, "Hacking the feds is not as easy as hacking the university or an email account," as she'd flipped the end of a snaky lock into her mouth. But if she was as good a hacker as everyone said, then she'd have figured out how to hack into WITSEC by now.

Where the heck were they? "Siri," she spoke into her phone. "Coffee near me." Kimball, Nebraska. Wherever that was.

Cruising along, humming to herself, she kept the speed just five miles an hour above the limit. After twenty minutes, Siri guided her off the interstate onto a side road. *That's it?* Up ahead, a boxy little motel with a sign for "Twenty-Four Hour Last Stop Coffee" reminded her of the Bates Motel from *Psycho*. Creepy. She coasted into a parking spot near the front of the deserted gravel lot.

"Rise and shine." She shook Jack's shoulder. "Coffee time."

"How long have I been asleep?"

"About five hours," she fibbed. "Do you feel better now?"

"Then why is it still dark out?" He stretched and then tossed her jacket to her. "I feel like breakfast."

"You look like breakfast. Scrambled eggs, to be exact."

"Thanks, cowgirl. You look fresh as a lettuce, as always."

"Do you think Amber will still be up?" she asked. "It's an hour later there."

"What time is it?"

She checked her phone. "One thirty."

"What day is it?"

"Wednesday. Why?"

"Amber opens Happy Hair on Wednesdays. She's there by six."

Happy Hair was the salon where Amber worked part-time to make extra money. Even though by some miracle she'd had a part-time job at the University development office and was qualified for high-tech jobs, she preferred shampoo sets and foil highlights.

"I'll try her after breakfast."

Last Stop Coffee Shop was a clapboard diner so isolated that it made her feel like it wasn't just the last stop but the last place on earth. In spite of the fact that it was freezing outside, her palms were sweating as she grabbed the cold metal door knob. When she opened it, the door creaked on its rusty hinges. She stepped onto the cracked linoleum tile floor and into the harsh fluorescent lights of the diner. Jack followed behind her, his hands on her back as if using her as a human shield.

The diner was deserted except for a cat sleeping next to a woodstove.

"Hello?" she said into the void.

"Be right there," a woman's voice answered. "Take a seat anyplace."

Jessica slid onto a barstool at the counter. The stool's plastic upholstery had a hole it in, and white stuffing was poking out. Jack took a seat next to her.

A matronly woman with a wandering eye appeared from the back, a glass coffee pot in one hand and two cups dangling from the fingers on the other. "Coffee? It's fresh."

"Yes, please." *Ahhh.* It felt good to be out of that little sardine can. Jessica stretched her legs, then her neck.

After they ordered breakfast, Jack folded his arms on top of the counter and laid his head on top. "What are we doing here?"

"We're on an adventure," she said, trying to sound encouraging.

He buried his head into his arms. "Where is here?" His voice was muffled. "And what are we going to do when we get there?"

"I have a picture of Nick." Jessica tapped her phone to look at it. "We're going to ask around." She glanced at the picture. Nick was at the Center, hanging a prized Kandinsky on the wall in his favorite gallery. He looked so happy. "Unless you have a better idea?"

"Get back in the car and head home?"

The waitress—or maybe she was the owner—served them some of the fluffiest pancakes Jessica had ever eaten. Jack had a full American, with sausage, bacon, eggs, and pancakes. He scarfed it down and drank five cups of coffee along the way. Jessica did her best to keep up—with the coffee, anyway.

In spite of the gallon of coffee and cup of sugar with it, a food coma set in immediately after she finished the full stack with extra real maple syrup. Her head was spinning from lack of sleep and too many carbs.

"So what's your plan, cowgirl?" Jack said in a good-spirited tone. "You were a Girl Scout, right? You've got to have a plan."

"Excuse me," Jessica said when the walleyed woman was in earshot. "I'm looking for my brother. He is estranged from the family, and I want to get back in touch. His old roommate said he moved to Wyoming, maybe Casper?" She held up the phone with the photo of Nick.

"Honey, Casper is a good three hours from here."

"Well, maybe he came through here." She stretched out her arm so the woman could look at the picture.

"Handsome fella." The waitress smiled. "Nope. Haven't seen him."

The waitress/owner disappeared into the kitchen.

"Great plan," Jack scoffed. "We're just going to wander around Wyoming asking everyone we meet if they've seen the *handsome fella*? What's the population of Wyoming?"

She scowled at him.

"One down, half a million to go. And we're not even in Wyoming yet."

Jessica ordered another cup of coffee. What the heck. She could just float into Wyoming.

At the border of Nebraska and Wyoming, as if on cue, the silhouette of a snow-dusted ridge jut up out of the boring plains into the moonlight. Not quite the rugged peaks of the Rockies, where Jessica grew up, but a welcome sight after a thousand miles of nothing. Finally, she was back in the embrace of the land.

Four hours later, they were in a Walmart parking lot in Casper, Wyoming, sleeping in the car with the engine running so they didn't freeze to death and waiting another two hours for daylight. Finally, at seven, dawn broke over the mountains. Jessica yawned and stretched her arms.

Holy smokes. In the distance, snowcapped mountains glowed pink with a golden crown atop radiating streaks of yellow riding on violet clouds. Glorious. Her chest tingled. She hadn't seen mountains since last summer in Montana. God, how she'd missed them.

As soon as the Walmart opened, armed with the picture of Nick, she resolved to ask every clerk and stocker if they'd seen him. Half an hour later, she had. Nope. No one had seen him. Nick had probably never been in a Walmart in his life.

Jessica tromped through the slushy parking lot and back to the car. Jack was dozing. When she opened the door and then hopped in the passenger's seat, he opened his eyes. "Well?"

"Nothing." She tapped her phone. "I'm calling Amber."

"I did it," Amber said without even a hello. "I found him."

"Where?"

"Can I call you back? I'm in the middle of a perm." Amber said something to someone on the other end. "Once I get Mrs. Homer under the dryer, I'll call you back." She hung up.

Dang it, Amber. Just tell me where he is!

For the next fifteen minutes, both Jessica and Jack sat staring at her phone, waiting for Amber's call.

The phone buzzed and skittered across Jessica's knee. She grabbed it. "Where is he?"

"Just a sec," Amber said, making paper-shuffling

noises on the other end. "I'm going back into WITSEC. Once I figured its system out, it was actually pretty easy. But it took me days to get in."

Jessica tapped her foot.

"Okay. Nick's at a ranch in Wyoming."

"What ranch?"

"Ford's Cutthroat Lodge outside Casper." Jessica sat at attention. She was wide awake now. "Wait. Something's happening."

"What do you mean?" Jessica swallowed hard. "Happening on the website?"

"Some kind of urgent alert just came up on the screen." More shuffling noises. "Root roo."

"What?" Jessica's breath caught. *What's going on?*

"The marshals were just called out to that ranch on an emergency," Amber said. "Someone got shot."

"Nick," Jessica whispered.

9

———

Arms folded over her chest, Lexi slouched further into the chair. She hated this room, with its overstuffed chairs, cheerful throw pillows, stinky fart smell, and Mental Health Day poster. This morning, her therapist had added a dozen pink roses in a red vase. It was sitting in the center of the low coffee table like a roadblock, separating them as they faced off over Lexi's PTSD.

Her cheeks burned as she told the shrink about hitting the floor when she'd heard a loud noise while examining the room where Jimmy was killed, and then the nightmares and socking a witness in the face. She was a basket case. And if she couldn't pull herself together, she'd probably get fired.

"How did it make you feel when your vulnerability was on display in these two professional situations?"

The therapist's smug smile made Lexi want to smack him.

How did it feel? What kind of stupid question is that? It felt like shit; that's how it felt. "Not good," was all she said.

"That's only natural." The therapist raised his eyebrows. "Tell me about your dream," he said, his pen hovering over his notebook. "Your recurring nightmare."

Lexi's phone buzzed in her purse. She'd turned it off at the therapist's insistence, but she still heard it vibrating. She stared down at her messenger bag. "I probably should get that." She glanced over at the paunchy middle-aged man with graying temples. "It might be work."

"This is *your* hour, Lexington. You have to take care of yourself." He smiled at her like she was a sick puppy. "We have to work through your survivor's guilt. It's only natural—"

"But it could be important—"

"This is important." The therapist opened his notebook and flipped through the pages. "You are important. What could be more important than taking care of yourself? You yourself said, and I quote . . ." He read from the notebook, "'I need to get myself sorted out so I can do my job right.'"

Now the bastard was using her own words against her. She put her elbows on her knees and her head into her hands. If she was going to tell him about her dreams, at least she wouldn't have to look at him while she did. She took a deep breath and held it. The only sound in the room was the clock on the wall ticking as the second hand made its way around and around, over and over again.

"It's the same every time." She closed her eyes. "I'm with my platoon in the desert. There's a loud noise . . . like an explosion. I hide behind a tanker truck." She dug her fingernails into her palms. "When I come out, everyone is dead . . . but not just dead." She sucked in air. "Eviscerated. Like they were turned inside out."

"And how does that make you feel?"

"How do you think?" She glanced up at him.

"I want to hear you say it." That smug smile again. She wanted to wipe it off his furry face.

"Bad."

"Because you blame yourself?" The therapist laid the pad and pen on his lap. "Just because you were there doesn't make it your fault."

"You know what? This session is over." She stood up, grabbed her coat off the back of the chair and her purse off the floor, and stormed out.

"But we have a half hour left," the therapist called after her. "I know it hurts. But I'm just trying to help."

"Like hell you are," she said under her breath, tugging her coat on as she marched out of the office and out of the building.

The morning sun struggled to burn through the dense cloud cover. The air had that frosty look, like it might snow again. Smelled like snow too. Damp and cold and sweet.

Her therapist's office was on the main drag, right above Ranch Outfitters, one of the many Western wear stores in Casper. Lexi was probably the only person in town—in the whole state of Wyoming—who didn't own a pair of cowboy boots. She'd had to park at the other end of town. For such a small town, it was hard to find parking downtown. Something else to hate about her shrink's office.

Stomping along the sidewalk, she glanced over at the bronze statue, the pride of Casper. A forlorn cowboy, head bowed, with a lamb—or was it a calf?—slung over his horse. Even the horse looked sad. It was called "Twenty Percent Chance of Flurries," an homage to Wyoming cowboys in winter going out in blizzards to rescue their livestock. *Sigh.* She knew how they felt. Instead of calves or lambs, she was protecting wolves and thieves.

Her phone vibrated, and she stopped to fish it out of her bag. *What now?* She stared down at the screen. *Son of a—*

Five calls from the head of WITSEC security and one voice message. *Shit. Something's wrong.* The only time she heard from Zack Pinto was when the situation was too hot for Drake and the locals, which meant it must be pretty bad. Hands shaking, she tapped her phone and listened to his message.

"Where the hell are you, Colt? Get your ass out to

Ford's Cutthroat Lodge on the double. If I have to call you again, I'm shipping you off to Siberia. I mean it, Colt." He didn't sound happy.

She let out a string of choice swear words. The kind that would make her mama wash her mouth out with soap. She dropped her phone back into her bag. She hoped to God the mob hadn't gotten to Nick. If she lost another witness, she'd . . . she didn't know what she'd do.

As she crunched through the snow to her car, she wondered if Siberia could be any worse than this. *Twenty percent chance of flurries.* Wasn't being banished to this miserable place two years ago punishment enough for her sins?

Her Charger was like a protective shell. Once in the driver's seat, she inhaled and exhaled, panting to calm down. She glanced into the back seat. *Thank God.* A solitary Diet Dew lay on its side, still tethered to the plastic six-pack holder. Reaching around to grab it, she caught a glimpse of a haggard face reflected in the rearview mirror.

She gasped. *What the—* She didn't even recognize herself. Something about those crazed eyes. Maybe her therapist was right. Maybe she should take some time off.

Snap. Fizz. The reassuring sounds of popping the top on her Dew. She guzzled half the warm pop, slammed the can into the cup holder, and wiped her mouth on her sleeve.

Where would she be without work? In the sinkhole of her past. Not just Afghanistan, which was bad enough, but the shame and hunger of her adolescence after her daddy got laid off from the mine. That time she got caught shoplifting tampons and spent two nights in jail. Afraid of the blood but more afraid to tell someone about it. Embarrassed she was a girl. Embarrassed she was poor. She'd been fourteen. It went downhill from there. Thinking about it made her skin crawl. *Pull yourself together, Lexi.*

She turned the ignition and the engine roared to life. *Come on, baby. It's you and me against the world.* At least the Charger responded to her touch. She sucked down the rest of her warm pop and then stepped on the gas. Whatever was waiting for her at Ford's Cutthroat Lodge still couldn't top the worst day of her life. She took her consolation where she could.

As she flew onto the highway, she heard that weasel therapist in her head. "How does it make you feel?" *Feel? What does that even mean?* The steering wheel hard under her palms? The cold leather of the car seat burning through her thin pants? The air rushing in and out of her nostrils? Those things she could feel.

What about watching all her friends, her buddies— the closest thing she had to family—blown to bits in front of her eyes? And being the only survivor? How did that make her feel? Enraged? Sick? Numb? Suicidal? Or just lucky? Yeah. She was one lucky bastard.

She wiped her eyes with the backs of her hands and

nearly swerved into oncoming traffic. Instinctively, she jerked the car back into its lane. Funny. She wanted to survive. And to die.

Fifteen minutes later, she was pulling into Cutthroat Lodge's long, tree-lined driveway. It had been freshly plowed, but still the Charger shimmied, just barely in her control. Emerging from the forest into the clearing, she spotted the lodge up ahead along with a cop car and three men huddled nearby. When she got closer, she recognized the uniformed officer and his hat.

Dammit. Another obnoxious cowboy sheriff. Hank Dillon. She'd had to deal with Hank plenty of times. Too many. What was it with these guys playing Wild West? She really couldn't deal with him right now. Especially on top of Wayne.

Wayne Ford. Ex-marshal. Ex-lover. Owned Cutthroat Lodge.

Before stepping out of her car, she checked her face in the rearview mirror. Who was that wizened woman looking back at her? She tucked her hair behind her ears, yanked her stocking cap over her ears, zipped up her parka, and stepped out into the frigid air.

"Good morning, gentlemen," she said.

"Why, if it isn't Marshal Filly." Hank grinned.

She scowled.

"My bad." He laughed. He never got tired of that joke. "This here is Frankie." Hank pointed to a scrawny teenager. "He found the body this morning when he was plowing. And this is Mr. Ford." He gestured toward Wayne Ford, the owner.

"I know Wayne," she said, glancing at the handsome older man. She didn't mention that she knew him in the biblical sense. When she'd first gotten to Casper, Wayne was persuasive and she was lonely. He'd forgotten to tell her that he was married.

Wayne moved closer and lowered his voice. "We don't want any scandal. We'd like to keep this as quiet as possible. Hunting accidents are bad for business." Wayne had damned near declared bankruptcy a few months back. And then a rich uncle bailed him out. Must be nice. Having a rich uncle.

"It was a hunting accident?" Her jaw relaxed just a bit. Maybe it wasn't her witness after all . . . unless he'd taken up hunting. With his fancy designer clothes and obsession with fine art, he didn't seem the type. *Who knows? Maybe he collects animal heads too.* He wouldn't be the first hoity-toity rich dude who liked to kill stuff. "Who's the victim?" She held her breath waiting for the answer.

"We don't know that," Hank said. "No ID. I just got back from seeing the body. The coroner's still out there. Puts the time of death sometime between ten and midnight."

"Hunting accident." She scoffed. "With game wardens crawling all over?" She narrowed her brows. "No hunter goes out without his license around here."

"You'd be surprised." Hank adjusted his hat. "But in this case, I'd say you're right."

"Any guests missing? Did you see the victim?" she asked Wayne. "Did you recognize him?" If it was Nick, he would have.

"I haven't been out there. Frankie told me what happened, and I immediately called the sheriff." *And WITSEC.* Not that he could say that out loud in front of the others. Wayne was a retired marshal himself. He knew all about WITSEC protocol. He still kept his ear to the ground and called Lexi if he heard anything.

"Hunting accident." She hugged herself. Maybe someone just wanted it to look like a hunting accident. "Frankie, can you tell me where you found the body?"

The scrawny kid pointed toward the woods. "Up there." He turned to Wayne. "You know, where Wayne Junior shot his first elk."

"Could you be more specific?"

"That's about a quarter mile off the county road—at that spot where Henry Whitehorse crashed his car into a tree two years ago." Wayne pointed up the hill.

"And where would that be?" she asked.

"Between popular hunting spots and major crash sites, not much need for actual maps amongst the locals." Hank chuckled. "I know the spot. I can take you up there, Marshal." The sheriff turned to the kid. "Mind if we borrow your snowmobile?"

"Key's in the ignition." Frankie shook his head. "Careful not to flood it."

Hank threw one leg over the machine and then reached around and patted the seat behind him, canines glistening as he smiled. "Hop on."

Great. I've got a wolf leading me to a kill site. Reluctantly, she climbed onto the snowmobile.

"Hold on," Hank shouted over the roar of the engine.

There was nothing to hold on to—except Hank. She had no choice. She put her arms around his chest, keeping as much distance between her torso and his as possible while trying not to fall off the confounded machine. Growing up in Tennessee, she hadn't seen much measurable snowfall.

Cruising along an old logging road was kind of exciting. But when Hank sliced up over the snowbank and headed out cross-country through the trees, things got interesting. The darn machine bounced up and down like a bucking bronco. She would have bruises on her tailbone. Not to mention scratches from branches whacking her in the face. She closed her eyes and put one hand over them, holding onto Hank's jacket with the other. Her face stung from the cold and the thwacking, and her butt hurt. She hoped to heck they'd get to the crime scene soon.

Yeah. The dudes said it was a hunting accident. But her gut—and that missing ID—told her otherwise. *Please, please, please don't be my guy.*

The snowmobile soared up over another snowbank. Hank let out a hoot. Lexi hollered too but not for the fun of it. She clung harder to him to avoid flying off the back.

When they jolted to a stop in a small clearing, her head hit his, and then she did fall off into the snowbank. *Good Lord.* She struggled to right herself and stand up, and then she shook the snow out of her gloves.

Up ahead, a man lay face down in the middle of what looked like a giant cherry snow cone. The petite coroner and her assistant were kneeling next to the body. Lexi recognized them from the last crime scene. A snowcat waited on the far side of the clearing with a sled for the body.

Lexi felt like she was wearing cement overshoes as she trudged through the deep snow toward the victim. Every step pulled her hip joints out of their sockets.

As soon as she got a good look at the exit wound, she knew. No way this was a hunting accident. The corpse wore a camouflage parka with a big bloody hole in the back but had no rifle . . . and no coat or hat. *It was an execution.* If she had to guess, a .44 at close range. *Question is, did the murder take place out here in the middle of this forest? Or was the body moved out here?*

Her heart sped up as she got closer. She screwed up her courage. "Can you turn him over so I can see his face?"

"We were just about to load him up," the coroner said. With her rosy round cheeks, button nose, and floppy Elmer Fudd hat, she looked like a cute pet bunny. "Come take a look."

"They said the time of death was last night?" Lexi asked, taking a couple steps closer.

"I'd say around midnight, give or take a couple hours." The coroner slipped a small notebook into the pocket of her ski jacket.

Lexi glanced around. "The fresh snow makes it hard to see any prints or blood."

"Right." The coroner stood up. "My guess is he was moved."

"That wound looks like a shot at close range." *That's no accident. That's a cold-blooded murder.*

"I concur." The coroner motioned for her assistant to turn the corpse.

Even blue-lipped, dead-eyed, and frozen, Lexi knew that face. "Son of a—" Not again. That same brown smudge on his lip. "Shit."

"You knew him?" Hank asked, coming up behind her.

She nodded and turned away.

10

———

"In three miles, turn onto Route Thirty toward Medicine Bow." With her forefinger and thumb, Jessica stretched the image to get a better look. "Then it's another eleven miles until the turnoff to Ford's Cutthroat Lodge." Tapping her phone again, she checked the time. "8:11."

"What difference does it make?" Jack was back at the wheel. "Lover boy will either be there or he won't. He's either alive or he's—" He glanced over at her but didn't finish the sentence.

Dead. She'd already lost Nick once. She wasn't going to lose him again. "Can't we go any faster?" The highway had been plowed, but it was still treacherous driving. Hit a patch of ice and off into the ditch—or into oncoming traffic—you go.

"I'm speeding as it is." Jack floored it and the MG rocketed past a semitruck. "And these aren't the best driving conditions." The tiny car fishtailed back into the right lane.

"I guess you're right." She hugged herself. *Either Nick was there or not. Alive or . . .*

For the next ten minutes, she gnawed on each fingernail in turn.

"There!" She pointed to the sign for Ford's Cutthroat Lodge. "Turn there."

Jack turned onto the one-lane road. At least it had been plowed recently. Still, hard-packed snow and patches of ice threatened the little sports car's stability. Not the best car for a Wyoming winter . . . or a Chicago winter for that matter. The Jack she remembered didn't care about status when it came to cars or anything else. Prison must have changed him. As the little roadster skated up the driveway and nearly slid off into the ditch, she wondered if the change was for the better.

Ford's Cutthroat Lodge was a mammoth three-story log building with a humongous wraparound porch. It reminded her of Many Glacier Lodge, where she used to work summers. Except, whereas the old railroad lodges in Glacier National Park showed their age, this magnificent lodge was dressed to the nines. If Nick was here, he'd be in his posh element. *Lucky ducky.* She'd have to work years to save up enough money to spend a week at a place like this.

The inside of the lodge was as impressive as the outside. The logs were polished to a shine, and a gorgeous natural stone fireplace lit up the cheerful lobby. Even the dead animal heads staring down at her seemed at home. Cutthroat Lodge was one of those fancy hunting lodges for people who wanted an outdoor experience but didn't like to get dirt—or blood —on their hands.

"Can I help you?" A man dressed in wool pants and a flannel shirt intercepted them before they reached the registration desk.

"We're . . . I'm looking for someone who's staying here." Jessica fiddled with the fringe on her jacket. "Nick Schilling . . . or Charis. He likes his privacy, so sometimes he checks into places under different names, but this is him." She pulled her cell phone from her jacket pocket, tapped it, and scrolled through her photos until she found a selfie she'd taken with Nick the weekend at the Parker Hotel before he'd disappeared. "Him." She held the phone up.

The man leaned closer, glanced at the photograph, and then smiled like she'd just shown him a cute cat picture. "I'm Wayne Ford, the owner." He held out his hand. "And who might you be?"

On autopilot, she put her hand in his. *Has he seen Nick or not? If Nick is dead, he wouldn't be smiling, right?* "I'm Jessica James. Nick's . . ." *His what? Girlfriend? Fiancée?* " . . . friend."

"I'm Jack Grove." Jack held out his hand to the owner. "Not his friend. Just the designated driver."

The owner squinted and blinked.

"Can you tell me if Nick—the man in the photo—is a guest here?" Jessica asked.

"I'm sorry, Miss James. We don't give out information on our guests." The owner gestured toward the fireplace. "But we do have some fresh-baked cookies. Feel free to help yourselves."

"I just want to know—"

He cut her off. "Why don't you try calling your friend?"

"I would, but—"

He interrupted again. "If he wants you to know where he is, he'll tell you." *Irritating man!* The owner smiled. "Isn't that right, Jack Grove?" He winked. "Hasn't the little lady heard of a bird in the hand?"

Jack's lips twisted into a knot, but he didn't say anything.

Little lady . . . I'd like his fat ass to meet the pointy toe of my cowboy boot.

"Make yourselves at home, now. I have to run." The owner turned on his heels and disappeared into an office behind the registration desk.

Sigh. Now what? Wait all day and see if Nick shows up?

"Might as well refuel," Jack said, heading for the plate of cookies laid out on a table next to the fireplace.

Who was Jessica to refuse a freshly baked cookie? Anyway, maybe the sugar would help her think. She followed Jack to the cookies, grabbed two and a napkin, and then dropped into a deep leather easy chair near the fireplace. The warmth from the fire took the edge off, and her muscles started to relax.

A man sitting across the room reading a newspaper looked up over his paper and smiled. "I couldn't help but overhear your conversation with the owner," he said, closing his newspaper. "Jessica, right?" He pointed to the chair next to her. "Do you mind?"

She shook her head. *Maybe this guy's seen Nick.*

The burly fellow plopped into the chair next to her with a groan. With his dark suit, short tie, and heavy accent, he reminded her of a Hollywood gangster. "So you're looking for your boyfriend?" He eyed Jack, who was stocking up on cookies. "Your other boyfriend?"

"Not my boyfriend . . . just a friend." She dug out her phone again and showed him the picture. "Have you seen him?"

"So you're Jessica . . . Jessica from Chicago." He leaned back and rubbed his bald head with the palm of his hand.

"How did you know I'm from Chicago?"

"I pay attention." He wiped his palms on the knees of his pants. "And I saw your license plate." The dude was rough-looking but had a gentle manner . . . an unnervingly gentle manner. "Did your Nick leave you at the altar? Is that why you're trying to find him?"

"Not quite." She didn't know how much to tell this stranger. After all, Nick was in witness protection. "But . . ." She lowered her voice. "We were almost engaged." She glanced over at Jack, who was busy pouring half a jar of sugar into his cup of coffee.

"And he got cold feet and flew the coop?" The dude chuckled.

"Have you seen him?" She held up the picture again. "He was coming out for a vacation to clear his head before the big day . . . a bachelor party of sorts," she lied.

"I wouldn't call it a party . . . more like a wake." He twisted a thick gold ring around his pinky finger.

Who is this guy? "Why do you say that?" She sat up like a lightning bolt. "Do you know Nick? Is he in trouble? Is he . . ." She couldn't say it. It dawned on her that this might be a mafia hitman sent to kill Nick. Her palms were sweating. Would he kill her too?

The dude waited for a well-dressed woman wheeling her bag across the lobby to pass by them and out the front door. Then he leaned closer. "From what I've seen," he whispered, "a lot of folks are looking for your *friend*. But don't worry. They won't find him. And neither will you."

"What do you mean? Who are you?" She didn't mean to raise her voice.

"Oh, how rude of me." He sat up and extended his hand. "Danny Quarrels. A friend of the family."

"Nick never mentioned you." She eyed him suspiciously. *First the guy pretends not to know Nick, and now he's 'a friend of the family.' What is he playing at?*

"I'm a friend of his dad's . . . well, a friend of a friend."

"Is Nick here?" Not that the guy would give her a straight answer.

"Not anymore."

"Where is he?" Her heart sped up. She was getting close, very close.

"I couldn't say."

"Can't or won't?" She narrowed her eyes. What was this Danny Quarrels after?

"Does it matter?"

Is he with WITSEC? Is that why he won't say where Nick is? Was Nick here but he's been moved? "Please, I just want—"

"Why don't you get that little Russian gal out here to help you?" He flashed a knowing smile. "I'd say she's already sent some backup. Too bad about what happened to him."

Jessica broke out in a cold sweat. Her heart was racing. "You know Lolita?"

He nodded. "Everyone knows Lolita."

How in the hell could he know Lolita . . . unless he's Bratva? But what does Lolita have to do with Nick and WITSEC? What does he mean 'backup'? Vanya?

"And the backup?" Jessica asked. "What happened to him?"

"Hunting accident."

"Hunting accident?"

"Dead guy with a golden smile. You know him?"

"Golden smile?" She sounded like a stupid echo. "Like a gold grill?" *Oh no. Not Vanya.*

"Yup. Happened last night. Those hills back there are still crawling with cops." He jerked his thumb toward the back of the lodge. "You can't be too careful during hunting season."

Her head was spinning. *What in the heck is going on? Did Lolita send Vanya out to find Nick? To protect him? Or to kill him? No way.* Lolita wouldn't do that. Neither would Vanya. They were her friends. If Lolita had sent Vanya, then it was to protect Nick . . . and her. Her stomach flipped. *Did Vanya get killed protecting Nick?* Her eyes burned. She fought back tears. *Poor Vanya.*

Detective Cormier was right. This whole thing was too dangerous. She was way over her head. It was her fault Vanya was dead . . . and it would be her fault if Nick got killed.

"Now, if you'll excuse me." The burly dude stood up. "I have to make a call. Cell service sucks balls out here." He held out his hand again. "I've heard so much about you. It's nice to finally meet you in person."

She was speechless as she watched Danny Quarrels disappear down the hallway.

She pulled out her phone and tapped Lolita's number. No answer. Voicemail full. *Crapulence.* "Answer your phone!" Why would Vanya have come to Wyoming? It didn't make sense. No. It couldn't be. It just couldn't. She wiped away a tear with the back of her hand.

"What was that all about?" Jack asked, finally breaking away from the cookies to join her. "What's wrong? Are you okay?"

"I don't know." She dropped her phone in her lap and put both hands to her cheeks as if to hold herself together. "But I'm about to find out."

CURSING TO HIMSELF, Danny Quarrels crammed into the tiny phone booth. He barely had room to reach in his pants pocket for quarters. What century was this, anyway? As he fumbled with the coins, he hoped he wouldn't have to kill her. Such a pretty girl. He'd never had to off a girl before.

Schilling was a lucky so-and-so with a lovely lady like that following him across the entire country. Most dames would have given up by now and latched onto some new sugar daddy. Then again, that Jessica chick had come with that snarky little pipsqueak. Maybe she'd replaced Nick with him. *Nah.* A fine lady like her would never settle for a one-bite snack when she could have an entire banquet.

He dropped the coins in the slot, waited for a dial tone. He really should get a calling card. Then again, with Nick gone, he probably wouldn't be staying in this godforsaken place much longer . . . unless the boss wanted him to kill the girl. Another hunting accident? With those big eyes, she did remind him of a doe.

There once was a girl from Chicago. Her eyes were as round as a deer doe. She froze in the headlights, was whipped up like egg whites, and thrown to the end of the rainbow.

The boss accepted the collect call. "Did you get it done?" he asked without even a "hello" or "how ya doin'?"

"I'm close." He shifted the receiver to his other ear. "But the girl showed up. Nick's girl, that Jessica chick. She's asking around. Want I should put a lid on it?"

"Just make sure she doesn't mess up the plan. Take her out if necessary."

"Okay, boss." He traced the phone buttons with his finger.

"What did you find out?"

"Nada. But I'm working on it."

"Find out what Schilling knows about my business with his dad. And what he plans to say at the trial. I'd hate for you to have to kill him. He's practically my nephew."

"What if Lolita Durchenko shows up?"

"Why would she?"

"The Butcher was here after the goods."

"The Butcher was in Wyoming?"

"Don't worry. I took care of it."

"Good. If anyone gets in the way, put them down. Or better yet, use the girlfriend as leverage to get Schilling to back off." Teeth chuckled. "Yeah. If Schilling won't cooperate, grab the girl. Do what you have to, you hear?"

Danny cringed. He didn't relish the thought of putting down a lady, especially such a young, pretty one. But if that's what had to happen, he'd at least try to make it quick and painless. Funny how life could turn on a dime. Like a good hunter, Jessica had tracked Nick halfway across the country. Now the hunter was about to become the prey.

PART II

11

L exi took her phone into her bathroom and shut the door. "Who did you say is looking for him?" She turned on the faucet for good measure. Her cottage was small enough and the walls thin enough; she didn't want to risk the witness overhearing her.

She'd moved into the one-bedroom log cabin a year ago. The woodstove in the living room kept it toasty warm. After living in an apartment in downtown Casper, she'd decided to take advantage of what Wyoming had to offer: open spaces and stunning sunsets. So she'd rented the guesthouse of a rich Wyoming rancher. She kept to herself, and so did he. Just the way she liked it.

"Jessica James, a friend from Chicago." Wayne's deep voice still rattled her. "She had a guy with her.

Both in their late twenties, or the guy might have been early thirties. I thought you'd want to know."

Holy hell. If his friends could find him, no wonder the Russian Mafia had too. "How in the world did they find him?" It was a rhetorical question given Wayne Ford surely didn't know the answer.

"Maybe he called her and told her where he was. I had witnesses do that to me." Wayne had taken earlier retirement from the marshal's service. Either he'd had enough of protecting bad guys or was tired of getting shot at.

Wayne had a point. Witnesses had been known to blow their covers by calling girlfriends or ex-wives. "Maybe." She bit her lip. If Nick had a girlfriend, he hadn't mentioned her.

"What about the dead guy?" Wayne asked. "The sheriff said you knew him."

"The sheriff has a big mouth." She closed the lid and sat down on the toilet.

"Lexi, you sound upset. Why don't we meet for a drink later?" Wayne never gave up.

"Not happening." She glanced at the bathroom door. Even if she wanted to hook up with Wayne, she couldn't. She had to babysit her witness.

"Because of him?" The whine in his voice wasn't attractive.

"Because of who?"

"Your hunky witness."

She rolled her eyes. "Give me a break."

"Where did you take him?"

"As an ex-marshal, you of all people know I can't tell you that. Especially after what happened at your ranch."

"It wasn't my fault." He was whining again.

"I know." She stood up. "It was mine."

"Don't blame—"

"Bye, Wayne." She tapped the red button to end the call and then turned off the faucet.

Gazing at herself in the mirror, she combed her hair with her fingers. *Maybe a dab of lipstick.* As she rifled through the top drawer of the vanity, she wondered why she cared. Who was she trying to impress? *Screw it.* She slammed the drawer shut.

"Was that about me?" Nick asked when she returned to the living room. He was lounging on the couch, reading some art magazine. He seemed awfully calm for someone on a hit list. His fancy tan loafers hung over the edge of the sofa. Was wearing shoes and no socks a thing in Chicago? Didn't his feet get cold? She had to admit, the bit of smooth bare ankle peeking out from under the hem of his jeans was kind of sexy.

"Nope." No way she would tell him that his *friend* from Chicago had tracked him down. He might want to see her. Might decide to leave the program. It was her job to keep him alive, at least until he could testify at Teeth's trial. She gathered up the empty pop cans scattered around the room and the empty pizza box off the coffee table and took them to the trash. Sometimes she wished she wasn't such a slob. If she'd known she was going to have to bring him home, she would have tidied up the place. But who could've foreseen that the Mafia would find him? Hopefully, she'd hear back from Drake soon about Nick's reassignment to a new location—and a new handler. She couldn't babysit him forever. He was cute but not that cute.

She plopped onto the burgundy corduroy La-Z-Boy —a hand-me-down from her mama after her first tour of duty—and leaned it back as far as it would go. It had been quite a day. First her mealymouthed therapist, then a dead Russian mobster, and now some heartsick girlfriend. This case was getting royally screwed up. If she didn't get Nick out of here soon, she just might have another dead witness on her hands. She instinctively touched her sidearm. *Not on my watch.*

Moving her thumb back and forth across the corduroy nap helped her calm down. She picked at a spot on the fabric. The armchair was nearly bald, worn down from decades of fretting fingers . . . mostly her mama's, worrying about her daddy breathing in clay dust all day at the mine. Eventually the dust had done him in. His death had hollowed her mama to the core. As if she'd been in a hurry to join him, a week later, her mama fell and broke her hip, then moved in with Lexi's sister. That's when Lexi had inherited her mama's sad chair.

The same dust that had settled over her mama's heart ignited a fire inside Lexi. Every wall she climbed, every target she shot, every lap she ran around the barracks—not to mention every single push-up and jumping jack she did all her years in the Army—they were all expressions of rage. Rage at Weakley Mining Company, rage at Weakley County, rage at the whole darn state of Tennessee, but mostly rage at her daddy for having no other choice than to work at the mines.

After years of listening to kids on her block call her daddy "Casper the Ghost" because he came home from work every day covered in dust, she swore she'd get out of Weakly County even if it killed her. And it almost did.

The Army was her ticket out. They'd trained her to be a marshal. Without a college degree, she'd never have made it without that training. But the Army also had taken more from her than Weakley ever could. By the time she entered the marshal service over five years ago, all she had left of those she loved most was this ratty old La-Z-Boy. Her daddy was gone, and she'd missed his funeral, unable to get home in time from Afghanistan. Her fiancé, Gabe, was gone. Her mama had worried herself into a heart attack that brought on dementia, so she might as well be gone too. And Lexi hadn't talked to her sister in over a year.

Her phone buzzed. *Drake.* The call she'd been waiting for. She jumped up and headed back into the bathroom. Her one-bedroom cabin was so small; it was the only place she could get some privacy. She turned on the faucet, sat down on the toilet lid, and answered her phone. At least now she'd find out where to take Nick and have her place to herself again. Nick hadn't even been there for an hour and she already felt crowded.

"Bad news," Drake said. "We don't have a place yet. You'll have to keep him there."

"What?" She stood up and paced back and forth in the tiny space. "But—"

"Sorry, Colt. We've got no choice." The tone of his voice told her not to argue.

"We've got another problem." She stopped and stared at herself in the mirror. "Some girlfriend showed up at the ranch asking after him." She leaned in to get a closer look at the purple bags under her eyes. "If his cover isn't blown already, she'll blow the lid right off." Nothing a little concealer and lipstick couldn't fix.

"Dammit, Colt." Drake's exasperation was all too familiar. "Get her out of the way."

"And how do you expect me to do that?" She dropped back onto the toilet. "Shoot her?"

"I hope you're not serious." He sighed. "Figure it out."

"What about the Russians?"

"Are you sure the corpse was Boris the Butcher?"

"It was Boris Solonik all right—crescent moon scar on his left cheek, broken nose, gold grill on his teeth, and bushy eyebrows were dead giveaways. And I'm pretty sure that if he was on a hunting trip, Nick was his prey."

"If Bratva sent the Butcher, they'll send someone else."

"Question is, who killed him? It looked like a mob-style execution."

"One of Teeth Marsiano's hitmen?" he asked. Obviously a rhetorical question.

"If so, we've got the Russians, the Italians, and the girlfriend swarming around Nick like flies on horse manure." She exhaled. "Guess that makes me the flyswatter."

"Just keep the witness safe for the next week. We'll have a new location by then."

A week? "I'll do my best."

"Your best better be good enough." He hung up.

She frowned. What did he mean by that?

When she came out of the bathroom, Nick was napping on the couch, the magazine open across his chest. She stood in the middle of the living room and looked down at him sleeping. He was easy on the eyes. But another week together, in a house too small for even one person, was a bit much.

Nick opened one eye. Flustered, she averted her gaze. Obviously, he'd been faking it.

"Do you always take your phone calls in the bathroom?" he asked, sitting up.

She tried to think of a smart-aleck response but couldn't. "Only when I have houseguests."

"Thanks for putting up with me." He folded the magazine shut.

"When you had minutes to gather up essentials, you took an art magazine?"

"Reading calms me down. Anyway, I had it in my pocket when the marshal service picked me up six months ago." He reached inside his jacket. "That and this." He held a small red velvet box in the palm of his hand. "I guess the magazine is more useful to me now."

"What is it?"

He snapped the box open. A gorgeous jade ring reflected the overhead light.

Wow. The girlfriend was a lucky lady. Or maybe not, since she wouldn't see Nick again until the trial, which could be years from now. That is, if Lexi did her job. "Pretty," she said.

"You want it?" He snapped the box shut again and held it out to her.

What the— "No way. I can't take that."

"Why not?"

"You're in my custody, for one thing."

"I'm also intruding in your life . . . and your home." He ran his fingers through his thick hair. "It's the least I can do." He shoved the box toward her.

Lordy. That ring must have cost a fortune. She tightened her lips. Sad that the only man who ever wanted to give her a ring was a witness she'd just met. She shook her head. "Thanks, but I can't."

"Suit yourself." He slid the box back inside his jacket pocket. "Let me know if you change your mind. It's not any good to me now."

"You must have cared a lot for her," she said, almost to herself. *I wish someone cared that much about me.*

"I did . . . I do." He leaned back into the couch and closed his eyes. "She was . . . is smart, funny, nerdy, and beautiful." When he opened his startling blue eyes again and gazed at her, her ears burned. "Will I ever see her again, Marshal?"

Good heavens. Is he going to cry? Dude must have it bad. She squirmed. "I don't know."

"Tell me the truth." He put his hands together as if in prayer.

Not if I can help it. "I don't know," she repeated. "Probably not."

Tears rolled down his cheeks.

Damn. Now what? She sat next to him on the couch and put her arm around him. "I'm sorry." His wool jacket was warm, and he smelled of juniper. His shoulders heaved under her arm. She felt for the guy. She knew what it was like to lose everything and start over.

He leaned into her and buried his face in her neck. She wrapped her other arm around him and held him, rocking gently. It should have felt weird, but somehow it felt good. *Is that wrong? I mean, the dude's in pain and I'm getting off on the smell of his hair.* She inhaled.

He lifted his face and gazed at her with those eyes. *Lordy.* She shuddered. As their lips met, she tightened her grip around his torso. He tasted like salt. *This is wrong . . . wrong . . . wrong . . . so wrong.* Her hand desperately sought out his soft hair. Overtaken by some haunted animal, she moaned and slid her leg over his thighs. *Wrong . . . so wrong.*

Wrong address. Again. He knew the marshal's name was Colt. So why couldn't he find her? *How many Colts are there in eastern Wyoming?* Danny wrapped his fingers around the steering wheel of the rented SUV and squeezed. *Where in the hell did Marshal Hot Lips go?*

Come on, Quarrels, think! He knew he should have followed the marshal when they left the ranch with Schilling. If it hadn't been for that Chicago chick showing up, he would have. Now he'd have to tell Teeth he'd lost him. *He'll have my head on a platter.* He had to find out where the marshal took Schilling before Teeth found out he'd lost him.

Anyway, why hadn't Teeth already pulled the trigger? He could have given it to Schilling back in Chicago when he'd had the chance. What was Teeth waiting for? Did he really think he could persuade Schilling not to testify if he asked nice? Nick might be like his nephew, but as he'd learned in catechism, "The blood of the covenant is thicker than the water of the womb."

Danny chuckled. At least he'd had the good sense to drop that disposable cell into the punk's MG. Maybe he and the girlfriend would lead him to Schilling. He had an unsettling thought. Maybe she wasn't Nick's girlfriend. Maybe she and the punk were working for

Bratva. They didn't look like Russian Mafia. But since the Oxford Don's granddaughter had taken over, Bratva hadn't been the same. Women shouldn't be mob bosses. What tough guy was going to take orders from a dame? Danny never would. *That's for damn sure.*

There once was a dame worked for Bratva. Her hair shiny black Cleopatra. Got it caught in a vice, pulled at it twice, and screams heard from here to Kamchatka.

12

Jessica paced the length of the cavernous lobby of the Cutthroat Lodge. Even under her fringe jacket, the hairs on her arms stood on end. Nick had been here. He wasn't the dead guy. What if Vanya was the dead guy? She grimaced. Lolita hadn't answered her phone. Jessica had been calling since yesterday when she heard about the dead guy. Her stomach flipped. *Poor Vanya.*

But at least Nick was still alive. *Where is he now?* She stopped and stared out the picture window at the snow-covered mountains in the distance. They reminded her of the peaky meringue her grandmother used to make to top lemon pie. Suddenly, she wished she were home. Not back in Chicago. But in Montana . . . at Alpine Vista Trailer Park with her mom. She closed her eyes and inhaled the smell of her childhood, the caramelly smell of burning wood.

She'd wanted to go looking for Nick yesterday when they first got there and found out he'd been at the ranch. But Jack had insisted on getting a room, a shower, and a good night's sleep *in a bed*, before he'd go anywhere. She'd made him get up early, which wasn't as bad as he made it out, considering the time difference.

"Now what, cowgirl?" Jack grabbed the last mini muffin off the plate and took a bite. "Man cannot live on bite-size muffins and caffeine alone."

Jack was right. Usually, she'd be the first one to the table, but all this worrying made her lose her appetite. She glanced at the grandfather clock near the registration desk. They'd been spinning their wheels for half an hour already.

"We need a plan," she said, warming her hands by the fire.

"How about breakfast?" He joined her at the fireplace. "I need some real food."

She chewed at a jagged nail. "But Nick—"

"How about we just make it a vacation?" Jack smiled. "I can rent us a romantic cabin in the woods. What do you say?"

It wasn't the worst idea she'd ever heard. Maybe she should cut her losses and forget about Nick. Anyway, how was she going to find him? And even if she did, then what? She tapped her phone awake and sent a text to Amber. If WITSEC moved Nick, then maybe Amber could hack in and find out where they'd taken him. A light bulb went off in her brain.

"What is there only one of in a small town?" She tapped the screen again. "Someplace everyone has to go at some point?"

"What's going on in that big brain of yours?" Jack moved closer and peered over her shoulder. He was starting to smell spicy again.

"Marshal Eva Mendes drives a bright blue Charger, right? How many of those can there be in Casper, Wyoming?" She frantically tapped her phone, googling information about Casper.

"What? We're going to stake out the entire town of Casper and its environs until we find a blue Charger?" He rubbed his hands together in front of the fire. "What if she's a survivalist who only comes into town once a month for supplies?"

"The marshals must have an office." She searched Google for the Federal Marshals' office in Casper. "We can stake out the office. Then when she comes in, we follow the Charger. Eventually, she'll take us to Nick."

"Eventually . . . unless they already moved him to Texas or Nebraska or California. What makes you think she's even still on his case?"

"I feel it in my gut."

"Are you sure that's not just hunger?"

Aha! The district headquarters was in Cheyenne, but there was a local recruitment office at the courthouse in Casper. "How about breakfast in downtown

Casper?" She sent the address to herself. "You fly, and I'll buy."

Half an hour later, they were seated in a booth at a swanky diner across from the courthouse. Jessica slid in close to the window, on the lookout for a bright blue Charger. Jack was busy staking out the menu.

The snow piled on both sides of the street sparkled like ground glass. Without taking her eyes off the street, she slid her shades out of her jacket pocket and put them on. The smell of fried onions and garlic made her mouth water, but she wasn't going to risk scanning for vegetarian options. "Order something for me." She put both elbows on the windowsill and cradled her chin in her hands, a sentinel on guard.

"What do you want?"

"Anything veggie is fine. Do they have banana nut pancakes?"

Her phone buzzed and skittered on the table. *Crapulence.* She tried to glance down at it and keep a lookout at the same time. With her luck, the minute she let down her guard, the blue Charger would sneak by and she'd miss it. "Can you answer that?"

"You want me to answer your phone?" Jack sounded incredulous.

Who did he think it was? *A secret admirer? Or my alcoholic mother?* "It might be Amber." Without looking down, she shoved the phone across the table. "Maybe she found something."

She tried to keep her focus on the courthouse, but Jack's conversation was driving her mad. He just kept saying, "Uh huh." Out of the corner of her eye, she watched him take out a small notebook from the back pocket of his jeans, one of those notebooks a detective might have. Yeah, Jack was that nerdy. He had a pint-size pen to go with it.

She was dying to know what he was writing. He must be talking to Amber. Who else could it be? Lolita? She thought of the burly dude at the lodge. What was his name? Danny something. How did he know Lolita? Was he WITSEC? Or . . . was he Bratva? If he was Bratva, then Nick was in deep trouble. She'd taken on the Russian mafia before. And if necessary, she'd do it again. *Hopefully I won't have to shoot anyone this time.*

Usually she had Lolita at her side, karate-kicking the bad guys. Her lips twitched. Were they even still friends? She squinted. They'd never had a such a heated argument before. Was Nick driving them apart? She didn't want to have to choose between her best friend and . . . and what?

"Uh huh." Jack was still scribbling. *Is he writing a freaking novel?*

"Who is it?"

"Shhh . . ." He held up one hand, still writing with the other.

She scowled. It was her phone after all.

Holy crap. She sat bolt upright. "The blue Charger." She pointed at the window. "Come on!" Without waiting for Jack, she dashed across the restaurant and out the door. The last time she'd seen that car, Nick was in it.

As soon as she stepped outside, a blast of frigid air scoured her face. *Dang.* She'd left her parka inside. Adrenaline coursed through her veins as she galloped after the car. Slipping and sliding on ice and snow, she wished she'd worn her snow boots instead of her cowboy boots.

The Charger turned into the parking lot of the courthouse. Jessica dashed across the street and nearly got herself killed. Cars honked and screeched to a stop. A bus whooshed by so close it blew off her trapper hat and doused her jeans with slush. Panting, she leapt onto the sidewalk in front of the courthouse and then promptly slipped and fell on her butt. *Ouch!* Stunned, she sat there for a few seconds before getting up, brushing off the seat of her pants, and limping around the corner to the parking lot. By the time she got there, the Charger was parked and no one was in sight. No Marshal Eva Mendes. No Nick. Nobody.

"Hey, cowgirl." Jack appeared from around the building, her green parka stuffed under his arm, as well as her hat, which had blown off into the street. Good old Jack. "Where are you going? I thought you were taking me to lunch. You stiffed me and left me with the check."

Jessica pointed at the Charger just a few feet away. "She's here." She hobbled over, her hip aching a little from the fall. Shielding her eyes, she peeked in the driver's-side window. "Whoa. She's addicted to Mountain Dew."

"I didn't know they still made that stuff." Jack joined her next to the car.

"Maybe she uses it as antifreeze. The stuff looks like antifreeze." She shivered and hugged herself.

Jack circled the car, admiring it. "Makes me think of my old Mustang."

"Can I have my coat?"

"Oh, sorry." Jack handed her the hat and coat.

She slouched into the coat and zipped it up, then brushed off the hat.

"Now what?" Jack asked. "We stake out the parking lot?"

"I'll stake out the parking lot. You go get your car so we can follow her when she comes out."

Jack shook his head. "I'm going to start calling you James Bond instead of Jesse James." He sauntered off at a snail's pace.

Scanning the parking lot for a place to hide that still had a clear view of the Charger, Jessica tugged her trapper down over her ears and then pulled some mittens out of the parka pocket. *Chicago is cold, but this is ridiculous. The windchill must be below zero.* She remembered her first whiteout on campus, when she literally couldn't see where she was or which building was in front of her. They had some impressive snowstorms in Montana when she was growing up—some years she could slide off the barn roof, the snow was so deep. But she'd never experienced anything like the "lake effect" until she found herself back east.

The back door of the courthouse swung open, and Jessica ducked behind a dumpster. She grimaced as the smell of rotting garbage nearly gagged her. Trying to hold her breath, she peeked around the bin in time to catch sight of a well-dressed woman in a long wool coat and leather gloves striding across the parking lot. Was that the marshal? With the hat and sunglasses, it was hard to tell. She watched the woman pick her way through the slush in high-heeled boots. She wasn't wearing very practical shoes for chasing fugitives.

The familiar MG pulled into the lot and parked in a spot two rows behind the Charger. *Good job, Jack.* Should she make a break for Jack's car or wait to see if the *well-dressed woman* got in the Charger? Nope. The woman pointed her key fob at a Lexus next to the Charger. The Lexus responded with flashing lights. That was Jessica's cue to walk—not run—to Jack's MG.

She bent down, climbed into the tiny car, and slid down in the passenger's seat, waiting for the marshal to make her appearance. That Charger was the marshal's; Jessica was sure of it. But was Nick with her? If not, would she lead them to him? Or had he been transferred out of state? *Sigh. Will I ever see him again?*

"Don't look now," Jack said, sliding down in his seat. "Sexy marshal at two o'clock."

Jessica peeked up over the dashboard, trying to get a good look. No Nick. Just the sexy marshal, wearing navy slacks, a sage-green bomber jacket, and big black rubber snow boots. Hatless, her brunette curls were pulled up and away from her face in the front and fell to her shoulders in the back. The juxtaposition between the drab clothes and her movie-star face was uncanny. With her valentine lips and arched brows, she looked like Liv Tyler or Anne Hathaway playing a cop in a film. Jessica wondered if the marshal had had as hard a time as she'd had being taken seriously in a male-dominated profession. It couldn't be easy to look like that and be a Federal Marshal.

"She's getting into her car," Jessica said. "Follow her." Hopefully, the marshal would lead them to Nick.

Jack shook his head and gave her the side-eye. "Okay, boss." He waited until the marshal had pulled out of the parking lot to fire up his MG. Fishtailing onto the main drag, he followed the Charger through down-town, speeding through a yellow light to keep up. "Fast enough for you?" He chuckled. Protests to the contrary, he was obviously enjoying this. "Just like Bonnie and Clyde." He glanced over at her and flashed his million-watt sexy nerd smile.

Good old Jack. He's game for anything.

"Just keep on her tail." Leaning forward as if she could propel the car through sheer willpower, Jessica gripped the dash, her eyes glued on the Charger two blocks ahead.

Jack maneuvered the little sports car through stoplights, around corners, all the way across town and into the suburbs, following just a couple blocks behind the marshal.

Wow. He's good. "You could be a professional driver."

"If the psychiatrist thing doesn't work out, I'll remember that," he said as he slowed to a crawl in the middle of a tree-lined street.

The neighborhood was quiet, with neat rows of modest houses. Some kids building a snowman. A pretty woman wearing sunglasses and a scarf driving an SUV, its tinted windows no doubt hiding the brood she'd just taken ice-skating or to swimming practice. *That's what Lolita would look like if she had kids.* Jessica smiled to herself. Hard to imagine Lolita with kids.

The Charger made a U-turn, stopping in front of a small brick ranch house up ahead. Jack pulled over to the curb. They watched as the marshal got out of her car and marched up to the door.

Crapulence. A man answered the door. She could tell that from his size. But the marshal was blocking the rest of him. She could only see the top of his head. Was it Nick? He had dark hair like Nick. But from that distance, she couldn't tell. The marshal disappeared inside. *Now what?*

"Now what, cowgirl?" Jack asked, as if reading her mind.

"Should I go to the door?" She gnawed on a jagged fingernail.

Jack shrugged. "We've come all this way . . . Might as well."

"Might as well," she repeated. She zipped up her parka. "Wish me luck." She opened the passenger door.

"I'm coming with you."

"Please don't." She leaned down and blew him a kiss. "Thanks, Jack. You're a good friend." She shut the car door and took a deep breath. *The moment of truth.* Crunching through the snow in her cowboy boots, she was about to cross the street when she spotted . . .

She froze in her tracks. *Oh my God! He's alive. What is he doing here?*

Confused, she ran back to the car and hopped in. "Look." She pointed. "Don't let him see us."

A wiry figure, smoke billowing out from under his hoodie, slipped and slid along the sidewalk in fancy leather boots. It was him; she was sure.

Lolita's cousin. *Vanya.*

13

____

"**W**hat are you doing here?"

Bobby "The Nose" Moretti sounded miffed. The Nose, a high-level mobster under WITSEC protection, wasn't known for his manners. At least not his good ones. His cover name was Bobby Moore. He'd been embedded in this two-bedroom brick ranch house in the suburbs of Casper for the last two years. *Pretty nice neighborhood for a crook.*

Bobby took a step backwards and let her pass. The smell of fried onions hit her like a wall, followed by the sickeningly sweet scent of floral air freshener. One of those plug-in numbers. She marched down the hall and made a right into the living room. She'd been here weekly to check on Bobby—so often, she could navigate the house with her eyes closed.

"We have to move you." Lexi sized up the contents of his living room. The furniture was rented. Only the

Persian rugs belonged to Bobby. Not that it mattered, since he wouldn't be taking them with him. "Pack your bag."

"What?" The Nose stood there in his bathrobe, fat feet bare, wet hair standing on end, a towel in his hand and water dripping off his big nose. "Now?"

"Yes, now."

"You must be joking."

She shook her head. "Nope."

"Give me a break." He threw the towel at a chair and missed. "I ain't movin' again. I like it here."

"Would you rather be killed?" She picked up the towel from the floor and handed it to him. "Get your butt in gear. I have orders to get you out of here now."

"Why?"

"You're in imminent danger." *A-hole.*

"What does that mean?"

"Means if you don't move your ass, you'll be leaving in a pine box."

"I was hoping for mahogany." He smirked. "How much time do we have?" He untied his bathrobe.

Lexi looked the other way. "Not enough." She thought of Nick back at her place and wondered how much time they had. The smell of his aftershave had come along for the ride. She inhaled deeply.

"How about you and me—"

"Nope." She swung around and glared at him. "Move your butt, or I'll let Teeth's guys blow your head off." *Doesn't he get the urgency here?* It was like he had a death wish.

"All right, all right. No need to get bitchy." He slipped off his bathrobe. Underneath, he was buck naked.

She tightened her lips but didn't budge. "Fifteen minutes. Then you're on your own."

He sauntered off toward the bedroom, trailing his robe like he had all day.

What a Pop-Tart. Like most of the guys she was supposed to protect, Nose really belonged behind bars. She knew the feds could never get the goods on a big cheese without the help of these pepperonis, but still, sometimes they were hard to take.

That's where Nick was different. Unlike the others, he wasn't a crook. He was a regular guy. Except he wasn't that either. There was something special about him. Not just the way he looked—which was yummy—or the way he dressed, but something about his gentle manner and top-shelf whiskey voice. She could get used to a guy like that.

"Okay. Where we goin'?"

Her hand flew to her gun. "Don't sneak up on me like that." She closed her eyes and exhaled. *Come on, Lex. Keep your mind in the game.*

Nose shrugged. "My earthly belongings." He held up a small duffel bag. He was now wearing his robe, which was hanging open, exposing his boxer shorts.

Sigh. "Bobby, go put on some clothes."

"I have on a robe." He looked down at his feet. "And socks."

"I'm not driving you anywhere until you put on *more* clothes." She shook her head. Why did these wiseguys have to be such jerks? Sometimes she felt like tipping off the mob to their whereabouts herself.

Bobby the Nose dropped his bag and disappeared around the corner. She dropped into a fussy chair in the living room and glanced at her phone. A text message from Nick. Her heart sped up. Was he in trouble? She tapped her phone and smiled when she read the message. "Miss U" was all it said. *Boy, is he on the rebound.* Sliding her phone back into her shoulder bag, she fought the temptation to text back in spite of the high-school-style butterflies in her stomach.

Bang. She hit the carpet. On the surface of her brain, she knew the noise was coming from the front door. But in a deeper, more subterranean part, she was back in Afghanistan, cowering behind a tank while her friends got blown up. Her hands were shaking, and her vision was blurred.

Gunfire. She fumbled for her sidearm. What was happening? Where was she? Overcome by nausea, panting, she crawled to her knees.

The gunfire got closer. A man yelling. Out of the corner of her eye, she spotted Bobby the Nose in his boxer shorts standing in the hallway, pointing a Magnum toward the front door. *Wait. He's not supposed to have a weapon. He's breaking his parole.* She shook her head to clear her thoughts. *Who's he shooting at? Or who's shooting at him?*

She jumped up, holding her Glock pistol out in front of her with both hands. She sprinted to the entryway. Bobby went down. *Holy Mother of God!* By the time she reached him, a pool of blood was circling his torso and rivulets had spread through the grout between the tiles. His mouth was moving, making smacking sounds.

Son of a— She glanced down at him but aimed her gun at the front door. The bitter cold was streaming in through the bullet holes. *Shit.* She had a dying witness on her hands and a killer on the loose. She knelt down and put her palm on Bobby's shoulder. "Hang on," she said, more to herself than to him. He had to survive. "Hold on. I'm getting help." Where was her phone? She had to call 911.

She ran back to the living room. Her shoulder bag was laying on the floor, its contents strewn across the beige carpet. She dove for her phone. Grabbed it. Stuffed her gun into its holster. She tapped 9-1-1 as she rounded the corner and slid past Bobby. *Poor SOB.*

Bobby groaned.

"Hang on," she said as she rushed past him. "This is Deputy Marshal Lexington Colt. A man's been shot. Get an ambulance to 1911 Cedar Street." She jammed her phone into her back pocket, yanked her gun out of its holster, and opened the front door. Gun drawn, she peeked out over the threshold. She looked left and then right. Nobody. Where was the shooter? Slowly, she walked out onto the stoop. She crept down the front steps and headed up the walkway toward the street, scanning the snow for fresh footprints as she went.

A couple doors down, a black SUV squealed out of the driveway and took off up the road. Lexi ran after it, trying to make out the license plate. She fired a warning shot. The vehicle turned the corner and was gone.

Dammit. She sprinted back to Bobby's place. Taking the front stairs two at a time, she slid over the threshold and almost slipped in the puddle of blood that had formed around Bobby's body. Still holding her Glock in one hand, she knelt down and put two fingers to his neck. "Come on—don't die on me, you bastard." Bobby was still now. An unnatural stillness. The warmth was evaporating from his body, lagging behind his spirit like the last hanger-on at a party.

"Party's over," Lexi said under her breath.

"Nick," a woman screamed. "Nick!"

Lexi's head jerked up along with her gun.

"Don't go in there," a man yelled. "Jessie, please. Come back."

A young blonde woman wearing a big parka and a funny hat stood in the threshold. Her mouth gaping, she pointed at Bobby.

Lexi stood up, her Glock trained on the woman. "Don't move."

The man appeared in the doorway. "What's going on?" He peeked over the blonde's shoulder.

"That's not Nick," the blonde said, her voice trembling. She started to cross the threshold.

"Don't take another step." Lexi kept her gun trained on the pair. If these two were the shooters, they wouldn't come back to the scene, would they? She glanced down at Bobby. His dead eyes stared back up at her. The sight of the red blood expanding across the taupe tiles threw her back into the Registan Desert, where the lifeblood of her fiancé, Gabriel Lopez, had sunk into the sand along with her dreams for their future, leaving her heart as scorched as the desert earth. She'd sworn she'd never love anyone or anything again. It hurt too much.

"Are you okay?" the blonde asked from the doorway. "Oh my God. You're bleeding."

Lexi looked down at her shirt and pants for signs she'd been shot. A red crescent stained her ivory blouse from her armpit to her waist. She touched her side. "It's not mine." She must have gotten Bobby's blood on her shirt when she bent down to him. "Who are you?" How did this woman know Nick? *Shit. Is this the girlfriend? The one he bought the ring for?*

"I'm Jessica James. Nick Schilling's, ah . . . friend from Chicago."

Dammit. She is the girlfriend. Wayne had warned her she was snooping around. *What would Nick do if he knew his girlfriend was here? Give her that engagement ring?* Her stomach soured.

"You're so pale," the girlfriend said, coming closer.

"Are you sure you're okay? You look like you've seen a ghost."

Ghosts were her constant companions, not that she'd admit it. Especially not to the girlfriend. "Stand back, please. This is a crime scene."

"Is that another witness?" the man asked, his hands jammed in the pockets of his wool peacoat. "The dead man?"

How in the hell does he know about my witnesses?

"I'm betting it was a Bratva hit or maybe Mr. Teeth." The girlfriend yanked her Elmer Fudd hat off. Her messy blonde hair fell to her shoulders.

Stunned, Lexi accidentally dropped her phone into the puddle of blood. *How in the hell does she know about Teeth? And how in the hell did Teeth's assassin find Bobby?* Holy hell. There must be a mole in WITSEC.

JESSICA BENT DOWN, picked up the marshal's phone, and wiped it off with a tissue from her jacket pocket. *Yuck.* She handed the phone to the marshal and nonchalantly dropped the bloody tissue on the floor. The marshal was even more attractive up close . . . a hot-but-wholesome kind of pretty. Was that a twinge of jealousy pricking her chest? Or maybe it was admiration. Probably not a lot of marshals who wore a silk shirt and blazer as well as this one.

The marshal looked up at her with steely eyes.

"How do you know about Bratva and Teeth?" She touched the hilt of the gun in her holster.

Whoa. Jessica took a step back. *She's not going to shoot me, is she?* "I saw a friend . . . actually, my friend's cousin . . . he's Bratva . . . well, ex-Bratva . . ." She was sinking into a hole she'd dug for herself. "I mean, my friend's cousin from Chicago."

The marshal scowled.

"He's a bartender. Well, he was a security guard, but he got fired. I mean, he used to be part of the Russian mafia."

"Slow down," the marshal said.

Jessica held her hands up. "Sorry."

"We saw him on the sidewalk and then drove around the block so he wouldn't see us." Jack stepped inside the entryway. "When we came back around, we saw holes in the door and freaked out."

"And who are you two?" The marshal straightened up. "Bonnie and Clod?"

"Clyde," Jack said, obviously hurt.

"Okay, Clyde. Why don't you and Bonnie here come inside and tell me what the heck you're doing here." The marshal gestured them into the living room, and they followed her. "Sit." She pointed at a floral couch.

Jessica did as she was told. Jack followed suit, sitting so close she could feel the warmth of his body against hers. The living room was freezing. *Someone really should close the front door.*

Sirens wailed in the distance.

The marshal sat down on the edge of a matching upholstered chair. For several seconds, she sat staring at them with a disapproving look on her face.

Jessica felt like she'd been called to the principal's office and was supposed to guess why. She fiddled with the fringe of her leather jacket sticking out below the green parka. Yeah. She was wearing two jackets. "Ragamuffin," her mom used to call her.

"So?" The marshal raised one eyebrow.

"So we were just driving up the street when we saw . . . our friend from Chicago."

"But you didn't want him to see you?" the marshal asked.

"We were surprised." Jessica glanced over at Jack. *I could use some help here.*

The marshal scowled again. "Your friend from Chicago. In the suburbs of Casper, Wyoming. Uh huh. Try again."

"We came to Wyoming to find Nick." She nudged Jack with her elbow. "Our bed-and-breakfast is right up the street."

"You're just driving up and down every street, looking for this guy Nick?" The marshal cocked her head. "Why don't you give it a try, Clyde."

Jack cleared his throat. "Jessica here is looking for her fancy-man fiancé." He made a weird spiraling gesture with his hands. "He's in witness protection somewhere in Wyoming, and you're the federal marshal protecting him."

Jessica elbowed him hard. "He's not my fiancé."

He winced. "Paramour."

"He's not even my boyfriend."

"So I have a chance?" he asked playfully.

If the marshal's eyes could shoot death rays, they'd both be goners. "I'm going to need your names and addresses." She slipped a small notebook out of her shoulder bag. "And a description of your ex-Bratva friend from Chicago. Then, after the crime scene team gets here, I'm going to escort you to the marshal's office." She got up and handed the notebook and a pen to Jessica. "And if they clear you, then you're going to head back home to Chicago and never come back."

"It's a free country, Marshal. And we haven't done anything wrong." Jack leaned back into the couch cushion.

"So I've heard. But if I catch you sniffin' around here again, I'll lock you up."

"On what charges?" Jessica asked.

"Let's see. You've already admitted being friends with the likely shooter." She cocked her head. "So how does 'accessory to murder' sound?"

"You've got it wrong," Jessica said as she scribbled her name and address on the pad. "Like Jack said, we're here to find my . . . my . . . my friend Nick." She handed the pad and pen to Jack. "And I really don't think Vanya could be the shooter. He's actually a nice—"

"Mobster?" The marshal waited for Jack to finish

writing and then collected her pad. "So where is this friend now?"

"When we came back around the block, he was gone." Jessica opened her palms.

"What kind of car was he driving?" the marshal asked.

"I didn't see a car." Jack turned to Jessica. "Did you?"

"I wasn't looking for a car." She shrugged. "Maybe he parked down the block?"

"So he just vanished into thin air?" The marshal shook her head. "An innocent man doesn't run."

"Unless there are bullets flying," Jessica said.

The sirens were right outside now.

"We'll finish this conversation at headquarters. I want to know how you and your *friend* found my witness." The marshal held out her hand. "Hand over your driver's licenses."

"But you already have our names and addresses," Jack said.

"Yeah. Let's see if you wrote down the real thing." She wiggled her fingers.

Jessica pulled her license out of her wallet and held it out to the marshal. Jack did the same.

The marshal slid both licenses into the pad. "You two sit tight." She stuffed the pad back into her bag and then headed to the entryway. "Don't move a muscle, you hear?" She disappeared around the corner.

Tires screeched outside, and the sirens cut off. *More police? An ambulance for the dead guy?*

"What are we going to do?" Jessica turned to Jack.

"Get the heck out of here." He leaned his elbows on his knees and put his head in his hands. "I went to jail for you once, and I don't ever plan on going back. You know I'd do anything for you . . . anything except go back to prison."

"But Nick—"

"No." He shook his head. "Not this time, cowgirl."

As soon as she was around the corner, Lexi let out a gasp. *That's the girlfriend. The woman Nick is in love with. Holy hell.* She put her hand over her mouth. *The one he bought the ring for.* Her eyes started to water, and she hugged herself. Why was her love life always so complicated? Why had she fallen for Nick? He was her witness. And he belonged to someone else. It was wrong. Just wrong. But she couldn't help it. Her heart didn't follow the rules. Never had.

Should I tell him that his girlfriend is here in Wyoming? Lexi bent over and put her hands on her knees to steady herself. No. She couldn't tell him. To tell him would be risking his life. She wasn't just being selfish. It was for his own good.

Sucking in air, she tried to quash the questions racing through her head. *Come on, Lexi. Get it together. You're at a crime scene.*

"Are you injured?" A voice from the doorway startled her. It was Noah Stark, her colleague. Nice enough guy. But she couldn't afford to appear weak in front of him.

"No." She straightened and adjusted her blouse. "It's his blood. Not mine." She took a deep breath and filled Noah in on what had happened.

"There are two suspects in the other room." She waved her thumb in the direction of the living room. "Can you wait for the coroner while I take them to headquarters? Drake will want to question them." *Drake. Dammit.* She hadn't called him yet. If there was a mole in WITSEC, they didn't have a moment to lose. All of their witnesses and the whole damned WITSEC program was at risk.

Two hours later—after Drake was satisfied the stupid kids had nothing to do with the murder or the mole—she escorted Bonnie and Clod to I-25 and pointed them south. They'd have to head east on I-80 out of Cheyenne. Hopefully that would be the last she laid eyes on either one of them. Especially the girlfriend.

Sigh. So that skinny, whiny Yank was the girlfriend. *What does Nick see in her?* She looked like a bag lady with that goofy Elmer Fudd hat and two coats. *Who wears red cowboy boots?* And those frayed jeans were wet up to her knees. She was a hot mess.

Lexi heard her Aunt Martha's voice in her head: *Bless her little heart.* Whenever Aunt Martha felt sorry for someone, she'd say, "Bless her little heart." Like warmed-over sweet tea on a sultry day, it was really more of an insult.

As Lexi watched the sports car speed off down the highway, she hoped she wouldn't have to add injury to insult. But if the girlfriend or her scraggly sidekick showed up again, she'd have to haul 'em off just to keep them out of the way.

She shuddered. She'd almost pulled on those idiot kids. She could have shot one of them. Or what if they'd gotten in the way of the bullet meant for Bobby? *Kids. Heck.* They couldn't be much younger than her. The guy might even be older. But somehow they seemed like kids. Kids who hadn't seen much of the world. Kids who still had stardust in their eyes. Kids who hadn't seen their friends get blown to bits in some godforsaken desert.

Wayne had warned her the girlfriend was in town. And last time she'd talked to Drake, he'd told her to get rid of the girlfriend before she got Nick killed. Those kids snooping around was dangerous. For them and for her witness.

They'd followed her from the courthouse. She'd seen the little car behind her but was in such a hurry— and so distracted by memories of her morning with Nick—she hadn't bothered about it. She should have.

Of course, if she had, she might have arrived to find Bobby dead, wearing nothing but his robe. Then again, her being in the house hadn't stopped the assassination. Except that Bobby was dead in his underwear because she'd insisted he put some on. She'd been right there in the next room, unable to stop it. She pounded the steering wheel. *Lexington Colt. Get your flipping head screwed on straight, you flipping head case.* She brushed a tear away with the back of her hand. She was a flipping basket case. And there was nothing anyone could do about it. She might as well drive into oncoming traffic and get it over with.

The poor SOB in the other lane didn't deserve to die today even if she did. Tucking her self-pity into a dark corner of her mind, she put the car in drive and pulled onto the entrance ramp to I-25. She didn't want to face Drake or anyone else at headquarters. Not after what just happened to Bobby. *On. My. Watch.* But she had no choice. She had to check in at headquarters and fill out a report on Bobby. And then tell Drake about the damn girlfriend and her sloppy sidekick. She couldn't avoid a debriefing after what had happened at Bobby's. Drake was going to chew her ass big time.

Keeping her eyes on the road, she felt around in the back seat for a pop. *Shit.* She'd run out of Mountain Dew. What a day. What a flipping day.

14

———

Parched, Danny pulled into the parking lot of the Safeway. He needed to get a snack and a Pepsi if he was going to keep driving around looking for the marshal. He was still kicking himself for not following her when she'd left the ranch. The sun was low in the sky. He glanced at his watch. Not even four. Sunset came early this time of year. He'd love to just go back to the Cutthroat Ranch and enjoy a nice dinner and relax by the fire. His stomach growled. That place did have good food. But a snack and a Pepsi would have to do.

Forget about the Pepsi. A Budweiser or a nice shot of whiskey—that's what I need. That and the full-course meal they served at the ranch. His mouth watered thinking about the pie he'd have for dessert. But if he didn't find Schilling soon, Teeth would go ballistic. Luckily, Teeth was a thousand miles away. So no pie yet.

He opened the door of the rented SUV. He had one foot on the slick asphalt when he saw her. The blonde Chicago chick. *Bingo!* He couldn't believe his luck. He shut the car door and watched her walk to a small Japanese car. *Hey. That's not the car she was in earlier. Where's her boyfriend, the skinny nerdy dude?*

If he couldn't find the marshal, then the girlfriend was the next best thing. She was persistent. He'd give her that. And maybe, just maybe, she'd lead him to Schilling. *Then bingo.* He patted his jacket pocket. He had something for Nick. *Won't he be surprised.* Not as surprised as Bobby the Nose, standing there in his undershorts. Danny chuckled and rubbed his chin. He'd heard all about it from pals. He didn't think she'd do it. *But she did . . . she did.* The little lady had guts, whoever she was.

The Chicago chick put a six-pack on the passenger's seat and dashed around and hopped in the driver's seat. Hands on the steering wheel, muscles tensed, he was ready to pounce.

No Pepsi. Damn. His mouth was dry. Man, he wished he had a six-pack. *Oh well.* He'd been sober for almost two years now. He wasn't about to mess that up just because he was stuck in Nowheresville, Wyoming, chasing some dead rich guy's kid.

Danny got violent when he drank, a violence he couldn't control. Violence was a scalpel in the right hands, steady hands . . . not the hands of a drunk. Whenever he drank, he regretted it. *Sigh.* Even back in high school, he'd been a violent drunk. And it had caused him a world of hurt.

He pulled back out into traffic, following the silver Honda at a safe distance.

The Chicago chick got on the highway heading south, and so did Danny. The rented SUV was a dog when it came to speed—luckily, they weren't drag racing. But it handled pretty good in the snow. He was glad about that, given the road conditions. As the sunshine decreased, the ice increased. If he didn't have to find Schilling, he'd be spinning brodies in the Safeway parking lot.

The Honda signaled just before the first exit to Casper. Danny moved into the right lane and coasted onto the off-ramp a few seconds after it did. He hoped he wouldn't have to spend the whole damn night in the car. He checked the gas gauge. If he did, at least he wouldn't run out of gas. No way he was turning the car off in this cold-ass weather. That chick better lead him to Schilling. She'd better not be taking him on a wild goose chase . . . or he might just have to cook her goose.

There once was a goose from Seattle. It had a darn sexy waddle . . . A telltale tattle?

He glanced in his rearview mirror to make sure Bratva hadn't sent another goon to make sure he didn't deliver the package. After what happened to the last one . . . He chuckled. Open hunting season on the Russian brotherhood. Maybe he'd be the one to bag a heavy tonight. That'd be fun. Make Teeth happy too.

The Honda pulled off onto a one-lane side road. Did he dare follow it? There weren't any other cars on the road. Surely, she'd spot him.

He stopped and waited until the Honda was out of sight. Then he coasted onto the side road and watched as the kid fishtailed up the road. The snowpack was slippery. He chuckled. Good thing he got the SUV. That little tin can she was in was no match for these roads.

Where was that Chicago chick taking him? And what happened to her sidekick and his little sports car? Last time he'd checked, the GPS on his phone was halfway to Omaha. Guess he was the appetizer. Now she was looking for the main course. He smiled.

There once was a chick from Chicago. Who ate little punks with risotto. She swallowed them whole, like a carrion crow, but spat out their spirits with gusto.

Danny's curiosity was piqued. He wanted to know what the blonde chick from Chicago was going to do when she met the gritty marshal from Tennessee. Yeah, Teeth had filled him in on the trigger-happy marshal. Story goes, she'd popped the last guy Teeth sent after a snitch in witness protection. That was a year ago. No questions. Just shot him in the face. Tough broad. But she didn't stop yesterday's bloodbath back in Casper.

Poor Bobby the Nose. He's wasn't such a bad guy. Danny rubbed his chin. Must have been another one of Teeth's guys. Funny, Teeth never mentioned it. He could have easily put it on his to-do list. Yup. Bobby shouldn't have snitched. In this business, loyalty was more important than brains, talent, or muscle. Good thing, too. Because loyalty was the one thing you could control. Maybe Danny didn't have as much muscle, brains, or talent as some, but he wasn't a snitch.

Danny pulled the SUV off to the side of the road again and into an unplowed turnout. He'd let the Chicago chick get more of a head start. Not much chance of losing her out here. There was one narrow road, and it was easy to see tire tracks in the fresh snow. He had time. He could wait. Anyway, until he gave the goods to Schilling, he was stuck here. Might as well have some fun.

Sage Brush Road. Jessica knew she could count on her hippy hacker friend. Amber had searched the WITSEC database until she finally found the marshal's address. *Clever girl.*

Well, this is Sage Brush Road, such as it is. Pretty desolate. The marshal must like her privacy. The narrow county road with snow berms on either side reminded her of home.

The temperature was dropping fast as the sun went down. Then the roads would be icy, and she'd be navigating in the dark.

The rental car skidded, and she tapped the brakes. *What if WITSEC uses decoy addresses?* Maybe she was on a wild-goose chase.

She wished Jack hadn't left. His parting words echoed through her head. "Not this time, cowgirl." Ever since Nick had died . . . disappeared . . . she'd come to rely on Jack. Today, she'd learned she couldn't take him for granted.

She white-knuckled the steering wheel to keep the rental car from slipping off the road. She couldn't afford a bigger car or one with four-wheel drive . . . Heck, she couldn't really afford this tin can.

Where in the world am I going?

The sun was setting, and the winter wonderland was turning a gorgeous pinkish-orange. *Maybe I should turn around. Maybe I should get back on I-25 and head home . . .* Home to Montana. *I could be in Whitefish by tomorrow morning.*

With the snow-covered evergreens in silhouette against the gray-violet mountains, she could be driving into Alpine Vista Trailer Park right now. She thought of her mother, all alone in that double-wide, drinking herself to death. Jessica promised the heavens that if she found Nick, she'd go visit her mom.

The evergreen trees heavy with snow that bent ever so slightly made her miss the mountains where she grew up. The whole world looked pure and reborn . . . until the pristine snow turned to gray slush and everything turned to crap.

Wait. Is that smoke?

In the distance, a stream of white smoke danced upward against the frigid violet sky. Where there was smoke, there must be fire . . . a woodstove fire. Folks out here couldn't count on the grid to keep them warm. Growing up in Montana, Jessica knew all about the necessity of being able to survive off the grid—which might have been why she'd fled to the city as soon as she could. Struggling to survive made people harsh. But, as she'd learned after six years in Chicago, so did living in the city. At least nature's bounty made it possible to survive out here, provided your body was strong. In the city, you needed an able body, street smarts, and a good job. Surviving in the country was backbreaking, but surviving in the city could be soul-crushing.

Now what? She stopped in the middle of the road. Off to the left, an open wrought iron gate invited her into a long driveway. Back off the road—lined up like papa, mama, and baby—sat a big farmhouse, a new barn, and a tiny log cabin.

Jessica twisted in her seat to get a better view. Sure enough, it was there. The blue Charger, parked in front of the cabin.

Should she just drive in? She rubbed her hands together in front of the heat vent. The marshal had said she'd lock Jessica up if she set foot in Wyoming again. She glanced around. This was the only entrance. On either side of the driveway, snow-covered fields spread out to the foot of the mountain range in the distance. Three pretty horses with their long winter coats huddled together in a windbreak. *Crapulence.* There was no way to drive in without being seen. She'd have to go on foot . . . and even then . . . Too bad she didn't have a white parka and white trapper hat for camouflage.

She understood why Jack had left, but she kind of wished he'd stayed. Sometimes Jack could be as clingy and annoying as a deer tick, but most of the time his presence was soothing. He was like a well-worn sweatshirt, the go-to favorite . . . out of habit as much as anything else. Then there were those moments when she had to fight the urge to kiss him. Jackass, with his floppy hair, smart mouth, and lopsided grin. He'd only been gone a few hours, and already she missed him.

Maybe she should give up her search and go back home . . . back to Chicago. She could do worse than Jack. And as everyone kept telling her, if Nick wanted to be found, he would have found a way to contact her. Anyway, what was she going to do? Sleep here in this ice-cold car all night, waiting for the marshal to lead her to Nick? For all she knew, Nick was halfway across the country by now. What good was staking out the marshal's house?

She had half a mind to march up to the front door and plead her case, woman to woman. Surely the marshal had been in love before and would understand, right? *In love.* Is that what she was? She rolled her mind's eye. She was just entertaining romantic fantasies about Jack, and now she's thinking she's in love with Nick. *Dang it, cowgirl. Make up your mind.*

Make up your mind indeed. If she kept the car

running, eventually she'd run out of gas. But if she turned it off, she'd freeze to death. She had to make a decision. Was she going to confront the marshal, or turn tail and give up? If only Detective Cormier hadn't told her about the engagement ring in Nick's pocket, she might have been able to let it go. It wasn't even that she wanted to marry Nick. Probably. She just wanted to know whether he'd planned to propose. No one had ever proposed to her.

She leaned her head into the steering wheel. It was absurd, really. She'd come all this way, had a federal marshal almost draw on her, and had been warned off searching for Nick a dozen times. What would she say if she found him? *I don't know if I want to marry you, but do you want to marry me? Is that why you had a ring in your pocket?*

And what if he did want to marry her? What then? Would she marry him, give up her job, and go into hiding with him? Not just her job . . . everything. Would she give up everything? Her past, her life, her strained relationship with her alcoholic mother? Was she losing her mind?

Paralyzed by indecision, she sat in the rental car with the motor running, staring across the white field at the log cabin, her eyes following the swirls of smoke from the chimney as they dissipated into the atmosphere. Sometimes she wished she could just disappear.

Long shadows and the orange glow on the horizon

told her it was now or never. She tugged her trapper down over her ears, stuffed her hands into the oversized mittens, and zipped up her parka. If only she'd brought her snow boots. You'd think growing up in the mountains, she'd know better.

Armed with only her phone and her wits, she slid across the county road and started up the driveway. Trying not to fall, she dug her heels into the snowpack as she stomped up the road. Eyes burning, head down, she trudged forward, pushing against the wind. *It's freaking cold.* Even her eyelashes and nose hairs were probably turning blue. At least the frigid air stinging her face and lungs kept her from thinking too much about what she was doing. One nail takes out another, as her dad used to say.

The brush along the drive was encased in jagged ice crystals. In the distance, the snowcapped mountains had turned pinkish. And the sun setting over the ranch house and little cabin looked like a pastoral scene out of a romantic landscape painting. Under other circumstances, she'd say it was beautiful. Now, she was freezing her butt off and probably about to be arrested. She'd be lucky not to get frostbite in her toes. *Stupid cowboy boots.*

By the time she reached the homestead, she was shivering so hard her teeth chattered. She'd only planned to peek in the windows, but she might have to screw up the courage to knock on the door just to get out of this cold. The big house was dark. Hopefully no one was home. Slowing her pace, she approached the cabin. Unlike the house, it was glowing in the twilight. Looking so cozy and warm. Maybe the marshal would take pity on her. Invite her in for a hot toddy or at least a cup of tea.

She was close enough now that she could see into the front window of the cabin. Even at this distance, she could make out a figure—a man—sitting in a chair near a fireplace. *Nick?*

She was almost to the front steps when, through the window, she spotted the marshal enter the living room with her hair down, wearing a bathrobe. She was carrying a bottle of wine. Jessica stood still and watched.

The man held up a wine glass, and the marshal filled it. He was still in silhouette, a shadow flickering in firelight. He took a sip. The marshal drank straight from the bottle. Was she laughing? Who was the man? The scene was so intimate; it couldn't be Nick.

When the man stood up, she got a good view of him. Her heart nearly jumped out of her chest. It was him. She'd found him! She put her mittened hand to her mouth to stifle a gasp. Then she froze in place. Paralyzed. She watched as Nick put his arms around the marshal and kissed her, a long passionate kiss. *No. No. No.* When he opened the marshal's robe, Jessica turned and ran.

She hightailed it out of there as fast as she could, tears pricking her eyes. She slipped and fell and got up again. Running, her heart racing, she felt like she might throw up. But she didn't stop.

She just kept running. Even when she fell and banged her knee, she kept running. She slipped again, this time falling face first, splitting her lip. Even the metallic taste of blood couldn't stop her.

If she had to, she'd run all the way to Montana . . . home . . . to curl up in a fetal position in her childhood bed and lick her wounds. She got up and started running again.

15

L exi had only seen a flash. She was, after all, a bit distracted by Nick's fiery kisses. Still, she'd recognized that green streak going by outside the window. It was the girlfriend's stupid green parka. Damn girl should be halfway across Nebraska by now. What was she doing here?

She grimaced. *Girlfriend.* Nick had given up the girlfriend a little too easily, hadn't he? He'd even offered the girlfriend's ring to her. Her gut told her to watch out for this guy. So did her heart. But the rest of her body betrayed her, surprised her even. She craved him like a crackhead craved another hit. And now it was making her careless. Risking the life of a witness. Plus if Drake ever found out she'd slept with Nick, she'd be canned for sure. She pulled out of his embrace.

"What's wrong?" he asked.

"Possible intruder." She threw her coat on over her

robe and jammed her feet into her snow boots. As an afterthought, she grabbed her gun belt and cinched it around her waist.

"Where are you going?" He followed her to the door.

"To investigate." When she opened the door, a blast of cold air hit her legs. She turned back to Nick. "Stay here."

What would she do if she caught up to the girlfriend? Arrest her? For what? She'd have to bring the girlfriend back to the cabin. That would be awkward with Nick there. And not just because of their fooling around. No. Nick had agreed to cut all ties with his former life in order to get protection. He couldn't have contact with that girl from Chicago. Plus, Drake had instructed her to lock up the girlfriend if necessary.

Anyway, Lexi had warned the girl. She'd given her a chance to go back home.

Even once her eyes had adjusted to the dusky light, she couldn't see the girl. She did a 180, scanning the property, looking for the girl. *Where did she go?* Lexi examined the ground. Sure enough. Tracks. She followed them to the driveway. The girl was on the run. Yup. Divots in the snow where she'd fallen a couple of times. The girl was in a hurry. Why? Was someone—or something—chasing her? Nope. Besides tire tracks, the girl's were the only tracks in the pristine snow. One thing about snowy Wyoming, it was easy to see footprints.

If the girl had found her place, so could the mafia. Dammit. She kept her address secret for a reason. The stupid girl probably led Bratva or Teeth's goons right to the cabin. Shit. She had to get Nick out of there ASAP. *Right now*. She couldn't wait for Drake to relocate him.

She turned and ran back toward the cabin. If that idiot girlfriend did lead them here, then mobsters could be descending on her at any minute. She heard a car and looked up in time to see a silver Honda Accord fishtailing up the county road.

No sports car? Clyde must have had the good sense to go back to Chicago. Why didn't he take the girl with him?

She inhaled the sharp air and took off sprinting. Bad enough she'd lost two witnesses. She wasn't going to let some lovesick girl make her lose another, especially not Nick.

DANNY KNEW there was trouble when he spotted that Chicago chick running like a bat out of hell and slip-sliding all over the place. What in the heck was chasing her down that driveway? Couldn't be good. That was his cue to find a better hiding place. He backed further into the turnout until he was right up against the snowbank. Trouble was, he could barely see the road through the trees.

Muscles tense, he waited for the headlights.

Should he follow the Chicago babe? Or should he wait and see what was chasing her? If that Jessica chick had found Nick, she wouldn't be hightailing it out of here. She'd be enjoying the reunion right about now. He grinned. Always follow the girlfriend . . . or the wife. Broads were bound to mess up.

There once was a broad from New Jersey whose figure was nothing but curvy. She snitched on her man, ended up in the can, and some said she still was unworthy.

A set of headlights zipped past on the county road. Had to be the Chicago chick, right? There was no one else out there.

The moment of truth. Would he follow the car or check for the hideout? Something scared that girl away. Something or someone. A bodyguard? The marshal? He was going to find out.

Grateful he had four-wheel drive, he barreled through the snow. A cloud of the powdery stuff swallowed up the vehicle. He cranked it into low and crawled out onto the road.

He glanced up the road. He couldn't be sure, but it looked like the little Japanese car. *Geesus.* The girl must have a death wish. The car nearly rammed into the snowbank before it started hauling ass. Whoever it was, they were going to get themselves killed driving like that on these roads. Obviously, something was up at that house up ahead. And he had an idea what it was. He smiled to himself. Time to have some fun.

He threw the SUV into high gear and gunned it.

He sped up the driveway. "I'll be damned," he said with a chuckle. In the beam of his headlights, he saw the marshal running through the snow in her bathrobe.

All this commotion had to mean Schilling the snitch was inside. *Bingo.*

LEXI JUMPED into the snowbank just in time to avoid being hit. An SUV sped past her. The flipping thing nearly killed her. Crawling out of the snowbank, she took off at full tilt toward the cabin. The impact of each footfall vibrated up her legs. Her lungs burned from the frigid air. She lost her footing on the ice and landed with a thud. *Ouch.* Her hip was going to have one hell of a bruise. Scrambling to her feet again, she gritted her teeth and ran through the pain.

The SUV swerved and slid to a stop in front of the cabin. *Shit!* That idiot girlfriend. She'd led them right to Nick. A big guy in a suit got out of the SUV and sauntered up to the door like he had all the time in the world.

Her hand on her Glock, Lexi didn't stop running until she reached the vehicle. She slowed to a speed walk as she assessed the situation. *Dammit!* She had to get the drop on the assassin before he killed Nick.

The thug used his elbow to break the glass on the front door. He stuck his arm through the window, presumably to reach the deadbolt. Thank God she'd locked the door on her way out.

Gun drawn, she approached the front porch. "Freeze. Hands in the air." Feet apart, holding the Glock in both hands, she got a bead on the killer. *Head or heart?* She was close enough. *Head.* "Turn around. Slowly."

The killer put his hands in the air and turned around. She recognized him as one of Teeth's guys. So it was Teeth that was having her witnesses killed. "Slowly," she repeated. "Walk over to your vehicle. And put your hands on the hood."

As the hitman walked in slow motion toward the SUV, Lexi did the same. She had to get his gun. *Dammit.* She needed her cuffs. She'd taken down guys his size before. And she'd just as soon shoot him as look at him.

"Alright, Marshal," the dude said. "Take it easy."

"Shut up. Hands on the hood." With her Glock still aimed right at his temple, she followed in his footsteps. The closer she got, the more confident she was that she could blow his head off if necessary.

The big guy made to turn around.

"Hands where I can see them," she shouted. "Spread your feet. Hands on the hood." She had to frisk him and take his weapon. Or weapons.

"I'm going," he said. "No need to get huffy." He stood next to his car.

"Hands!" she yelled, moving closer.

"There once was a gal from Kentucky," he said, putting both hands on the hood.

She was right behind him. So close, she could feel the heat of his massive body. With one hand, she kept the Glock pointed at his head. With the other, she patted him down. No easy feat.

With one quick backward jab, he kicked her in the kneecap. *Shit.* She lost her footing. Her gun went off. She didn't know if she'd shot him or not. She hit the ground so hard, it knocked the wind out of her. Her Glock flew out of her hand and landed a few feet away in the snow.

"Moving too fast, she'll land on her ass," the hitman taunted her as he hopped into the driver's seat. "But next time, she won't be so lucky."

All she could do was watch as he backed out and sped away.

Now that the mob had found him, she had to move Nick immediately. She had no choice. *Dammit.* She'd have to call Drake and tell him what happened.

She pulled herself to her feet, retrieved her gun, and marched into the cabin.

"Get your stuff," she called out. "We're leaving." Motel 6 on the edge of town was probably the best bet. Since it backed up to Casper Creek, there was only one approach. She would stand guard all night until Drake found a new location. "Get your ass in gear. Now!"

Jessica could hardly see the road through her tears. *How could he?* Then again, why not? It wasn't like they were engaged or anything. They'd barely gotten back together when he was . . . shipped off to WITSEC. She didn't like to think about when the detective had told her Nick was dead. At that moment, her world had ended . . . but somehow this was worse. Guilt on top of jealousy on top of regret. She wiped the tears with the backs of her hands as she gunned the accelerator. *Good riddance.* Why had she come looking for him anyway? How stupid could she get? What a waste of time.

She was crying so hard, she had to pull over onto the shoulder of the road. She slowed down—but not enough. The car hit the snow berm and jolted her forward and back. By the time she got control and stopped the car, her hands were shaking. Her heart was racing, and her breath was short. Nothing like a car out of control to get the adrenaline surging. Stunned, she sat there panting, staring through the frosty windshield at the snowbank. The snow reflected the moonlight like a broken mirror.

She wiped her nose on her sleeve. Her shirt collar was wet with tears. How had it come to this? She should have just gone home with Jack. She'd risked what she had with Jack for this?

Jack . . . he would never do something like that.

Something like what? Really. What had Nick done? Who wouldn't do the same? He thought he'd never see her again, after all. And unfortunately, the federal marshal assigned to him was as hot as they come. Her stomach churned, and she wondered if she'd have to pull over to barf. *Dang him. Why did he do it?* If he really loved her, he would have waited no matter how long it took.

She shivered. She'd been sitting there no more than fifteen minutes, but it felt like hours. She had to find a place to sleep. Her mom had always said, "Things will look better in the morning." From her experience, the smeared makeup and stained blouse that were funny the night before were a nightmare in the morning. She pulled back onto the road and headed toward Casper.

On the edge of town, she spotted a sign for a Motel 6.

In a daze, she pulled into the parking lot. *Now what?*

With the motor running, she just sat there. She didn't want to be here.

She searched her phone for cheap airfares. The cheapest required a week-in-advance purchase, and a ticket for tomorrow cost the same as her monthly rent.

Crapulence. She couldn't call Jack and ask for another loan. He'd probably give her one, but she just couldn't bring herself to ask—especially since she could have been in his car right now, getting driven home for free. She could call Lolita. But then she'd have to admit she'd been wrong about Nick. Why were flights so expensive? It was cheaper to stay in this crappy motel for another week and then fly back than to fly out tomorrow.

What choice did she have? No way could she stand staying here for a week, constantly being reminded that Nick was shacking up with Eva Mendes across town. Tapping the screen as fast as she could, she would max out her credit card buying a ticket home if that's what it took . . . *Home.* Was Chicago really home?

Montana was just a day's drive away. If she left now and drove all night, she could be there by morning. Was it worth another "I told you so" from her mother? *Caught between the rock of maternal guilt and the hard place of perpetual debt.* She slid her phone back into her pocket.

Alright. She pulled it out again. She bit the bullet and bought the cheapest ticket she could find. Now she'd have to hang around this crappy Motel 6 for another week. But at least she was getting out of here. Had he ever loved her? She leaned her head against the steering wheel and gave in to a flood of tears.

Thump! Thump! Someone was rapping on the window of her car. *Yikes.* She nearly jumped out of her skin. *What the . . .*

It was the marshal. She motioned for Jessica to get out of the car. *Crap. Looks like I'm not going back to either Chicago or Montana, but to jail.*

Jessica waited for the marshal to take a step backward and then opened the car door. "Can I help you, Officer?" She tried to sound innocent.

"Look, Bonnie, I told you to leave Wyoming and not come back." The marshal's legs were bare above her snow boots.

She must be freezing. "I know. But—"

"This badge means no buts." The marshal opened her coat and pointed to a badge attached to her gun belt. "Where's Clyde?"

"He went back to Chicago." Jessica hugged herself.

"You should have gone with him." The marshal's voice was stern.

"I had to find him." Jessica bit her lip. "I saw him in . . . in . . ." *In what? In your house? In your arms?*

"Saw who?" The marshal's steely eyes bore right into Jessica's skull.

"My . . . my . . ." Jessica stammered. *A picture's worth a thousand words.* She reached into her pocket for her phone.

The marshal pulled her gun from the holster. "Take your hand out of your pocket. Slowly."

Holy crap! Does she think I have a weapon? Jessica removed her hand and put her arms above her head. She sucked in frigid air and tried not to hyperventilate. Was she going to jail?

"I warned you," the marshal said. "Now I'm going to have to take you in."

Jessica lowered her arms and put her hands

together in prayer. "Marshal, please. I was only looking for my friend Nick."

"Looking for friends in WITSEC is dangerous business," the marshal barked. "It could get you killed, and it probably will get them killed."

Jessica stared at her hands. "I'm sorry." The marshal was right. She never should have come looking for Nick. She was an idiot. She'd put him in danger and messed up everything.

"We have to take extreme measures to keep our witnesses safe." The marshal lowered her gun but didn't put it back in its holster. "New identities. No connections to their past—"

"I just wanted to talk to him one last time," Jessica said softly. "To get closure." She realized how stupid she must sound. "I'm sorry."

"It's too risky." The marshal's cheeks were bright red.

The marshal was acting tough, but she must be chilled to the bone with no pants on. And if she cared so much about Nick's safety, why was he at her house? "If I could find him, so can Bratva or the mafia."

The marshal finally holstered her gun. "That's exactly my point. We can't take any risks."

"Is that why he's staying at your place?" she blurted out.

"It's not what you think." The marshal glared at her. "It's temporary."

"A marshal getting involved with a witness . . . isn't

that *verboten*?" Jessica was a fine one to talk. She'd gotten involved with Nick when she was his student . . . that was definitely forbidden. "I'm not blaming you. Nick's always been a player." The words stabbed at her heart. It was true. He'd been a player when they'd met four years ago. Why would he be any different now? *A leopard doesn't change its spots.*

"I tell you what." The marshal shifted from foot to foot. "I'll give you one more chance to get out of the state if you promise to quit looking for Nick."

"Quit looking?" she repeated. Could she really make that promise? She'd always be looking . . . even if she wasn't actively looking, she'd be on the lookout. She'd see a tall man in a suit jacket and blue jeans out of the corner of her eye and wonder if it was him. She nodded.

What the . . . Jessica stared past the marshal with wide eyes. Her mouth fell open.

Lolita's cousin Vanya was sneaking up behind the marshal, holding a handgun by its shaft. When Jessica opened her mouth, he shook his head. She snapped her mouth shut.

Should she warn the marshal? Or keep her trap shut? She didn't know who to trust. They both had guns pointed in her direction.

Just as the marshal started to turn around, Vanya brought the butt of his gun down on the back of her head. She collapsed into a heap on the icy asphalt of the parking lot.

"Vanya?" Jessica lowered her arms. "What's going

on? Why'd you do that?" He'd just assaulted a federal officer. That couldn't be good.

"I was just trying to help." Vanya shrugged and smiled, his gold grill gleaming. "Looked like you were in trouble."

"Is she dead?" Jessica knelt down beside the marshal and felt her pulse. "She's alive."

"I hit her very soft," Vanya said. "Just a little tap. She will have headache, that's all."

In the dark parking lot, his accent sounded like something out of a gangster movie. Her heart sped up. What if he was working for Bratva? What if they'd sent him to find Nick? To silence Nick . . . to kill him? She shuddered. "Why are you here?"

"Lolita sent me." Vanya tapped a cigarette out of a pack of Marlboros and clicked his titanium lighter. He took a couple of drags and exhaled a cloud of smoke.

"Lolita?" She was trying to comprehend what was going on. Lolita had gone undercover last spring when her uncle anointed her head of the outfit. Vanya still treated her as the queen. Could she really be running the Russian mob from business school? She was smart enough and shrewd enough, but she was one of the good guys. *Right? I'm just being paranoid. But then what's Vanya doing here?* "Did you kill that man?"

"She's a man?"

"The witness. The guy in his underwear."

Vanya chuckled. "Oh, that poor bastard." He shook his head. "Let's go." He dropped his cigarette and crushed it under the toe of his Italian lace-up. "Sleeping Beauty will wake up soon."

"We can't just leave her here." Jessica stared down at the marshal, who didn't look like she was in a very comfortable position.

"You want to take her with us?" Vanya narrowed his eyes. "Not a good idea."

"Take her with us . . ." Jessica repeated under her breath. *No. Not a good idea. But what?* She couldn't just leave the marshal lying here in a freezing parking lot, unconscious, with her legs exposed to the elements. If the marshal didn't wake up soon, she'd get hypothermia.

"Let's blow this joint." Vanya gestured with his gun.

"I'm not going to leave a federal marshal to freeze to death." Jessica put her hands on her hips and squared off with the wiry Russian.

"Let's go." Vanya stepped over the marshal's body and grabbed Jessica by the elbow. "Come on. They're waiting."

"Who's waiting?"

"You'll see." He grinned. "Hurry, before she wakes up." He tugged at her arm.

"Okay. Hold your horses." She pulled her arm free, then unzipped her coat and shrugged it off.

"Whatcha doing?" Vanya asked. "You think it's summer in a winter dress?" He chuckled and said something in Russian.

Jessica bent down and covered the marshal's legs with her parka.

"*Psikh*. Loony." Vanya shook his head. "Pick up your coat and let's go."

"We can't just leave—"

Vanya interrupted, his tone as dark and treacherous as the asphalt. "I'm not asking." He pointed the gun at her. "I'm telling."

16

Nick wrote the note on the motel stationary. What else could he do?

I'm leaving WITSEC to be with my girl-friend. I'm sorry.

He slid the note into an envelope and then glanced over his shoulder. Surreptitiously, he tucked the letter in behind it. He sealed the envelope and left it on the little table. Lexi would find it when she got back. He clenched his fists so hard his fingernails pressed into his palms. *What will she think? That I'm a no-good criminal and a damned cad, that's what.*

Shivering, Lexi held her head and sat up. *Where am I? What happened?* Why was she lying in the middle of a parking lot? She rubbed her hands together and wiggled her frozen toes. *How long have I been out?* With her numb fingers, she touched her sidearm. At least whoever coldcocked her didn't take her gun.

The asphalt stung her legs as she glanced up at a mostly burnt-out neon sign. Motel 6. Nearby sat a Honda Civic. Not her car. *Right.* The one she was following.

Maybe those kids from Chicago really were a sort of Bonnie and Clyde. She remembered finding Bonnie—the girlfriend—in that Honda. Had Clyde left town? Or was he waiting to hit her over the head? He didn't look like the type to brain a federal marshal. *But who knows.* She hadn't gotten a good enough look at whoever hit her to be sure. She held her head in both hands. A vise squeezed her brain. And she swore she could smell burnt toast.

What in the world? She recognized the ugly green parka wrapped around her legs and kicked it off. Crawling to her hands and knees, she knelt on top of the coat for a few seconds, waiting for her head to quit spinning. Whoever clocked her did a good job. She probably had a concussion. She got to her feet and stood there for a few more seconds, trying not to keel over. *Concussion be damned.* Dragging the girlfriend's parka, she leaned against the Honda. Holy Mother of God, her head hurt.

Right. She'd locked Nick in a hotel room. She glanced up at the balcony. A light was on. Nick was probably still waiting for her to come back. How long was she out?

She pulled her phone out of her pocket. *Dammit.* The screen was cracked. Probably from when she'd fallen. At least it still worked. Almost five-thirty. *Shit.* She must have been out for twenty minutes. Why hadn't Nick come looking for her? Then again, she'd told him to stay put. *Good boy.*

Licking her lips, she focused on walking to her car to get a Mountain Dew. That would make her feel better. The world looked like it was underwater. Not a good sign. She should go the hospital.

She staggered to her car, opened the back seat, and felt around for a pop. Her hand touched something cold and sticky. *Come on! Give me a break.* Her last can of Diet Dew had exploded, leaving a fluorescent iceberg on her back seat.

Why in hell couldn't she be back in the south, where your pops didn't burst open unless you hurled them at fence posts?

She took a deep breath, hoping to quell the nausea. *Ahhh.* She groaned.

Her blurred vision wasn't helping the queasiness. *Come on, Lexi. You just have to make it upstairs.* Upstairs to someone else's boyfriend. Bonnie was right. Her relationship with Nick was inappropriate. She'd never gotten involved with a witness before. So why now? Obviously, it was clouding her judgment. She touched her head. *Ouch.*

Her shrink would say it was PTSD or because she wanted revenge on her dead daddy or some horse shit. If he were alive, her daddy would laugh and say "good old-fashioned animal lust." Of course, he'd be talking about himself and not about her. In his eyes, she was always an innocent little girl. She'd been acting like it since she got back from Afghanistan—chaste as a nun. Since she watched Gabe get blown limb from limb in that gawd-awful desert. She hadn't been with a man since. She wouldn't risk her heart again. Why had she let her guard down now? Trouble. She knew he was trouble.

Her shrink would probably consider it progress. Getting back in the game. Taking the risk. But with a witness? Why did it have to be Nick?

He was attractive. More than attractive. Still, lots of good-looking guys hit on her, and she'd managed to ignore them. What was so special about Nick? It was more than his looks. It was his manner. The way he looked her in the eyes with his full attention, like she was the only thing in the world that mattered. His calming energy was like a tranquilizer soothing her frazzled nerves. He made her feel better. Better about herself, her life, her past. How could she feel this way about a guy she'd just met?

Anyway, Nick had to be involved with some pretty shady characters. Most dudes in WITSEC were pretty bad news. For all she knew, he could be as guilty as most. That would be just her luck—to fall in love with a witness *and* a crook. Even worse, he was still in love with his girlfriend. If there weren't a million other reasons, that was reason enough to call it off.

Hell. Call it off. It wasn't really even on. *Was it?* Whatever it was, it had to stop. She couldn't be sleeping with a witness. It was against regulations. She could lose her job. More importantly, it could compromise his safety. And hers. But the real danger, she knew, wasn't losing her job or her life, but her heart.

Through sheer willpower, she'd made it across the parking lot and to the staircase. She stopped and put her hands on her knees. If only the dizziness would stop. Lordy, her head hurt. She sat on the bottom stair just to get her equilibrium. She wished she could just crawl into bed with Nick. *Dammit.* Thanks to the girlfriend, she was going to have to move Nick yet again. What were the chances the damn girlfriend would be staying at this hotel? She was supposed to be halfway across Iowa for cripes' sake. *Damn her.* She put her head in her hands.

Finally, the dizziness subsided. She stood up and took ahold of the handrail. It was ice-cold even through her gloves. She had to concentrate on lifting her feet. One step at a time. She thought of Gabriel. His bristly hair, the soapy-clean smell of his neck, the way his uniform looked just a little too small for his muscular frame.

She'd first noticed Gabe during a basic-training exercise at Fort Leonard Wood. That was almost ten years ago, when she'd first joined up. On that sweltering July afternoon in Missouri, with the humidity near 90 percent, the new recruits were out running time trials to see who would be in what group. Because her time was already better than the "female" range, she was training with the guys. The fastest of them turned and winked at her as he whizzed by. He was cute but cocky.

On the second day of training, which was even hotter than the first, the dark-haired private fell behind the pack. Something was wrong. He'd slowed to a crawl and was gasping for air. Instead of sprinting past him as she should have, she stopped to see if he needed help. Unfortunately, the drill sergeant stopped too.

With a stern look, the sergeant shouted the army motto into the guy's ear. "The best way to make fitness training easier is to work harder. Lopez, pick up the pace." The sergeant turned to her. "You too, Colt."

The private bent over, gulping in air. His hand trembled slightly as he reached in the pocket of his shorts and pulled out an inhaler.

"Colt, get moving," the sergeant barked.

"But—"

"What are you waiting for?" the sergeant asked, obviously not expecting an answer.

"The core value of personal courage is standing up for what you know is right, especially if it is not popular with others." It was a quote from the pamphlet outlining the army's seven core values, which they'd been given the day before.

The handsome young recruit sucked on his inhaler and looked up at her with gratitude in his dark eyes. That was it. She was hooked.

Gabe, why did you have to go and get yourself killed? If only he were here now, she wouldn't be in this mess.

She inhaled deeply, and the burnt toast smell turned into the stench of burning flesh.

Wincing, she pulled herself to the top of the landing. Was it the concussion, or were there tears in her eyes? She was trapped in a fishbowl looking out. Or was she outside the bowl looking in? Inside out, that's how she felt, like her nerves and blood vessels were on the outside of her body, exposed. It didn't help that the world was bathed in a watery green light and her headache was getting worse.

Her shrink said she had to come to terms with her past and let it go or she'd never be able to live fully in the present. Maybe the arrogant weasel was right. Her past was definitely screwing over her present. But the pain in her head was very much in the present. It made her want to vomit. She needed to lie down. She needed a Mountain Dew. She needed to figure out who was killing *her* witnesses.

Was it that Bratva Chicago "friend" of the girlfriend? The one who'd been there when Bobby the Nose was shot? She'd described him as skinny with a gold grill. The big jackass shooting at her back at the cabin definitely wasn't skinny. Could there be more than one hitman? Maybe they were working together. And how did they find all these witnesses? No easy feat. *Unless.* Unless there was a mole in WITSEC.

First, The Art Dealer in Chicago. Then Jimmy Giordano in Montana. Then Bobby the Nose in Wyoming. Three dead witnesses in less than a week. And, then, there was the dead Russian. Boris "the Butcher" Smirnov wasn't in witness protection. Still, no way was it a coincidence he'd been found dead near where she'd stashed Nick.

So what did Italian mafiosi from New York and Chicago have to do with a dead Russian from Long Island? Maybe some kind of gang war? But why would the Russians target snitches? Especially since those snitches would put their enemies behind bars.

And why was Boris the Butcher in Wyoming at the ranch anyway? Did he come here to kill Nick? Maybe someone had killed him before he got the chance. But who? Was the murderer staying at the ranch too? She'd already examined their guest list, but no names jumped out. The guys back at the office were checking on it now too, but they'd probably get nowhere. If the killer was a guest at the lodge, chances were he was using an alias.

Nick was involved with both the Italian and Russian mobs. Maybe all of this revolved around him. If it did, he was most certainly next on the hitman's list.

Cringing, she staggered to their motel room. She knocked on the door. She didn't want to startle him or catch him with his pants down. As she pulled the plastic key out of her pocket, she had a sinking feeling. She slipped the key into the door and pushed it open.

"Nick?"

No answer. She checked the bathroom. His toothbrush was standing inside a glass on the sink. "Nick?" But that was the only sign of him. *Dammit to hell.*

Nick was gone.

Arrr. She jammed her fingers into her hair and pulled. Now what?

Calm down. Maybe he just went out for some air. *In the dark? When it's twenty degrees?* He could have gone to the ice machine. That must be it. She'd told him to stay put. Anyway, where else would he go?

On her way out the door, she saw it. She turned back. An envelope laying on the table. She rushed over and snatched it up. **MARSHAL COLT** was written in all caps on the front. Her heart was racing as she ripped the end off. *This can't be good.* A note. *To Marshal Colt.* Written on motel stationary. She stood gaping down at it.

I'm leaving WITSEC to be with my girlfriend. I'm sorry.

What the hell? Lexi crumpled the note and jammed it and the envelope into her jacket pocket.

The idiot girlfriend and her asshole sidekick. *Stupid idiots.* They were going to get themselves and Nick killed.

She'd seen the girlfriend's rental car in the parking lot. So the girlfriend had to be nearby. She and her *attack dog* must be staying at the motel.

Lexi could feel her pulse pounding in her brain. Energized with adrenaline, she went to the front desk and got a master key. She knocked on every door of the motel and checked every room. *The girlfriend and her accomplice must be staying here.*

If they were, they weren't in their room.

Where in the hell are they? Dammit. She returned the master key and then hobbled back across the parking lot to her Charger. *Yup.* The girlfriend's car was still there. But where was the sidekick Clyde's sports car? That little f-er had brained her real good. She was going to find them and convince Nick to come back into WITSEC. Not only for his own good, but for his girlfriend's. *Damn her.*

Lexi slid into the driver's seat and called into headquarters. "Ted, find out if anyone from Chicago has checked into a hotel or B and B in Casper in the last three days."

She turned the heater on full blast. Cold air smacked her in the face. She could barely move her frozen fingers, but she couldn't wait for it to get warm. She had to find Nick before someone else did. Someone even more dangerous than the girlfriend.

PART III

17

"Slumming it?" Jessica glanced around the King Parlor Suite. The stains on the nubby striped carpet reminded her of working as a maid in Vegas. Faded Western-themed curtains drooped from overpainted casements. Once-proud buffalo-print chairs in the living area sat around a scratched coffee table. *Yup.* The shabby room had seen better days . . . maybe during its grand opening a hundred years ago. "Not your usual penthouse suite."

"What do you mean?" Lolita smiled. "It's the best Casper has to offer. The historic Prairie Hotel."

"Emphasis on the *historic*." Jessica peeked into the bathroom. Puke-green vintage tile walls, a tongue-pink bathtub, and a scuffed black-and-white checkerboard tile floor. "Wow. Cool."

"Lukewarm, but it will have to do." Lolita leaned

back in one of the buffalo chairs and twisted her long legs over its arm.

"You're not planning a poker game, are you?" Jessica glanced over at Lolita's cousin, who was watching an old western on TV and chain-smoking cigarettes.

"And why not?" Lolita picked at one of her wicked red fingernails. "A girl's got to pay her travel expenses."

"So explain to me again why you're here and why you sent Vanya to get me ... at gunpoint?"

"I already told you. I was worried about you." Lolita sat up. "Would you like some bubbly?" She went to a mini fridge in the corner of the room. A microwave sat on top of it. Not exactly the swanky wet bar she usually had on hand. She pulled two small bottles of prosecco from the tiny freezer compartment. "Sorry. I don't have any whiskey laid in." She popped the corks, slid two champagne flutes from a padded bag atop the microwave, and poured.

"I'm not buying it." Jessica plopped into one of the overstuffed buffalo chairs. "Why are you really here? And don't tell me you came all this way to host a poker game in a crummy hotel. And how did you find me, anyway?"

"Amber hacked your phone. I have some news." Lolita handed her a glass of bubbly. "I'm afraid you're going to wish you had something stronger."

"What about me, cuz?" Vanya looked like a stray dog left out in the rain, begging for garbage.

Lolita handed him both bottles. "Finish these." She didn't bother giving him a glass.

"What news?" Jessica steeled herself. What news could make Lolita come all the way to Wyoming? It couldn't be that Nick was dead. She'd just seen him . . . in the arms of Federal Marshal Eva Mendes. Thanks to Vanya, she'd just left the marshal for dead in a parking lot. But Nick was very much alive. In fact, if Lolita's gunslinging cousin hadn't dragged her here, she just might be at the cabin confronting Nick at this very moment. *Yeah, right.* What would she have said? "How dare you go into WITSEC, change your identity, and throw me over for a hot marshal"?

"Seems your professor-cum-art dealer is all that and a bit more."

"Cum art dealer," Vanya repeated with a snort.

Lolita gave him the evil eye. He got a sheepish look on his face and then lit another cigarette.

"What's he doing here?" Jessica whispered, pointing at Vanya, who'd gone back to his cigarettes and television. "Did Bratva send him to find Nick?"

"Cousin Vanya is my bodyguard." Lolita lounged across the chair again, sipping her prosecco.

Jessica narrowed her eyes. "Why do you need a bodyguard?" Unless her friend really was working for Bratva. "And why did you have him drag me off at gunpoint?"

"You know Vanya." Lolita chuckled. "He can be overly enthusiastic."

"I hear you," Vanya said, not taking his eyes off the television. "As you say in America: eager beavers catch the worms."

"Early birds," Lolita corrected.

"Eager beavers catch the early bird?" Vanya asked, glancing over at his cousin.

"And I'm the worm?" Jessica drained her glass. "Or is Nick the worm?"

"Speaking of Nick . . ." Her friend got up and returned to the refrigerator. "That's why we're here." She pulled another small bottle from the freezer and popped the cork. "About Nick." She refilled both of their glasses, sat down across from Jessica, and, elegantly crossing her long legs, continued. "Amber found something." Sage-green cat eyes twinkling, she sipped her prosecco. Like a cat, Lolita was toying with her.

"Well, spit it out."

"What does it mean, 'spit it out?'" Vanya asked.

"Spill the beans." Jessica sat on the edge of her seat. "Break the news . . . let the cat out of the bag."

"Spilling, spitting, breaking the bag." Vanya shook his head. "No wonder it's so hard to learn English."

"The camel deserted his tasty dessert in the desert," Lolita said.

"What?" Vanya looked confused.

"Never mind the tongue twisters. What did Amber find out about Nick?" Jessica tightened her lips to avoid cursing.

"To produce more produce, the farmer taught his sow to sow." Lolita winked.

"Just tell me already!"

"Now, now. No need to get testy."

"Tell me what you know." Jessica put her champagne flute down a little too hard on the coffee table.

"All right." Lolita picked up the glass, wiped the rim on the hem of her dress, and took it back to its case. "No need to break my travel crystal."

"I saw Nick. He's alive." Jessica didn't know whether to mention what else she saw. "If Vanya hadn't kidnapped me, I might be with him now."

"Believe me. Be thankful that you're not." Lolita returned to the sitting area with a bag of chips. "This will tide you over until we get you some real food." She handed over the unopened bag.

Jessica tore the bag open and stuffed a handful of chips in her mouth. "Happy now?" she asked with crumbs escaping her lips.

"Ecstatic." Lolita marched over and turned off the television. "Time for show-and-tell."

"Vanya, tell our Montana friend what you found out." Lolita gestured for her cousin to take a seat. He grabbed the bag of chips and dropped onto the saggy sofa.

"I thought Amber found something." Jessica blew at her bangs. Sometimes her friend could be so exasperating.

"First things first, *milaya*," Lolita purred, pacing back and forth like a caged tiger.

Jessica knew that look. Her friend was hatching a plan. But what sort of plan? It wasn't like they could spring Nick from WITSEC. And even if they could, after what she saw, would she want to?

Vanya pulled a big handful of chips from the bag. "Teeth Marsiano has a gopher in WITSEC—"

"Mole," Lolita interrupted.

"Mole," Vanya repeated. "Anyway, word on the street. Teeth is hitting witnesses. And the professor is next on the list."

"So are you the hitman?" Jessica sucked in a breath. "Or are you following the hitman?"

Vanya glanced over at his cousin and popped another potato chip into his mouth.

"Vanya is following you," Lolita said.

"Gee, thanks."

"Someone has to watch out for you."

Something didn't add up, but Jessica didn't know what. And if Nick was in imminent danger, she didn't have time to find out. She needed to get back out to the cabin and warn him. "Shouldn't we warn Nick . . . or the marshal?"

"You don't know how these guys work." Lolita took another lap around the room. "I do."

"That's right, cuz," Vanya chimed in. "We know these guys."

"We have to warn Nick." Jessica's tone was getting

desperate. Back at the Motel 6, with Vanya's gun pointed at her, she'd abandoned her rental car. She had no way to get back out to the cabin. "Where are Teeth's guys now?" For all she knew, they'd followed her out to the cabin and had already found Nick. She grimaced. And with the marshal lying unconscious in a parking lot . . . "So where are Teeth's guys now?" she repeated.

"*Milaya.* When Amber hacked WITSEC, she found something else." Lolita stopped pacing. She kneeled next to Jessica's chair and looked her square in the eyes.

The look in those green cat eyes made Jessica shiver. "What?"

Lolita put her hand on top of Jessica's. "Nick *is* one of Teeth's guys."

18

Where in Hades was he? Locked in a tiny room with a bed, sink, and toilet. Must be in the middle of nowhere. When he pounded on the door and yelled, no one came. Was Tiny just going to leave him here to die?

Nick paced back and forth in the small room. The smell of bleach and stale cigar smoke reminded him of his father's club . . . minus the bleach.

When he was a teenager, his old man would make him put on a tie and jacket and take him there to indoctrinate him into the ways of wealthy New Yorkers. His father had been the kind of guy who didn't take no for an answer. So Nick kept his mouth shut and let his old man drag him along to the Metropolitan Club. His father was none too pleased that young Nick was more interested in the portraits of past presidents that hung on the walls than the living, breathing movers and shakers hobnobbing with his old man. Of course, his father had found a way to get his hooks into Nick eventually.

Now, even from the grave, his father had snagged him in one final intrigue. Nick ran his fingers through his hair. Fingering the tiny key in his pocket, he stopped at the one and only—barred—window and looked out. Was he on a farm somewhere? In the moonlight, a vast snow-covered field glowed. A pinkish full moon was diffused through a snowy cloud. *The dawn came up like thunder.* A line from Kipling. Would he live to see the dawn? He checked his watch. Not quite six. *Where is Tiny?*

If only I could call Lexi. But Tiny had taken his phone. *Lexington, look at the letter. Don't believe the note.* Tiny had threatened to kill both Jessica and Lexi. He had no choice.

Nick closed his eyes and inhaled. *Coconut.* She smelled like coconut . . . and strawberries. For a woman so sweet on the outside, she was sure bitter on the inside. The contrast was intoxicating. He hadn't felt this way about anyone since . . . He dropped into a wooden chair next to the small table in the corner of the room. Would he ever see her again?

He put his head in his hands and tried to remember her face. *Dulce.* The image of her was fading away like the reverse of photograph paper in a developing tray. Instead of getting sharper, her image was getting dimmer. Fading into nothingness.

Argh. He pounded his fist into the table. What had his father gotten him into? From beyond the grave, his old man was dangling the one thing he couldn't resist: a mystery. *What's the safe-deposit box? Another donation to the Center?*

He leaned his elbows on the table and put his head in his hands. Why was he even thinking about the Center? *Face it. That life is gone.* He pulled the velvet box from his jacket pocket, opened it, and stared down at the ring. *Everything is gone. The Center, my art collection. And Dulce ... sweet Dulce.*

Still clutching the ring in one palm, he splashed water on his face at the little sink in the corner. The ring made a little splash before sinking to the bottom of the bowl. Nick depressed the handle. A flash of jade swirled around and then disappeared—like the rest of his past —down the toilet.

When he stared at himself in the bathroom mirror, he saw his father's face looking back at him. *I'll make a man out of you yet.* He stood there, his face wet, not the sort of man his father wanted but a man nonetheless. He closed his eyes. That coconut smell again.

Lexi, have you found the clue yet? He hoped to Hades she had. She was a federal marshal. And a good one. She'd know what to do.

Clunk. The door handle was loud. Nick's breath caught. The moment of truth. Was Tiny going to kill him now or later?

19
____

Just over an hour ago, she'd seen Nick in the arms of the pretty marshal. And then she'd seen Vanya pistol-whip the marshal in an icy parking lot. Jessica tried to put the painful image out of her mind. But like fighting the urge to tongue a sore tooth, it was no use.

And it'd be no use when she got home. She worked every day at the Center, which was so jam-packed with memories of Nick, she'd never be able to forget him. That place was his baby. But he'd walked away from it just like he'd walked away from her. Either he was in deep danger, or he was as fickle as the Montana wind. Years ago, her gut had told her he was bad news. She should have listened. Was he really working for Mr. Teeth?

She took another turn around the room.

"Quit making holes in the rug," her mom would say.

Not that the rug didn't already have holes. The luxury suite in the Prairie Hotel was anything but luxurious, unless maybe you were a prospector back from the mines or a cow herder looking for your yearly bath. The radiator had creaked and complained all night. The room was too hot, with no way to regulate the temperature. The windows were painted shut, so there was no way to get fresh air. And the faint smell of mildew beneath the perfume of carpet cleaner was driving her nuts.

Lolita had invited her to share the suite—more like insisted. At least it saved her the expense of the Motel 6 and the rental car, which she'd turned in. Vanya had offered to give her a lift wherever she wanted to go . . . except to see Nick. Now she was killing time, waiting for Lolita and Vanya to get back from shopping for the poker party.

She still couldn't believe Lolita was going to host a high-stakes poker game in this dumpy hotel in the middle of nowhere. Leave it to the Poker Tsarina to lure in Wyoming fat cats. She checked the fridge. *All right.* Lolita had gotten her a couple bottles of Coke. Maybe she'd get through this dreary day after all. She rummaged through her backpack for her Swiss Army knife, popped the cap off the Coke, and took the first glorious sip. Nothing like Coke out of an ice-cold bottle. Forget about those plastic bottles or tin cans.

Speaking of the Center, might as well get some work done. Maybe it would distract her from Nick . . . and the marshal . . . and Vanya hitting the marshal in the head. *Ouch*.

Jessica pulled her computer out of her backpack and flopped into an overstuffed buffalo-print chair. She really should grade her students' papers. But she couldn't face them. Grading was demoralizing. But the deadline to turn in grades was tomorrow. She really should have done it before she left Chicago. She was going to need something stronger to face her students' papers.

If only Lolita had gotten some Jack Daniels to go with the Coke. Sitting with her computer open on her lap, she set the bottle on the floor and started typing. Just a quick look at the internet before grading. Hoping to get ideas for the classes she taught at the Center, she searched the internet for art education programs. Much more fun than grading. *Interesting*. An advert for a post-graduate program in Art Crime and Cultural Heritage Protection caught her eye. *Art crime*.

She'd certainly encountered her fair share of stolen paintings and professional forgeries. But she'd never considered a career in art crime. *Ooh . . . the program's in Italy*. Just what the doctor ordered. A trip to Europe to forget about Nick. Not that she'd ever be able to afford it. She imagined exploring the Italian countryside and learning about art crime. *Must be nice*. She'd never been off the continent. The first time she'd ever been on an airplane was when she left home for graduate school. She was probably the only philosophy PhD in existence who still hadn't been to Europe. As her dad always said, "If wishes were horses, then beggars would ride."

Okay. Enough horsing around. She opened her email and stared at the folder marked DEGRADING. She clicked it open. Might as well start with Yanis, the pimply-faced kid who'd thanked her after her last class. His paper was sure to be the best.

Three hours later, she was nearly done grading when a knock on the door interrupted her Track Changes. *Lolita must have forgotten her key.*

Jessica slid her computer off her lap and went to the door. "You're not Lolita."

"To become who we're meant to be . . ." A tired-looking Jack tipped his hat and bowed. ". . . we must forget who we are."

"What are you doing here?" She wouldn't admit it, but she was happy to see him.

"Lolita—"

"I should have known," she interrupted.

"I was halfway across Iowa last night when I got her call." Jack followed her to the sitting area and flopped down onto the sofa.

"Let me guess." She sat next to him. "The Poker Tsarina needs a dealer?"

"The question is what do *you* need?" He unbuttoned his moth-eaten wool peacoat. "I've heard that even cowgirls get the blues." He flashed his crooked smile.

"Did Lolita tell you that Nick is working for the

Mafia?" She stared down at her red cowboy boots. "Or was . . . until he turned witness."

"I knew he's a snake." Jack smirked. "Nick Schilling. Always full of surprises."

"Is that why you came back? To rub it in and say, 'I told you so'?" She tightened her lips.

"No." He troubled the silk band on his fedora. "I felt bad about abandoning you in the wilderness." He glanced over at her. "Not that you can't take care of yourself."

"I believed in him." She gave him a weak smile. "Convictions are more dangerous enemies of truth than lies." Her voice cracked reciting the line.

"*Human, All Too Human*," Jack said.

She'd missed the Nietzsche quotes when he was away in prison. "I should have run the other way as soon as I found out he had a double life."

"How were you to know the snake had a triple life?" Jack sloughed off his coat. "Anyway, your trust in people is one of your most endearing qualities . . . Of course, it's also your worst fault."

"Virtue is the flip side of vice." She got up and went to the refrigerator to see if she'd missed any alcohol hiding in there.

"Is that Nietzsche? Or a cowgirl-philosopher original?"

"Even snakes can shed their skins." She cocked her head and then set about rummaging through the fridge. *Aha.* Lolita was holding out on her. Tucked into the back of the small freezer, behind a pint of rum raisin ice cream, was a pint of Stoli. She should have known Lolita would have vodka in her freezer. "Pick your poison. We've got vodka, Coke, or ice cream."

"If you've got a glass, I'll have all three." Jack jumped up and joined her at the minibar.

Together, they made two tall vodka Coke floats. First, she poured a healthy dose of vodka in each glass, followed by a splash of Coke. He followed with a large dollop of ice cream on top. The white blobs sank to the vodka bottom and then reemerged like icebergs hitting the *Titanic*.

She took a sip. Sweet cream followed by bubbly Coke, then the vodka burn. "Not bad." She held up the glass. The ice cream melting down into the drink created a snow-globe effect.

"No whiskey?" Jack took his Coke float, along with the pint of vodka, back to the couch. He alternated between the float and swigs of vodka straight from the bottle. After his second swig, he handed the bottle to her.

"Beggars can't be choosers." The lip of the bottle was cold, and the vodka stung her throat. "Or, as Vanya would say, debtors. Crapulence. I haven't told you about Vanya and the marshal." She told him everything. Seeing Nick kissing the marshal. Speeding away in the rental car. Sitting in the parking lot, crying. Buying a plane ticket. Getting interrogated by the marshal, who'd somehow found her. Vanya braining the marshal with the butt of his gun. The marshal unconscious on the ice. Vanya forcing her to go with him at gunpoint. Lolita telling her that Nick was really working for Teeth.

"The secret to life is danger." Jack grinned.

She shook her head. "You're ruining Nietzsche. That's not the way it goes."

"Don't bogart that bottle." Jack reached for the vodka.

She took another swig and then handed the bottle back to him. The vodka burn took her back to her first dinner date with Nick. She'd taken him to Pavlov's Banquet, where the tables were better dressed than she was. They drank frozen vodka shots, ate blini, and watched old couples slow dancing.

"He doesn't deserve you," Jack said, as if reading her thoughts.

"And I suppose you do." She took another big swig. Her mouth tingled and sparked.

"That's not what I meant." His bronze cheeks turned pink. "I just meant that you're . . . you're . . . special."

"Geez. You're starting to sound like a Hallmark card."

He flipped his hat back onto his head and lowered the brim over his eyes. "Even Hallmark gets it right sometimes." He sulked.

Crapulence. She shouldn't have insulted the jackass. He was just trying to be nice. "I guess I should have listened to you from the beginning." She blew at her bangs. "You always said he wasn't trustworthy."

"People like him live in another world from people like us." Jack tossed his hat onto the coffee table. "They have a different code of ethics, different norms of behavior."

"But the mafia?" *And infidelity?* "Aren't some values universal? Like abiding by the law and playing by the rules?"

He smirked. "After all the Nietzsche you've read, I can't believe—"

"Okay. Maybe not law or rules, but what about matters of the heart?" She finished the last of her Coke float. "Love . . . isn't love universal?" she asked, licking the cream off her upper lip. Nick technically might not have been unfaithful, considering he thought their relationship was over. But he sure had moved on awful fast.

"You don't think culture affects love too?" He raised one eyebrow. "The marketing gurus are counting on it. Why do you think they spend so much time studying demographics?"

"Desire, maybe . . . but not love." She wondered if she knew how to separate the two. She so easily confused desire with love.

"I know a lot about desire but very little of love." Jack's lip twitched, and he stared down at his sodden desert boots. "You're the only one . . ." He glanced up at her, his long lashes fluttering.

Like a dagger through the heart, she had a sudden urge to kiss him. She squeezed his knee, and he moved closer until their bodies were smashed up against each other. He gazed at her with such affection and longing, she couldn't resist. She leaned in, her lips almost touching his, when the door to the suite swung open. Lolita and Vanya bustled in carrying overflowing shopping bags. *Arrr . . . what timing.* Jessica jumped up to help.

The cousins' cheeks were red, and they both had the bright-eyed look of skiers fresh from an invigorating run down the slopes. The leather uppers on Vanya's Italian lace-ups were withered and ruined. They were speaking Russian and laughing as they dropped the bags near the mini refrigerator, which was the closest thing the suite had to a kitchenette.

"Jacko, you made it." Lolita rubbed her hands together. "Great. You can deal on Saturday."

"Out here in the Wild West . . . I hope there's not a shoot-out." Jack chuckled.

"Wouldn't be the first time," Jessica said, picking a raisin out of her drink. "You should ask the players to check their guns at the door."

"If I did, no one would play." Lolita was unloading bottles of booze and lining them up on top of the microwave. "Anyway, where's the fun in that?"

"Not so long ago, you almost bled out thanks to gunplay at one of your poker games." Jessica went to examine the liquor cache.

"I guess being shot is like giving birth. Eventually you forget how painful it was." Lolita folded the paper bags and stuffed them behind the refrigerator. "Anyway.

As I recall, at a certain poker game, it was Nick's little gun that saved you from those frat boy rapists."

Jessica winced. Remembering the night she'd met Nick made her want another drink. "Mind if I open this?" She picked up the bottle of whiskey. *What's wrong with me? I don't even know my own heart.* Did she love Nick, or was it just desire . . . or worse, the need for approval? And what about Jack? *What a mess.*

Bam. Bam. A loud pounding on the door made her jump. *Who the heck could that be?* "I'll get it." She downed the shot of whiskey and then went to the door.

Crapulence.

Federal Marshal Eve Mendes, arms akimbo, gave her the evil eye. "Where is he?"

"Who?" Had she come looking for Vanya? She probably wanted to haul him off to jail for knocking her unconscious . . . and Jessica along with him. "How did you find me again?"

"Not many guests visiting Casper from Chicago. Now, where is he?"

Jessica glanced back into the room. "Vanya?" she whispered.

"My witness." The marshal glared at her. "You know who."

"Nick?" Jessica swallowed hard. "Isn't he at your place?"

"Mind if I come in and look around?" The marshal didn't wait for an answer. She pushed past Jessica. "Maybe your friend who hit me on the head is inside?"

Without a word, with her hand on her holster, she stalked the parameter of the room, checking the bathroom, the closets, and even under the bed.

Vanya and Lolita watched from the sitting area.

After the marshal had looked behind every door and checked every inch of the suite, she stopped in front of the cousins. "So, which one of you SOBs hit me in the head?" Taking her hand from her gun for the first time since she'd come into the room, she touched her head.

Vanya flashed his gold-toothed smile.

"If I wasn't in a hurry, I'd take you in." She pointed at the wiry Russian. "Try something like that again and you won't live to tell about it." She strode to the entrance and turned back to Jessica, who was still standing at the threshold. "I told you to get out of Wyoming. Thanks to you, Nick is missing. Or worse. If you know what's good for you—and him—you'll take your toys and go back home." The marshal disappeared down the hall.

Jessica stood staring at the open door. Why didn't the marshal arrest Vanya? Things must be really bad. Nick must be in imminent danger. And it was her fault. She'd never forgive herself if he got hurt . . . or worse.

20

Lexi slapped the siren on top of her car and stepped on the accelerator. Should she put out a BOLO on Nick? The note said he was leaving WITSEC to go back to the girlfriend. She cringed. He was a free man, not a fugitive. Tightening her grip on the steering wheel, she held the car on the icy road through sheer willpower.

The way he kissed her. She tingled all over just thinking about it. Either he was a real player, or he was *not* thinking of the girlfriend. Anyway, he wasn't with the girlfriend. Was he still looking for her? On his way back to Chicago? Did he even know the girlfriend was in Wyoming?

Something just didn't feel right. What if Nick hadn't left of his own free will? She slammed her palm against the wheel. The car shimmied, and she jerked it back into her lane. She'd screwed up one too many times, and now her job was at stake—along with her witness. *And lover.* She pushed the thought from her mind. Whatever her feelings for Nick, she couldn't let them get in the way of her work.

Please let me find him. I promise I'll keep it professional from now on. No more messing around. Please. If only I find him. Alive. I'll promise to be good.

Nick may have been missing, but at least she'd found the ex-Bratva Chicago "friend." Prime suspect in the murder of Bobby the Nose. Why would a Russian gangster kill a witness against an Italian crime boss? It just didn't make sense. There had to be some gang feud going on. Something weird going on between the Russians and the Italians.

She depressed the button on her two-way radio. "Hey, Ted. Get a car to the Prairie Hotel. Room forty-seven. Arrest the man with the golden grill in his mouth. He shot Moretti." Ignoring the sputtering on the other end, she dropped the microphone back into its cradle.

Luckily, the Casper airport was only five minutes from downtown. The Charger skidded to a stop in front of the terminal. She waved to the officer patrolling the entrance. "Federal Marshal Lexington Colt," she said in her most official voice. "Looking for a fugitive." She flashed her badge. She couldn't admit she'd lost a witness and had no flipping clue where he went. Her gut said he didn't go willingly. What if the big F-er who'd been shooting at her had gotten to him?

That damn girlfriend had led the thug straight to them. *Why in the hell did I have to pick the damned Motel 6?*

The officer nodded. "Got ya covered, ma'am."

"Marshal," Lexi said under her breath. "Not bleeping ma'am."

The Casper airport looked like a two-lane bowling alley. It didn't take long for Lexi to hit every ticket counter in the place, armed with a photograph of Nick.

The only destinations out of Casper airport were Denver and Salt Lake City. Once in the morning. Once in the afternoon. And occasionally once in the evening. But if Nick had flown out earlier this evening, he could be to Denver and halfway to Dallas or really anywhere by now. And unless she could catch the afternoon flight she'd have to wait until tomorrow.

A woman too old to have her hair in pigtails nodded when she saw Nick's picture. "Yes. He and another gentleman just boarded flight 5724 to Denver." The United agent tapped on her computer. "I wouldn't forget that face."

I bet. Lexi leaned on the counter. "So the plane hasn't left yet?"

"Let me check." She picked up the phone. "Has flight 5724 left yet?" She nodded. "Okay." She hung up the phone. "I'm sorry. It just took off."

"Dammit." Lexi pounded her fist on the counter. "This other gentleman—describe him."

"Husky fella. Looked like a boxer . . . like his nose

had been broken a couple of times. Not too tall. Dark fringe around a balding head."

"What was he wearing?"

"A dark suit." The agent's eyes lit up. "You know, he didn't have an overcoat. I thought that was odd."

Lexi nodded. "Was Denver the final destination, or are they changing planes?"

The agent's fingers flew over the keyboard. *Clack. Clack. Clack.* Her forehead was creased in concentration. Her eyes moved quickly, scanning the screen. More typing. More scanning.

How many people left out of Casper on a Thursday? How could it take so long to find him on a passenger list? Lexi forced herself to take deep breaths.

"Aha!" The agent smiled and flung a pigtail over one shoulder. "I found him."

"And?" Lexi wanted to jump over the counter and shake it out of her.

"New York's LaGuardia." She looked very pleased with herself. "Landing at 11:57 New York time."

Dammit. "When's the next flight to New York?" Lexi glanced up at the screen on the wall above the agent's head. Quarter to eight. She'd probably have to wait until tomorrow.

More typing.

Lexi tapped on the counter with her fingers.

Without looking up, the agent gave her a fake smile. "I'm sorry, Miss . . . Miss—"

"Colt. Federal Marshal Lexington Colt."

". . . Miss Colt." She glanced up. "I'm working as fast as I can."

Lexi exchanged the finger-tapping for toe-tapping.

"Okay," the agent said triumphantly. "There's an 8:15 flight to Salt Lake City. From there, you'll catch the 11:10 to San Francisco and land in time to have a midnight snack before you catch the red-eye to JFK at 12:32."

"San Francisco? You mean I have to fly to the West Coast to get to the East Coast?"

"I'm afraid so . . . unless you want to wait until tomorrow. That's the quickest we can get you to New York."

"What about on another airline?"

"I checked. You're on three airlines as it is." She shook her head. "This is the very best we can do . . . unless you want to wait until—"

"No. I can't wait." She had an idea where to find Nick. But only if she got there in time. If she missed her chance, she might find him dead. "What time would I arrive?"

The agent tapped her keyboard again. "The red-eye arrives at 7:37."

"Tomorrow morning?" By the time she landed and then caught a cab into the city, she'd be too late.

"That's right. Local time. Would you like me to go ahead and ticket that for you?" She flung her other pigtail over a shoulder.

Lexi had an idea. "What about flights out of

Denver?" If she hauled ass, she could be to Denver in four hours. A straight shot on I-25 south.

"Denver?" The agent squinted at her.

"Nonstops tonight."

More incessant tapping.

"Well, there is a nonstop flight at 10:58 that—"

"Book it." Lexi slapped the counter. If she used her flashers and broke the speed limit, roads permitting, she *should* make it just in time. At least she'd be doing something and not just waiting around airports all night. There was nothing she hated more than waiting.

She grabbed the ticket and ran through the terminal like a running back at the fifty-yard line. Glad she left her car parked right outside, she nodded to the cop on duty and slid into the driver's seat. "Come on, baby," she said to the Charger. "Let's haul ass."

A PERK of being a federal agent, she could speed the entire way to Denver. Flasher on, she made it in record time. A personal best, in fact. Three hours and twenty-seven minutes. Just in time to park her car in overnight parking, sprint to the gate, and board the flight just before it closed.

No toothbrush. No clean underwear. No overnight bag. Armed with just her purse and her gun—another perk of being a federal agent—Lexi boarded the jet to New York.

Lexi cringed as the red-eye took off. She never did like flying. But after her tour in Afghanistan, any loud noises sent her through the roof. She white-knuckled the armrest until they reached their cruising altitude. The plane's shaking as it climbed had thrown her back onto the trembling desert sand in her worst nightmare . . . a nightmare that was all too real.

A twinge in her gut reminded her of the pain she kept buried deeper than any other. She didn't just lose Gabe in that life-shattering blast. She miscarried and lost their baby. The worst part was the shame. Like it was her fault. She grieved for a girl she'd never met, a girl not even born. It was like mourning a figment of her imagination, except the massive hemorrhaging had made it real . . . all too real. And at the time, she couldn't tell anyone. Her engagement to Gabe was a secret. And so was her pregnancy. She had to carry the pain all on her own.

She reached into her purse and pulled out the prescription bottle. She shook the little white salvation into the palm of her hand. She popped it into her mouth and then bit down hard. The bitter pill shattered into the familiar shards of anticipation. It never really took the pain away. It just made her numb enough to keep going.

The baseball-capped middle-aged dude sitting next to her had started yacking about airline safety as soon as she'd grabbed the armrest when they took off, and he was still going on and on as if statistics made any difference. *He has no idea.*

Usually, she would have tried to humor him, to smile and nod. But after far too many hours on the road, no meals to speak of, and the roller-coaster ride of four—now five—takeoffs and landings, she was in no mood. She stared straight ahead at the tray table, wishing it would end. Not just the flight, but everything . . . especially the dude's lecture about the safety of flying. She'd flown a helicopter, for God's sake.

For God's sake. More like forsaken by God. She'd lost Gabe. She'd lost their daughter. And she'd lost her faith in God. A loving God couldn't allow such suffering. Her mama would tell her everything happened for a reason. But what reason could there possibly be for letting her see what was left of the love of her life after he was blown to bits?

The flight attendant interrupted her nightmare and offered her a pop. Stupid plane didn't serve Mountain Dew, a Pepsi product, so she had to settle for Coke. The first sip tasted like acid. But after two cans, she was getting used to it. She was going to turn into a squirrel if she ate another peanut, so somewhere over Illinois she finally broke down and ordered an overpriced, shrink-wrapped ham sandwich. It tasted as bad as it looked, but it would keep her going through the night.

After an hour in the air, Baseball Cap had nodded off and slumped sideways with his mouth hanging open. Lexi didn't know which was worse—the dude's incessant yapping or his thunderous snoring. She leaned her head against the window to get as far away from his sour breath and pasty face as possible. *Three more hours . . .* She could continue feeling sorry for herself, or she could make a plan to find her missing witness. *Suck it up, Lex. You have work to do.* Too bad she hadn't brought her computer. She'd have to buy the internet pass, and do her research on her phone.

She reviewed the files on Nick's father, Richard Schilling, Victor "Teeth" Marsiano, and Boris the Butcher. To keep any more witnesses from being killed, she had to figure out the connection between Nick, the Russian mob, and the Italian mob.

Why take Nick all the way across the country to dispose of him? If they wanted to kill him, just gun him down him like they did to Bobby the Nose. *No.* They must want to get something out of him. If they wanted to shut him up and keep him from testifying, why not just kill him? She shuddered at the thought of the mafia torturing information out of Nick. Pruning snips meeting his long fingers. Whatever they wanted from Nick, it must have something to do with that letter from his father. Either that or Nick had gone willingly. Hell, like the other scumbags in WITSEC, he was probably mafia too.

Five bags of pretzels later, she'd read the complete files on the dead witnesses. She was still trying to connect the dots. One interesting thing. The three dead witnesses—Jimmy Giordano, Bobby the Nose, and The

Art Dealer—all went to the same high school. Prospect Heights in Brooklyn. They may not have been from the same mafia families, but they were from the same neighborhood. *Holy Mother of God.* So was Boris the Butcher. That couldn't be a coincidence.

But what did the connection between the four dead men have to do with Nick? Or was it his father? Something didn't add up.

The cabin lights were dim, and most of the other passengers were sleeping. There was something strangely exciting about working under the tiny overhead spotlight while the world slumbered around her. Huddled inside her winter coat, which she still hadn't removed, she searched the federal database for information on Nick's contacts in New York City. He'd grown up in New York, so undoubtedly there were many. But given his late father's connections to the Italian mafia, it seemed reasonable to start there.

Sure enough, there was a file on Nick's daddy. Richard Schilling. Seemed he'd been a bigwig behind the scenes in New York politics and had been known for his various affairs with fashion models and actresses. Nick's mother must have been a saint to put up with that horse manure. Lexi would have taken the pruning snips and—

She scrolled down screen after screen, squinting to read the files on her phone. Apparently, when Nick was declared dead and whisked off to WITSEC, his nephew had inherited the family fortune, including the art collection. She wondered how Nick felt about that. Seemed both father and son had a passion for art. *Yeah.* She'd listened to Nick give excited lectures on Russian art over dinner. And the dad had been involved in banking . . . banking, construction, and art dealing. What wasn't he involved in?

Wait. What's this? Aha. She needed to write this down.

Her purse was jammed between her seat and the wall. She pulled it out of the cubbyhole and rummaged through it, looking for a scrap of paper and a pen. All she found was a takeout menu from Panda Express and a ballpoint pen from a Holiday Inn Express.

On one edge of the menu, she wrote the address of the Swiss bank. *Finally.* She had a lead. She dug deeper into Nick's file. *Dammit.* She was locked out of the FBI file. Still, she planned to comb through every bit of information WITSEC had on him before the plane landed. She ordered another Coke. Her index finger was cramping from all the scrolling. And she really needed some sleep. "No rest for the weary," as her mother always said. And her mother should know.

How many more bags of peanuts could she eat? Wiping the salt off her fingers, she went back to examining the files. *Son of a—*

Her finger froze over an update added just two days ago. The feds were reopening the investigation against Nick. Seems it may not be just the father who was involved in money laundering. New evidence pointed to the son too. *What the...?*

Lexi leaned her head against the wall and closed her eyes.

Could she have been that wrong about the Nick? Did he leave of his own free will? What if the guy with Nick wasn't his kidnapper but his accomplice?

THE SOUND of running water woke Nick up. *Where am I? Is Lexi taking a shower?* Even as that thought flooded his somnolent brain, Nick realized he'd been dreaming of someone else. "Dulce," he whispered as he opened his eyes. Up until just a few days ago, he'd thought she was the one . . . Now he wondered. Anyway, what did it matter? He'd never see her again.

His eyes adjusted to the ambient light, and he could make out the silhouette of another double bed, a long desk table, a flat-screen television. He was in a hotel room, a high-end hotel room, not like that one back in the middle of nowhere. Lifting himself to his elbows, he surveyed the room. The bed across from his was neatly made, and a suit jacket, starched shirt, and pants were laid out on it like a soldier waiting for orders. The strong smell of Brut cologne slapped him in the face, finishing the job of waking him up. *Right. Danny Quarrels. His father's secret.* Unfortunately, it was all coming back to him.

Now he wished it was Lexi in the bathroom or that he could go back to his sweet dreams of Jessica. Instead, he was sharing a hotel room with one of Teeth's goons, Danny Quarrels, waiting for the nine a.m. meeting. At least he wasn't in the Siberia that was Wyoming. He smiled to himself. He was more comfortable being in a cramped New York hotel room with a mafia hitman than the rambling, wide-open spaces of the West. *Calling Doctor Freud . . .* Of course, he didn't need Freud to interpret his hot wish-fulfillment dream.

Nick glanced at the clock on the nightstand. *What the . . .* Five in the morning. Obviously, Tiny didn't need much sleep. It had been the wee hours when they'd finally gone to bed. Thanks to a delay in Denver, it had been after midnight when they got to the hotel—the Beekman, pride of the financial district. It was right near the bank they'd be going to as soon as it opened.

Sharing a room hadn't been Nick's idea. But Tiny had insisted. And the husky fellow—and his Magnum —could be very persuasive. Anyway, if there was one thing Nick had learned from his father, it was don't cross the Italian mob . . . *unless you want to become the meatballs in grandma's special spaghetti sauce.*

His father. The old man was probably looking down from heaven, laughing his ass off. Running Nick back and forth across the country. Except, his father wouldn't be looking down, but up . . . from Hades.

The bathroom door opened and Tiny stepped out, hair wet, with a towel wrapped around his waist. With his broken nose, craggy cheeks, and muscular frame, he looked like a champion wrestler who'd lost as many matches as he'd won.

"You're up early," Nick said, crawling out from under the sheets to see what Tiny was doing. So far, the mobster was playing nice, but like a scorpion, he could strike at any moment. Nick had slept in his boxers and undershirt again since Tiny hadn't exactly given him time to pack an overnight bag.

"Early bird gets the worm." Tiny snapped the towel off and rubbed it briskly on his stubbly hair.

Nick looked away. "I suppose that makes me the worm." He stumbled to his feet, grabbed his pants off the back of the chair, and headed for the bathroom in the hopes that by the time he came out again, Tiny would be fully clothed.

After a quick shower, Nick slithered back into the same clothes he'd worn yesterday—and the day before—his usual winter outfit . . . black turtleneck, blue jeans, and a herringbone wool blazer. The hot water had revived him, and he was ready for a big breakfast. He'd gotten used to big breakfasts pretty quick at the ranch, back when he thought Tiny was a real estate investor. Danny Quarrels looked like the type of guy who could eat a porcupine without needing a toothpick.

When Nick returned from the bathroom, Tiny was tightening his necktie. For a thug, he was a fancy dresser. Then again, Victor always did like his guys to look sharp. He'd been his father's business partner after all. Growing up, Victor "Teeth" Marsiano had been a constant fixture in their New York penthouse—Victor and his old man always trying to outdo one another with their expensive clothes. Only later had Nick found out that they were clean on the outside but dirty on the inside.

"Looking good," Nick said, dropping into one of the easy chairs near the floor-to-ceiling window. Another thing you could count on with Teeth: a nice hotel suite with a living room and a wet bar. Nothing second-rate about that guy.

"I gotta work at it," Tiny said, admiring his reflection in the armoire mirror. "Not like you." He chuckled. "With a dame in every port."

"What do you mean by that?" The last time he'd heard the word *dame* was in a Humphrey Bogart movie. Was this goon for real?

"I wasn't born yesterday." Tiny turned to face him. "I know you was bonking that sexy marshal." His grin cracked his rough face in two. "There once was a dandy from Sukkar, who moaned like bi—"

"Okay. Okay." Nick scowled. He didn't like people poking into his personal life, especially not mafia thugs. And he didn't like men who denigrated women.

"And then there's that blonde chick what followed you across the country—"

Nick sat bolt upright. "What blonde chick?" *What in Hades is he talking about?*

Tiny set to work firing up the coffee maker. "Pretty little thing." He shook his head. "You're a lucky so-and-so."

"What blonde?" Nick twisted the gold ring on his little finger. *No. It couldn't be.* No way. She couldn't have found him. How could she? Detective Cormier had reported him dead. Poor Dulce. He couldn't imagine the scene with the detective breaking the tragic news to Jessica . . . in the middle of their romantic weekend. The thought of it turned his stomach.

The smell of burnt coffee filling the room didn't help.

"That Jessica chick. The one that followed you from Chicago." Tiny poured coffee into two porcelain cups. "You know." He winked. "The one that says she's your girlfriend." He held up one of the cups. "Cream or sugar?"

"My girlfriend?" His stomach did another flip. "Jessica . . . Dulce . . ."

"How do you take your coffee?" The thug held up a packet of sugar. "Cream or sugar?"

Nick shook his head. "When did you see Jessica? In Wyoming?"

"Sure did." Tiny delivered a cup of black coffee.

"Where?" Nick got up and started pacing the room. "Where did you see Jessica?"

"Calm down, man." The thug sipped his coffee. "She showed up at that guest ranch."

"Jessica was at the Cutthroat Lodge?" He stopped in

his tracks. He couldn't believe what he was hearing. How did she find him? Had she really followed him across the country? Why didn't he know that until now? Did she still care for him? Was it possible? A million questions spiraled through his mind. He patted his breast pocket.

"Sure was." Tiny smiled and rubbed his chin. "Quite the looker. You're one lucky guy—"

"Where is she now?" He had to get back to Wyoming. He had to find her. What must she think of him? *Shit.* He shouldn't have flushed the ring. *Damn it to Hades.* His mind was racing. He started pacing again, faster this time. Walking helped him think.

"She's still in Casper. Her and Lolita."

"Lolita's there too?" Nick's mouth fell open. What was going on? How did Tiny know all this? "How do you know—"

"Look, man. Lolita Durchenko is on my to-do list." Tiny leaned forward in his chair and set his cup down on the coffee table. "Teeth has eyes and ears on that one."

"Why?" He knew the answer. Lolita was the granddaughter of the Oxford Don, the most important Russian crime boss of that century.

Tiny scoffed. "Everyone knows she's the new head of Bratva."

Nick narrowed his eyes. He'd heard the rumor. But he didn't believe it. Lolita was a smooth operator, but she wasn't a criminal.

"She's hosting a high-stakes game tomorrow." Tiny went to the wet bar and refilled his coffee cup. "Out there in a Wild West hotel suite."

"She's hosting a game in Wyoming?" *Why in the world would she do that?* He squinted hard, as if with a sharp look he could penetrate the fog in his brain.

Tiny pulled his cell phone out of his interior jacket pocket and tapped the screen. "Yup. Saturday night at ten o'clock in room 422 at the Prairie Hotel in Casper."

"Saturday? You mean the day after tomorrow?" Nick ran both hands through his hair. "I've got to get back to Wyoming." *I've got to find Dulce.* "If Lolita's hosting a game, that means she's still out there. Did you say Prairie Hotel?" Nick tapped his phone to record the information. "What room again?"

"Want another cup of coffee?" Tiny held up the pot.

"I don't want any more coffee. I want to know that room number." He glared at Tiny.

"422." Tiny grinned. "Why? You thinking of playing?" He laughed. "The stakes are too high for you. You make one false move, here or at the bank, and I blow your head off. And then go after that pretty little girl-friend of yours."

"You wouldn't dare."

"Wouldn't I?"

"You can't change shaving creams without orders from Victor." Victor was practically like an uncle to him. He'd always been kind to Nick, kinder than his own father.

The big man laughed again. "Let's just say I might be upgrading my Barbasol sometime soon."

Nick shook his head. He wanted to get to the airport and get on a plane back to Casper. He crisscrossed the room, picked up the receiver of the hotel phone, and punched the button for the front desk. He would get a limo to the airport and get on the next plane back to Casper.

"Look, man. Relax." Tiny pushed a meaty finger onto the receiver button. The line went dead. "You aren't going anyplace until we do what we came here to do. *Capisce*?"

21

By the time they landed at JFK, Lexi was covered in a thin film of exhaustion. She needed a shower, a change of clothes, and a good night's sleep. What she got was a cold splash in the face at an airport restroom sink and a long taxi ride into Manhattan.

The cab smelled of onions, and the black seat was ripped. Lexi sat in the back, shielded from the driver by plexiglass with a tiny hole to exchange money. She'd been in cities before but not the Big Apple. She was dog-tired and as keyed up as a rabbit in springtime.

The cab emerged from the dark tunnel. *Wow. Just wow.* The breaking dawn exploded behind the dusky skyline. It took her breath away. Jagged black teeth in a big orange mouth. The closer they got to the city, the more her tongue grated like sandpaper. Where could she find a pop at seven in the morning in New York City? And not just any pop, her pop. *It's New York for heaven's sake.* She should be able to get whatever she wants on any street corner.

"Do you know a good place for breakfast?" she asked the cab driver. "Someplace open all night?" She had to at least get some coffee if she was going to confront Nick. Had he left of his own free will? Or had the mob got ahold of him? If it was the mob, why didn't they just off him in Wyoming? They must want him alive. And if he left voluntarily . . . Well, if he left voluntarily, why? And why go to New York and not home to Chicago? Who was his traveling companion?

He glanced at her in the rearview mirror. "What kind of food do you like?"

"Mountain Dew." She'd almost forgotten they were talking about breakfast.

"Excuse me?"

"Biscuits and gravy. Chicken and waffles. Shrimp and grits." Now she was just making conversation. All she wanted was caffeine. The sooner the better.

"Soul food." The driver sounded pleased.

"American food. And high-octane pop."

"All the good places aren't open yet. Like Pies 'n' Thighs." He grinned. "Best place for soul food open now is the Remedy Diner."

"Sounds perfect." She needed a remedy . . . a remedy for missing sleep, a remedy for missing meals. But most of all, a remedy for her missing witness.

It took over another hour just to get across the

bridge and make their way into downtown Manhattan. She could have swam across faster. She checked her phone. Almost seven. Rush hour started early.

The bank wouldn't open until nine. Until then, she had no idea where to find Nick. But that didn't mean she wanted to spend the morning in a stuffy cab. The traffic barely moved. Not like Wyoming, where you sometimes could floor it for miles on the open highway without seeing another living soul.

Spending half the night crossing the country was bad enough. But the cab ride put her over the edge. By the time the driver pulled up to the curb, she was desperate for air, as if she'd been buried alive. *Fresh air . . .*

The driver pulled up in front of a big red neon sign atop an old-fashioned clock attached to the corner of a building. "Enjoy your breakfast," he said as he tucked a tiny piece of paper through the slot in the plexiglass. "That'll be $66.50

Geez Louise. The cab fare was as much as a full month of unlimited cable. She'd have to remember to take the bus back to the airport . . . hopefully, with Nick in tow. She could make him spring for the taxi. It would serve him right. Lexi fumbled with her credit card, trying to use the awkward paybox attached to the back of the seat. She didn't dare turn in these receipts, unless she wanted to be a meter maid in Timbuktu. This trip was all on her.

"Insert your card and follow the instructions on the screen," the driver said.

She managed to pay and exit the cab, thankful to be out of moving vehicles and under her own steam. *Finally.* Filling her lungs with what passed for fresh air, she stood outside the diner, absorbing the city's energy.

The Remedy Diner's cool black-and-white brick front and stainless steel doors with portal windows looked like something out of a movie. A place where Robert De Niro and Al Pacino would have a stare-down over pancakes. Inside, the dim lighting and earth-toned terra-cotta, tan, and beige decor contrasted with gleaming countertops and glowing display cases full of gorgeous cakes, creating a cozy-yet-chic vibe.

Lexi slid onto a barstool at the counter, where smaller cases displayed huge flaky croissants and fruit-filled Danish pastries. Her mouth watered, and her stomach growled, reminding her that she hadn't eaten since yesterday, except for that small unpalatable ham sandwich on the flight. The menu didn't disappoint. No biscuits and gravy, no chicken and waffles, no shrimp and grits. But the lumberjack special would do. And best of all . . . they served Diet Mountain Dew. She'd missed her faithful friend. The first sip was heavenly.

Sipping her pop, she read over the notes she'd made on various napkins and receipts. She scrolled through the files one last time to make sure she hadn't missed anything. To review, Richard Schilling had accounts at several banks in the city, which had been transferred to his grandnephew, who was his only known living heir after Nick was pronounced dead. This time, scrolling through the accounts, she noticed something she hadn't on the plane. Something odd. One anomaly. She sucked up the last of her Mountain Dew and ordered a refill.

Enlarging her phone's screen using two fingers, she peered down at one line in one of the bank files: a safe-deposit box that was still in Richard's name. It hadn't been transferred to the nephew. *Why not?*

The pieces were falling into place. That must be the box mentioned in the letter. The letter Nick left at the Motel 6 along with that stupid note about going back to his girlfriend.

She reached into her pocket and pulled out the note, the letter, and the crumpled envelope. She uncrumpled the note and reread it. In full marshal mode, with stone-cold vision unclouded by emotion, she noticed that the handwriting was shaky. The word *girlfriend* was smaller than the rest. She reexamined the envelope. **MARSHAL COLT.** In big bold letters. Why not *Lexi*? Or even *Lexington*? After what they'd been through, he'd written *Marshal Colt*. Why?

Because someone was watching, that's why. Someone had forced him to write that note. Her marshal's gut told her so. And her woman's heart couldn't help but hope it was true. But that meant Nick was in imminent danger. *Dammit.* If only she knew how to find him. Her only chance was the bank. Nick and his companion couldn't have gotten to New York in time to go to the bank yesterday. So if they were going, it would be today, probably first thing. As much as she hated waiting, she'd have to wait until the bank opened. And she'd have to stake out the bank all day—or all week—if necessary. It was her only lead.

No use calling the bank when they opened. She knew from experience that this was the kind of situation where you had to show up in person and flash your badge around.

The waitress delivered a thick ceramic plate loaded with pancakes, eggs, and ham. Lexi dug in with gusto. Halfway through her breakfast, she stopped to google the distance between Remedy Diner and the Bank of Switzerland. Not bad. Only fifteen minutes by taxi and about the same by subway. Should she dare the subway? She couldn't risk getting lost. Still, the bank wouldn't open until at least nine o'clock, so she had another hour.

What could she do in that hour? There must be some other way to locate Nick. She could contact headquarters and have them search all the hotels in New York. For what? Would one of Teeth's thugs check in under his own name? Or Nick's? Anyway, they could have him tied up in a basement anywhere in the city. Dammit. There must be something she could do. She felt so helpless.

A young woman wearing yoga pants plopped a curly haired little girl onto the seat next to Lexi. "Is this seat taken?"

Lexi shook her head. "It's all yours."

The girl squirmed out of her mother's hands and tried to climb up onto the counter.

"How old is she?" Lexi thought of her own little girl, who would have been about that age now . . . if she'd been born. Lexi stabbed the fork into her half-eaten pancakes and ditched her crumpled napkin on top.

"Feisty fours," the girl's mother said. "Worse than terrible twos."

"She's adorable." Tears welled up in her eyes. "Enjoy your breakfast." She went to the cash register, paid, and fled the diner before she started bawling. *It's 'cause I haven't had any sleep. That's why I'm so emotional.*

Stepping out into the brisk morning air did her good. She decided to walk a few blocks to shake off the sorrow. From Houston, she headed south on Essex Street. After sitting on planes for what seemed like days, moving felt good.

She lengthened her stride. Distracted by the sights, sounds, and smells of New York City—skyscrapers and flower stands, sirens and hawkers, bakeries and kebabs —the blocks flew by. She didn't want to get in a cab or the subway and miss out on the vibrancy of the street life. Even in Chicago, Miami, and San Francisco, she'd never seen anything like it. The crush of people. The mishmash of different languages. The exotic smells. The fast-pace of the stream of foot-traffic. She didn't dare stop or slow down, or she'd be trampled.

Following the directions on her phone, she tramped

through the slush until she got to Seward Park. The small green patch looked like a welcome mat for Lower Manhattan. She turned right on East Broadway and found herself in Chinatown. The sights, sounds, and smells got even more dense and intense. Busy sidewalks chock-full of colorful souvenir shops, bubble tea boutiques, and Chinese bakeries. Open markets offered bins of elongated cucumbers, thin eggplants, and green beans over a foot long. Lexi gawked at weird-shaped fruits, pungent dried fish, and bags of herbs hanging from awnings. When she passed by one stand with barrels of dried orange fish and trays of whole fresh fish on ice, she had to put her hand over her nose.

As the novelty of the city wore off, the claustrophobia set in. Lexi was used to the wide-open spaces of Tennessee and Wyoming. The jam of people and jumble of things was squeezing her like an orange in a juice press.

She stopped and leaned up against a building to catch her breath. She shouldn't have eaten the Lumberjack Special. *Lumberjacks. How many lumberjacks are there in New York City anyway?* She sucked in the foul air and forced herself back into the throng.

What if she couldn't find Nick? What if something had happened to him? She didn't want to lose another witness. And she didn't want to lose someone else she cared about. Yes. She cared about Nick. Maybe she'd even fallen for him.

Water. She needed water. She ducked into the

closest market, bought a bottle of cold water, and guzzled it down like a nomad lost in the desert. Never mind that it was spilling down the front of her coat.

The shopkeeper gave her a strange look as she handed the empty plastic bottle back to him and wiped her mouth with the back of her hand. "Dehydrated," she said. "Jet lag is real." He probably thought she'd been on an all-night bender . . . and in a way, she had.

Although she was weary and her legs were tired, she was too close to take a cab or the subway now. She'd passed the point of no return. She took a deep breath and steeled herself for the rest of the slog. Holding her arms close to her sides and clutching her purse, she pretended she was encased in a bubble, something like the popemobile, that would protect her from the masses. Trying not to look around, she concentrated on walking a straight line down the center of the sidewalk.

Her attempts to shroud herself were interrupted by her phone chiming. The distinctive ringtone told her it was Drake. *Shit*. What did he want? She hoped it wasn't time to move Nick. Gritting her teeth, she somehow managed to answer her phone on the fly without dropping it or her purse onto the dirty sidewalk. Not able to walk and talk at the same time, she slid through the crowd and ducked under an awning for a reflexology and brow-microblading dive. She *really* didn't want to talk to him. But she had no choice. *When Drake called, you answered*. No matter what.

"Colt." Drake's voice was cold. "I've been calling since yesterday. Why didn't you answer?"

Dammit. She hadn't checked her voice messages. He must have called when she was in the air. "Sorry. I must have been out of cell phone range." She winced. "You know how it is out here in the Wild West."

"Where are you?"

"What do you mean?" She cupped her hand around the phone.

"All those sirens and—"

"Oh. It's the TV." She just lied to her boss, and not a lie of omission either. A lie about flying across the country to search for a missing witness—whom she'd never reported missing in the first place. If he ever found out . . .

"I've made arrangements for you to get your witness out of there now."

Shit. She'd need to be a magician to get her witness anywhere. "Okay."

"I sent the plane tickets to your work email. You fly to Nashville this afternoon, rent a car, and drive to Paris, Tennessee."

"What?" Her mouth fell open. "Why there?" Paris, Tennessee, was twenty minutes from where she'd grown up . . . twenty minutes from the last place on earth she wanted to be. She thought of Gabe. Okay, the second to last place. Watching her lover get blown up was traumatic, but watching her daddy slowly fade away was no picnic either.

"It has the advantage that you know it and the Mafia doesn't." Drake sounded impatient as usual. "A local sheriff named Travis Dawson will be waiting for you."

Lexi inhaled loudly. "Not Travis Dawson!" Why had she said that? What could she say now that wouldn't sound idiotic?

"Why not Travis Dawson?"

Flipping Travis Dawson. She bit her tongue to keep from letting out a string of curses.

"Why not Travis Dawson, Colt?" Drake's voice was even colder than usual.

"He—"

"Colt!"

"He kissed me once behind the bleachers." And then they had sex and were caught by the principal. Travis was hailed as the king of school while Lexi was marked as a slut.

Silence. She could feel him rolling his eyes.

"Get over it, Colt. High school was a long time ago."

Not that long. "Couldn't we find another place? I mean—"

"Colt, get your witness to Tennessee now or look for another job."

The line went dead. He'd hung up.

"Fuuuuuuuuuuudge!" She slammed her phone against her thigh. *Now what?* If she didn't find Nick and by some miracle get him on that plane to Nashville, she would be fired.

Son of a— She'd never get him on *that* plane with

the tickets Drake bought leaving from Casper. She'd have to go online and change the tickets to fly out of New York. And then hope to God she found him, and soon. She let out a little whimper.

It was hopeless. She was toast.

And to top it off, she was lost. The street was a blur as she glanced around to find a landmark to enter into her cell phone. Her finger hovering over her phone, she noticed she had a new message from headquarters: the information on the guest list from Ford's Cutthroat Lodge. She'd have to look at it later.

Glancing up from her phone, she saw it. How had she missed it? She was standing across the street from the Bank of Switzerland. Stepping out into the street, she nearly got hit by a cab. The angry driver rolled down his window and shouted an obscenity. For a moment, she felt like she was back in the Army, where everyone swore like fiends and no one wrote them up. Until everything got blown to hell, she'd at least felt at home there. She sprinted across, hardly caring whether or not she got smashed.

She stood on the sidewalk in front of the bank's heavy gilded doors and tinted glass exterior, looking up. She couldn't even see the top. She swayed and caught herself before she toppled over.

Stopping the flow of traffic on a New York sidewalk wasn't a good idea. People were bumping her shoulders on both sides and cursing her as they passed. She inhaled sharply, pulled the giant wooden door handle, and stepped inside. She hoped to God she was right and Nick and his companion were coming here first thing to claim that safe-deposit box.

She scanned the lobby for Nick. He wasn't there. *Dammit.* She knew her plan was iffy, but still she had been hopeful. Anyway, she didn't know where else to look. This was her only lead. New York was a big city. Big and dangerous.

The gaping lobby, with its marble floors and huge potted plants standing at attention in front of large columns, reminded her of the Lexington train station. Behind a long mahogany counter, tellers waited for their first customers of the morning.

Needle in a haystack. Even if she didn't find Nick, she might find out why Richard Schilling had an unclaimed safe-deposit box in Nick's name.

While she strode across the lobby, she assessed which teller would be the most helpful: the pretty brunette with pink eyeglasses, the one with a matronly updo, or the petite man in a closely tailored suit and bow tie. *The hipster, the librarian, or Pee-wee Herman?* Luckily, a heavyset man with a comb-over opened his window just before she reached the hipster. She made a beeline for him. Middle-aged men were more likely to dismiss her credentials but also more likely to succumb to her charms, such as they were.

When she flashed her badge—and her best smile— and asked to see Richard Schilling's safety-deposit box, the teller scowled. Maybe she should have chosen Pee-wee Herman or the hipster.

"Have a seat, Officer," he said, pointing toward a sitting area up against the far wall. "I'll have to get the manager."

"Marshal," she said under her breath. Lexi took a seat on the end of the row of empty hard-backed chairs. Adjusting her coat, she crossed her ankles and waited.

Why Paris, Tennessee? Why Travis Dawson? Worse than the thought of seeing him again was the thought of seeing herself through his eyes. Just thinking about him set off her gag reflex.

"Mrs. Schilling?" A well-dressed woman appeared out of nowhere. "I'm Cynthia Chase. The bank manager. They're waiting for you in the back room."

"They?" Her cheeks burned.

The woman flashed a practiced smile. "Mr. Schilling and his bodyguard."

Lexi couldn't help but smile back. She'd flipping found him. As her daddy always said, "If you work hard enough, sometimes you get lucky."

22

———————

The vault was like a sterile cave. No windows. Everything shiny and white. Along three walls, there were lockers. Big ones on the bottom—Nick could only imagine what they held— and smaller ones up top.

The bank manager's heels clicked on the marble floor as she delivered the safe-deposit box.

Nick's heart sped up. What in the world would his father have left him in a secret safe-deposit box? Apparently, his father had rented the box two months before he'd died and never told Nick about it. Whatever it was, Victor wanted it and had sent Tiny all the way to Wyoming to bring Nick back to get it.

The manager placed the box in front of Nick on a rectangular bar-height table. "Take your time," she said. "Press this buzzer if you need anything." She pointed to what looked like a doorbell next to the vault door, then left the room.

Nick removed the tiny key from his pocket. He glanced up at Tiny, who was looming over him like a big gorilla watching a juicy caterpillar it's about to eat. He slid the key into the lock and twisted it. Pulse pounding, he opened the box. His breath caught, and he put his hand to his chest.

Overcome, he laughed out loud. "I can't believe it." A piece from the mysterious missing Romanov jewels. And not just any piece, but the Vladimir Sapphire Kokoshnik Tiara. He carefully weighed the tiara in his hands. It was heavy yet buoyant. Refracted light from the green sapphires danced across the white ceiling and silver vaults and seemed to expand the room. Interlocking gold circles studded with diamonds framed the sapphire pendants. *Breathtaking. Lovely. Extraordinary.*

"Is it worth a lot?" Tiny asked.

Nick chuckled. "It's priceless."

"Teeth wants the crown." Tiny was leaning against the vaults, picking his teeth with a toothpick. "His orders are to bring it back to him. He says it rightfully belongs to him."

Nick furrowed his brows. "And why is that?" He gently placed the tiara back in its velvet case. "It really should go to the Center for Russian Art. I think that's what my father must have wanted." Wouldn't it be something if the Center had this treasure on display? That would get the world's attention. The Center would become world-renowned overnight. Shame one tiara would get more attention than all of the Kandinskys and Goncharovas in the collection. People cared more about expensive jewelry than paintings. He had to admit, seeing the Kokoshnik tiara and holding it in his hands was exhilarating. What a piece of Russian history. A token of excess and revolution.

"If it's worth so much . . ." Tiny moved closer and stared down at the tiara. "Why didn't your old man sell it?"

"This tiara is a piece of history. You can sell a tiara, but you can't sell history." But why had his father kept this one piece separate from the rest of his Russian art collection? And what did it have to do with his father's business associate Victor "Teeth" Marsiano? Even from the grave, his old man managed to pull his strings.

"I bet Teeth will sell it." Tiny grinned. "Maybe he'll give me a cut."

"No one is getting a cut." Nick picked up the velvet case. "Why does Victor think he owns this tiara? What's his claim on it?"

"Some deal he made with your old man." Tiny shrugged. "I dunno."

Nick scowled. "What kind of deal? If it's the money —" Of course, once he'd been pronounced dead and whisked off to WITSEC, he'd also been cut off from his money. Still, there must be a way.

"Look. Pack up the crown and let's get going." Tiny reached for the tiara, but Nick snatched it up before he could get his beefy paw on it. "Teeth told me to bring him the crown, and that's what I'm going to do. And if you don't get a move on it, I might bring it to him on your head."

"This tiara belonged to the Grand Duchess," Nick pleaded. "She used it to buy her way out of Russia during the revolution when other members of her family were being murdered by the Bolsheviks. Like most of the Romanov jewels, it went missing . . ." He stopped and stared down at the tiara. *Was it worth risking his life for?* Maybe the tiara could buy him safe passage too. He tucked the tiara back into the box and closed the lid.

He licked his lips. How was he going to get out of this one? Everything seemed to be moving in slow motion. Fluorescent lights flickered. A vent blew cold air even though it was winter. The sound of high heels tapping on the marble floor. He tightened his grip on the velvet box. It seemed to radiate heat.

It's hot. That's why the old man hid it and then engineered this drama with Victor and the secret safe-deposit box. Nick's palms were sweating. *Leave it to him to entangle me in some illegal scheme.* Then again, maybe his father had bought the jewels. He'd purchased others from the Romanov collection. Were they bought on the black market? With some research, he could find out. His father had been an avid collector, but he didn't care much about his sources.

Nick thought of a time when he was fourteen and

his father had taken him to Italy on an art-buying excursion for the first time. Tagging along had made Nick feel so grown-up, and he'd been on his best behavior . . . He knew the consequences if he wasn't.

On a bright sunny day in Florence, his father had taken him to a dank garage in a creepy alley, where a man with a dark beard unrolled canvases on a plank suspended between two sawhorses under a makeshift spotlight. They didn't even have frames. His father paid the man cash for two paintings, which the bearded man rolled up like cigars, pushed into cardboard tubes, and presented to his father without ceremony. Then the man made a big production out of giving his father two thick envelopes that were sealed and embossed.

On the way back to the hotel, Nick had asked what was in the envelopes. His father had said, "With enough money, you can buy legitimacy." At the time, Nick didn't know what he meant. Only later did he find out that his old man had purchased black market paintings along with the all-important certificates of authenticity and title-ownership pedigrees. With enough money you could buy anything. Maybe even history.

Nick opened the box to take another look at the tiara. However he'd come by it, the public deserved to see this priceless piece of history. And what better place to put it on display than the Center? With only a slight twinge of guilt, he closed the case and tucked it under his arm.

"Teeth will be waiting for us," Tiny said.

Let him wait. "I need to give this to the Center's assistant manager."

Tiny chuckled. "You mean your girlfriend."

Nick scanned the vault. There was only one way in or out. How was he going to get away from Victor's goon and get the tiara to Jessica? Tiny was big and probably had a gun.

The tapping of high heels was getting louder. The door to the vault opened with a creak. *The manager must be coming back.* Nick was running out of time. He had to stall and come up with a plan. "You don't happen to have a plastic bag?" he asked the bank manager.

"No, but I have a set of handcuffs," a familiar voice said.

Nick swung around. Marshal Lexington Colt stood in the doorway, arms akimbo. "Lexi, what are you doing here?"

"I was about to ask you the same thing." The marshal's low heels clicked as she stepped inside the vault.

"The one that got away, huh, Marshal?" Tiny laughed. "My job here ain't done." He made for the door. "But if you lovebirds don't mind, I'll take off for now and catch up to yous later."

"Not so fast," Lexi said.

But the thug had already slipped out the door. Lexi looked from the door to Nick and back again like she didn't know which way to go. He shrugged and gave her a sheepish smile. She marched across the vault.

Hands on her hips, head tilted, she gave him the kind of look a jealous lover would right before throwing her drink in his face. Only instead of a drink, she had handcuffs.

"What's in the safe-deposit box?" She glared at him.

"Something my father left for me." He tucked the velvet case further under his arm.

"Why wasn't this safe-deposit box listed as part of his estate?" She leaned on the table. She looked tired.

"How do you know that?"

"I know a lot of things."

No, not coconut and strawberries. Coconut and raspberries. Nick inhaled her shampoo scent. He set the case on the table next to her and opened it. "The Vladimir Sapphire Kokoshnik Tiara."

She picked up the case. "This tiara is over a hundred years old?"

He nodded. "The Grand Duchess used it to buy her life during the Russian Revolution."

"It must be worth a lot." She touched one of the sapphires.

"Priceless." He twisted the ring around his little finger. *Now what?* Would she take him back to Wyoming? He needed to get back there as soon as possible. He needed to find Jessica and give her the tiara to put on display at the Center . . . and to explain why he hadn't called her.

"I guess it's worth the life of a duchess," she said thoughtfully. "But is it worth your life?" She snapped the case shut and dropped it on the table. "You're lucky you're not dead already."

"Thanks to you." Nick took a step closer. "Thank God you came." When he put his hand on her shoulder, she flinched and took a step backward. "I'm sorry I left. But Tiny insisted."

"I recognize him." Lexi crossed her arms. "One of Teeth's guys." She seemed angry. She couldn't be upset that he left. It wasn't his choice after all. *So what's eating her?*

Nick nodded. "I truly am sorry. I—"

"So you said." Lexi flipped her hair over her shoulder. "Let's go."

"Back to Wyoming?" He couldn't tell her why he was in a hurry to get back. She'd probably try to prevent him from seeing Jessica . . . for his own good. "Sure."

"No. Wyoming isn't safe." She made a sour face, like she'd gotten a whiff of vinegar. "We're moving you to Tennessee."

"Tennessee!" His jaw dropped. "I need to go back to Wyoming."

"Why?" She narrowed her eyes. "It's not like you'd put down roots."

"My stuff is there," he lied. The only thing he'd left was safely hidden under Lexi's mattress.

"The department will deliver it to Paris."

"Paris?" he blurted out. "I'm going to France?"

"Paris, Tennessee." She tightened her lips.

"There's a Paris in Tennessee?"

"Quit stalling. Let's go." She took his elbow.

"I've got to get back to Wyoming." When he looked into her eyes, she glanced away. "The tiara. I've got to deliver it to the associate director of the Center for Russian Art and Culture."

She gave him a quizzical look. "Your director is in Wyoming?" A light went off in her eyes, and she exhaled loudly. "Right. You're girlfriend."

"You know Jessica is in Wyoming?" Everyone knew but him. He pulled his arm away. "How long have you known? Why didn't you tell me?"

"You know the rules. It's WITSEC or prison." She unclipped the cuffs from her belt. "Which is it?"

"Prison?" *What in Hades is she talking about?* "You're joking."

"Do I look like I'm joking?" She dangled the cuffs in front of his face. "Let's go."

"Wait a minute. No one ever said anything about prison." He clasped the velvet case to his chest as if it were a life preserver. "I haven't done anything—"

"Conspiring with the Italian mafia, fencing stolen paintings and jewelry, for starters."

"What?" He couldn't believe what he was hearing. Was she making this up? Was this her way of getting back at him for Jessica? She couldn't be serious. "That was my father, not me."

"Intel says otherwise."

"What intel?"

"They're reopening the investigation against you."

"On what grounds?" Damn his old man. What had he gotten him into? Nick should have known better than to take those paintings from his father. But he'd been so fixated on making the Center a success. He should have known dealing with his father would bring him nothing but trouble. "It was my father. I had nothing to do with it. I'm not a criminal. I've never stolen anything."

"You stole my heart," she said under her breath. At least, that's what he thought she said. "Hand it over." She reached for the velvet box.

"But—"

"Now."

He held out the box. Lexi grabbed it with one hand and snapped a cuff around his wrist with the other.

What the . . . "You've got to be kidding me." His face was hot. "This isn't funny." He was starting to get angry.

"No. It's not." She shoved the velvet box into her purse and then snapped the other cuff onto her own wrist. "But it's for your own protection. Come on. We have a flight to catch, and I still have to change out tickets."

"You don't need the bracelet." Nick tugged at the cuff. "Just ask nice and you can take me anywhere."

"I thought I'd never see you again." Her lower lip trembled almost imperceptibly.

"Marshal . . . Lexington . . . Lexi." He looked into her eyes. "I'm not that kind of guy."

"How do I know what kind of guy you are?" She yanked on the cuff. "We barely know each other.

LEXI FELT bad about the handcuffs. But she wasn't going to risk losing Nick again. The cuff chafed her wrist and dug in whenever Nick moved. Falling into step, they exited the bank and walked to the corner to hail a cab. Whenever one of them broke the rhythm, she paid for it with a sharp dig from the cuff. Walking wasn't the only thing awkward about being handcuffed to Nick. She'd just as soon kiss him as run away from him. But for the sake of her job, she couldn't do either.

She removed the cuffs once they got to the airport. She didn't want to draw suspicion. An hour later, they were on a plane to Nashville.

Spending the two-plus-hour flight next to Nick—feeling his arm brushing against hers, inhaling his citrus and juniper scent, and avoiding his long-lashed gaze—was both exhilarating and exhausting. Whenever he moved or spoke, the tiny hairs on Lexi's arms stood on end. *Hormones. That's all it is. Chemicals, like sulfuric acid.* Or hydrated aluminum silicate, otherwise known as kaolinite. The stuff that had eroded her daddy's lungs at the clay mine. She spent the flight trying to smooth out her jagged breathing.

"Why do you think I'm a criminal?" Nick asked.

"Something I read." She snapped back.

"What?"

"Confidential. Can't tell you." She looked away.

"Why are you always so angry?" Nick asked.

Not angry. Betrayed. Nick had snowed the feds. And worse, he'd lied to her. She ignored him and fished in her purse for her cell phone.

"Lexi, I really care about you." The warmth of his body next to hers sent a shiver up her spine. "You know I'd never lie to you."

"Do I?" She glanced over at him. "You could be Jack the Ripper for all I know."

"I know something bad happened to you," Nick said softly. "The nightmares. The shakes. I'm here for you if you want to talk about it."

"You sound like my shrink."

"Please, Lexi. Don't shut me out." He put his hand on hers.

She held on to his hand, not so much a caress as a drowning woman latching onto a life preserver.

He pushed a lock of hair out of her face and tucked it behind her ear. "What happened to you to make you so bitter?"

"I'm sorry," she said.

He tilted her chin up. "Don't apologize."

"I'm supposed to be protecting you. But I can't even —" Her voice broke off.

"You're good at your job, Marshal." He stroked her hair. "Even you can't fight off the demons inside." He lifted her hand to his lips.

She held her breath, fighting back tears. She shook her head. "I should get some work done. If there's a mole in WITSEC, I've got to find them before they kill you. Or someone else." She pulled her hand away and tapped her phone awake.

"Guess I'll take a nap," Nick said.

"Good idea," she replied without looking up. *Demons inside. He had that right.*

She tapped open the file on the guest list she'd downloaded earlier. *Danny Quarrels.* That was no surprise. She'd just seen him with Nick in the bank. She knew she recognized him. Another Italian mobster. One of Teeth's henchmen. She scrolled farther down the list, stopping at *Angelina Christina Fontaine.*

Wait a second. Another person from Brooklyn? Out in Wyoming, at Ford's Lodge? This was getting weird.

She forked over the internet fee so she could google the name. *Good lord.* She had been a cheerleader at Prospect Heights High School and then a real estate agent in Brooklyn. That couldn't just be a coincidence. But what did it mean? She stared down at the picture of a teenage Angelina smiling, holding pom-poms above her head. Next to her was another girl who looked just like her. *Her sister?* Using her fingers, she made the picture bigger until the girl turned into a bug-eyed spider. *Hmmm. Something familiar about her.*

She glanced over at Nick. He was fast asleep. She continued her research. Angelina Christina Fontaine did have a sister, Annabella Carina, who was eleven months older, although in the picture they could have been twins. Why was Angelina Fontaine visiting Ford's Lodge? Was it significant that she went to the same high school as the murdered witnesses? And where did the Italian mafia fit in? Was Nick their next target?

He looked so peaceful with his long lashes brushing against his cheek. Dammit, Lexi. Get a grip. He was most likely a criminal. In which case, he was a big phony. Just her luck. *The first guy she's attracted to in forever, and he's a flipping crook.*

Crook or not, it was her job to protect him. And she was going to do her job. No more witnesses were getting killed on her watch. She had to get Nick settled and safe. Then she'd track down Angelina Christina Fontaine.

A voice came over the loudspeaker. "Please power down and store all electronics for landing." Lexi pressed the button on her phone and then dropped it into her purse.

As the flight touched down in Nashville, a familiar dread descended into the pit of her stomach. Every time she came home, she was once again plagued with her childhood "tummy aches"—which was the least of the reasons she'd sworn she'd never come back to Tennessee. When she left for the army, she thought it was for good. Becoming a federal marshal was her insurance. Now, the very thing she'd counted on to keep her away from home had sent her back . . . back to the past, a past she'd just as soon forget.

"I don't need to cuff you again, do I?" she asked, only half serious.

"I'll be a good boy," Nick said. "I promise."

As she followed him off the plane, she tried not to look at his perfect butt. *Dammit, Lexi. Stop it.*

The welcome committee of one was waiting for them when they got off the plane. The sight of him made her stomach flip: Travis Dawson in his sheriff's uniform. *Gawd.* Had Drake sent her back here as punishment?

"Why, if it isn't Sexy Lexi, come home to roost." Travis flashed a big toothy grin. "Or should I call you Baby Ghost?"

She choked back a curse and forced a smile. "Marshal Colt will do."

"We go way back." Travis held his arms out like he might hug her but seemed to think better of it when he noticed her companion. "Why stand on ceremony, Lex, darlin'?"

"I take it you and Federal Marshal Colt grew up together," Nick said, emphasizing *federal marshal.*

She didn't need Nick coming to her rescue. Although it was kind of sweet. *Dammit, Lexi. He's probably a crook and a liar. Forget it.*

Travis ignored him. "After you dump your garbage, we should catch up over a beer."

"Let's just get on with it," she said. "Where are we taking Mr. Schilling?"

"Old Hickory Trailer Park. You remember where that is, don't ya?"

She nodded.

"Trailer park?" Nick chafed.

"Why don't you get your rental car, drop him off, and then we can catch up?" Travis touched her arm.

She jerked out of his reach. "I'm not letting Mr. Schilling out of my sight until he's safely reassigned." *Anyway, I'd rather eat a dirt sandwich than catch up with you.*

"When you're a snake charmer, you're gonna get bit." Travis winked.

"Don't believe everything you hear about snakes." She unbuttoned her coat. Nashville was a lot warmer than Wyoming.

"Speaking of snakes . . ." Travis laughed. "Remember when you was so terrified of those cottonmouths in the Tennessee River?" He fake punched her shoulder. "Remember when you jumped into Devil's Hole, and we told you the swirling water was a nest of snakes gonna suck you under?" He was laughing so hard he had tears in his eyes. "You fell for it hook, line, and sinker." He snorted. "Flapping your arms like a big ol' goose."

"Cottonmouths don't make nests." She glared at him. If only she'd known that back then, she wouldn't have made such a fool of herself. "They're solitary creatures." She used her left hand to brush a lock of hair out of her face. "Like me," she said under her breath. "And they always open their mouths in warning."

"If she opens her mouth, watch out." Travis chuckled and punched Nick on the shoulder in a bromance sort of way.

"Watch who you're calling a snake." Nick narrowed his brows. "I used to collect snakes when I was a boy."

"I bet you did," she said.

"I'm gonna start calling you Cottonmouth." Flipping stupid-ass Travis was laughing his idiot head off. *Jerk*.

She glared at him. "That's *Marshal* Cottonmouth to you." *A-hole*.

23

———

Nick had never set foot in a trailer before. It was weirdly like a cross between a dollhouse and a bus, which really wasn't so bad once you got used to everything feeling disposable. Being with Lexi wasn't bad either, even if she thought he was a criminal. He could inhale her coconut-strawberry- . . . -raspberry freshness all day. But he'd have to be Houdini to get away from her in time to get back to Wyoming for that poker game.

Still, there had to be a way. He just had to knock her out, steal the tiara from her purse, get back to Casper, break into her house to retrieve what he'd left under her mattress, and get to Lolita's poker game . . . all by tomorrow night.

Good thing he was an optimist at heart, or he might have been discouraged.

Anyway, the whole thing was ridiculous. His father was the art fence, not him. And if the Center did launder money or hawk paintings for his old man, it was unintentional. *The sins of the father...*

Unfortunately, Nick hadn't suspected what was going on until it was too late. By then, his old man was dead and he'd been poisoned. Back then, the cops had told him Victor "Teeth" Marsiano was responsible and would try again. They'd promised to protect him if he joined WITSEC and turned over any records on his father's business and his father's business partner, Victor.

Everything had happened so fast. Maybe he shouldn't have joined WITSEC. Growing up, Victor had been like an uncle—a scary uncle, but still. Now he was on Victor's hit list.

"I'm not a criminal," Nick said.

"The feds will be the judge of that." Lexi led him through the dinky living room to the back bedroom.

"Lexi, you've got to believe me," Nick turned to her and put his hand on her arm. "You're good at your job. Trust your instincts. What does your gut tell you?"

She averted her gaze and pulled away. "In here."

Nick followed her in. He was serious when he'd said he'd follow her anywhere.

This must be the master suite. Just inside the bedroom door was another door to a tiny bathroom. Nick peeked inside. With its shiny linoleum floor and plastic faucets, it looked like a toy bathroom. An outsize window covered with a cartoon decal took up half the wall behind the toilet. Lexi tugged on the cuff, pulling him back into the bedroom.

Like the rest of the mobile home, the bedroom, with its peeling floral wallpaper, looked like it was made out of cardboard.

"Sit." Lexi pushed him down onto the edge of the bed.

"Nap time?" he asked hopefully. Once she was asleep, maybe he could get the key to the car from her purse and make his escape.

She smiled, her mouth slightly open. She had no clue how beautiful she was. She straddled his lap.

Wow. He didn't expect this. But aside from being pleasurable, it just might be the opportunity he'd been waiting for. He lay back on the bed. Lexi fell on top of him. He caressed her hair. She kissed him. Her lips were soft as rose petals . . . her hair brushed against his face.

She sat on his chest, took his hands in hers, and pushed his arms up over his head. *Okay. If that's how she wants it.* She pulled something from her pocket. Before he knew it, she'd cuffed him to the bedpost. She crawled off him, threw her head back, and laughed.

"Hey, what are you doing?" he asked. "You can't leave me here."

"Watch me." She did an about-face and marched to

the door. At the threshold, she turned back and waved. "Be a good boy and stay put."

Now what? All his muscles tightened. *Any chance the bedpost is as flimsy as the rest of this place?* He tugged at the cuff. *Nope.* "Lexi, come back . . . Lexington . . . Marshal Colt—"

Straining against the cuff was only making his wrist hurt. He forced himself to relax into the bed and breathe. The glass half full had become the glass half empty. He was now officially discouraged. He closed his eyes. *Let's face it. You'll never see Jessica again. And you'll never get the Vladimir Tiara to the Center. You'll be lucky not to go to jail . . . or be killed. What a chump.*

He laughed. He had to admit, Marshal Lexington Colt really was something. *Sigh.* Lying down reminded him how little sleep he'd had in the last forty-eight hours. Might as well take a nap. He wasn't going anywhere any time soon.

Bang. Bang. A loud noise woke him up. *What the . . . Is someone kicking the trailer door in?* His breath caught. *Shit.* Lexi had said he was next on the hit list. Had the assassins finally found him? He yanked at the cuff. *Merde. I'm going to die like a chained-up dog.* "Lexi, what's going on? Lexington . . ." He twisted his head around to examine the bedpost. *There must be some way out of here.* The banging was getting louder. "Marshal Colt? Are you out there? I'm a sitting duck in here," he yelled.

Breathless, Lexi came crashing through the bedroom door and then slammed it shut and locked it.

"What's going on?"

She fumbled with the handcuff key. "I've got to get you out of here now."

The cuff fell onto the floor. He jumped up off the bed. Voices from the next room were getting closer. Was it Tiny? Had he followed them? Or some other mafia goons? Until now, he hadn't really believed his life was in danger.

Lexi unholstered her gun. Holding it in both hands, she pointed it at the bedroom door. "Take the car keys out of my purse." She nodded toward the purse sitting on the dresser. "I'll hold them off. You get out of here."

"I'm not going to just leave you here."

"Yes, you are." She jerked her head toward the purse again. "Keys. Now."

He slid across the bedroom, grabbed her purse, and rummaged for keys. An explosion on the other side of the bedroom door sent bullets whizzing into the room.

"Get down!" Lexi shouted, firing back through the door.

He just stood there, holding her purse.

The sounds of gunfire and bullets flying seemed to be in slow motion. Lexi let out a yelp and fell back against the bed. She slumped to the floor and sat there, holding her side. A red flower bloomed across her white shirt.

"Go out the bathroom window," she said, gasping.

He hurried to her and knelt at her side. "I'm not leaving you here like this." He put his arm around her.

"Yes. You. Are." She spit out the words.

"But you're bleeding."

"Go now!" she screamed.

Jarred into action by the pitch of her voice, he ran into the bathroom. He heard the gunmen ramming the bedroom door. Using Lexi's purse, he broke the bathroom window. Only after he saw the broken glass did it occur to him that he could have just opened it.

The sound of gunfire sent him flying through the window. He landed on the ground with a thud. The wind knocked out of him, he rolled over, panting. He got to his knees. Stumbling to his feet, he launched himself into a run. The rental car was parked behind the trailer. Feeling for the keys in Lexi's purse as he ran, his hand brushed up against the velvet box of the tiara. Then, like a baseball player stealing home, he dove across the grass toward the car.

Come on. Come on. Come on. The key fob. *Yes.* He pushed the fob. The car beeped. He jumped into the driver's seat, pushed the ignition, threw it in reverse, and jammed on the accelerator. In the rearview mirror, he watched a guy in a gray suit run around the trailer. *Merde!* Nick stomped on the gas even harder. As the guy aimed his gun at the car's rear window, the car lurched backward and winged him. The gun flew as the guy fell. Without looking back, Nick zoomed out onto the street and took off. His heart raced as he sped through Paris, heading for the interstate. Good thing he'd always had a knack with geography and had paid attention on the drive from the airport.

If only Tiny hadn't taken away his cell phone, he could call 911. He'd call as soon as he got to airport. He hoped to Christ Lexi would live that long.

24

Jessica lined up the booze bottles in a neat row on top of the microwave. It wasn't Lolita's usual snazzy bar, but it would have to do. After all, the game started in less than an hour.

The suite at the Prairie Hotel wasn't the Ritz, but it seemed about right for a high-stakes poker game in the Wild West. Lolita had rented two folding tables and some chairs. Jessica helped set them up. They'd moved all the furniture out of the sitting area, and it was shoved up against the bed at the back of the room. It was a bit cozy . . . *Okay, cramped.*

Gliding around the room, Lolita was acting like it was the penthouse at the Parker Hotel back in Chicago. "You really should play, *milaya.*" Lolita stacked fancy poker chips in color-coded towers around the folding tables. "You could pay for your flight home . . . and that trip to Italy you've been mooning about."

"You have a lot of confidence in me." Jessica crammed as many pops and mixers into the small refrigerator as would fit. "What if I lose?"

Lolita laughed. "You never lose. Anyway, I'll stake you, so what does it matter?"

"It matters more if I lose *your* money."

"Not to me."

"Well it does to me." Jessica unwrapped three new decks of cards and dropped them in the center of the round table.

"Italy . . ." Lolita whispered. "Art, food, wine . . . hot Italian men."

Jessica smiled. "I *could* use the money."

The door opened, and Jack came in carrying two paper bags from Safeway. He kicked the door shut with his foot.

"Then it's settled." Lolita stood back, admiring the poker table. "I'll stake, and you'll play. Someone needs to put these cowboys in their place."

"If anyone can handle the cowboys," Jack said, dropping the grocery bags onto the table, "it's the cowgirl philosopher, Jessie James."

Jack put his arm around her shoulder and squeezed. "And if you're nice to the dealer, he just might slip you an extra ace now and then."

"Now, now," Lolita said. "We run an honest game. My reputation's at stake."

"Even out here in the wilds of Wyoming?" Jack winked.

"Everywhere."

The next forty minutes were a blur of putting stuff away and setting up for the poker game. A quick shower and change and Jessica would be ready to face the cowboys. Waiting for the water to get warm, she chewed on her fingernail.

Even if she usually won, she still got nervous playing. In fact, she hated it.

By the time the players started showing up, Jessica was cleaned and pressed into her favorite vintage dress: a long blue number with black velvet flowers. She'd polished her red cowboy boots with a hotel washcloth. She'd even used the blow-dryer on her hair instead of letting it air-dry for hours like usual.

Lolita stalked the room in her Catwoman black leather pants and a frilly silk blouse. Jack . . . well, Jack just looked like his usual scruffy self in his frayed blue jeans, wrinkled flannel shirt, and balding corduroy jacket. Still, with his five-o'clock shadow and the lock of chestnut hair falling across his eyes, there was something sexy about his devil-may-care dishevelment.

"Too bad about Vanya," Jessica said, making conversation to kill time. The marshal had called a colleague to come pick him up. He was cooling his heels in the local jail.

"He can take care of himself," Lolita said. "Although I did like having a bodyguard, even if it was just my goofy cousin."

"Aren't you worried?"

"As my dad says, don't do the crime if you can't do the time." Lolita winked. She didn't seem very concerned about her cousin. Something still didn't add up. Why would Vanya kill witnesses? Was he working for Sly Yudkovich again?

"Did your cousin kill that dude in the burbs?" Jack asked, as if reading her mind. "Is Vanya working for the Russian mafia again? I thought he'd given all that up."

"Don't be silly." Lolita flipped her hair over her shoulder. "Vanya's a good boy. He'll be out in no time." Why was Lolita so confident Vanya go free? Would Bratva break him out of jail? Maybe Lolita put up bail. Still, he'd have to face a trial. Unless . . . unless both Lolita and Vanya were still working undercover.

A knock on the door signaled that the time had finally come. The big game was about to start. Jessica's palms were sweating, and her throat was dry. She went to the "bar" and mixed herself a stiff drink. Half Jack Daniels and half Coke.

The first player through the door was Wayne, the owner of Ford's Cutthroat Lodge. "Say, aren't you the gal who was at the ranch the other day?"

She nodded. "Good to see you again."

Wayne was one of those guys whose age was impossible to guess because his skin was as tanned as a cowhide. His jeans had a crease down the front, like he'd had them dry-cleaned. And his striped snap shirt was crisp and starched.

To Jessica's surprise, the next player was a woman—

a petite, attractive thirty-something woman with a lively spark in her eyes. Usually Jessica was the only gal in the game. While she didn't expect sisterhood from a competitor, she was glad for another woman player.

Shania Ripton was a local real estate mogul from back east who'd made a fortune selling huge spreads to movie stars looking for mountain getaways. Her territory stretched from the Tetons in the northwest all the way to Laramie in the southeast, where she had an impressive horse ranch of her own. "

And rumor has it," Wayne said with a wink, "she protects her territory like a mama grizzly." Shania and Wayne seemed pretty chummy. Jessica wondered if they were a thing.

After sizing Shania up as an aggressive player, Jessica planned to sit to the left of her at the poker table. Always sit to the left of the most aggressive player at the table so you come behind them in the betting. As her mother always told her, "See which way the wind is blowing before you blow your entire stack of chips."

The rest of the players were roughnecks and roustabouts from the fracking camp on the Wyoming border. Men far from home who had so much money, they didn't know what to do with it. She had seen their type a couple summers back, when she was working at Glacier National Park. The job had given her a close and personal view of how repulsive—and dangerous— they could be. She gave them a wide berth as they paid for their buy-ins, collected drinks, and took their places at the table.

As soon as Shania took a seat, Jessica slipped in next to her. "Have we met before? You look familiar."

"I just have one of those faces." Shania smiled. Her voice was gravely, like that of a heavy smoker.

Jessica thought of her mother chain-smoking cigarettes and living on Vodka Collins and pepperoni sticks. She dragged her chips closer. "You play a lot?"

"Every chance I get." Shania fingered her chips, restacking them to her liking. "How about you?"

"Only when I have to." Jessica sipped her Jack & Coke.

Shania balked. "Honey, whether you have to or not, better to own it." She went back to playing with her chips. "Otherwise, these guys will eat you alive." She nodded toward the roustabouts.

"I've seen what they can do." Jessica swallowed hard, remembering what other roustabouts had done to girls on the Blackfeet Reservation a few summers before.

"Me too," Shania said. The glint in her eye was a sharp as a razor. "Men. You can't live with 'em. But you can't kill 'em."

Jessica let out a nervous giggle and then went back to work on her drink. She knew she'd seen Shania before . . . *but where?*

When Jack dealt the first hand, the excitement was palpable. The roughnecks hooted and joked. Wayne joined in. Shania sat back and watched, that steely glint in her eyes. *This lady is a force to be reckoned with.* Like Jessica, she obviously knew that observing other players was the key to winning. *You have to learn their tells and their betting strategies. You have to distance yourself and watch them like a zoologist studies animals.*

They'd only been playing for a little over half an hour, but Jessica was bleeding chips. Her stack had dwindled down to a third of what she'd started with. She blew at her bangs. How was she going to pay Lolita back? *Crapulence.* Instead of making the money to buy her plane ticket home—let alone that fantasy trip to Italy—she was getting deeper in debt.

On the next deal, she suppressed a smile when she peeked at her hole cards. *Finally!* She'd been dealt a good hand. She struggled to keep her poker face. Her hands were trembling as she pushed a small stack of red chips into the center. "Call and raise you a hundred." She gulped down the rest of her drink. As usual, before her glass was completely empty, Lolita was there with another. *The hostess with the mostest.*

Everyone called, and the pile of chips in the middle of the table kept growing. Jessica peeked at her hole cards. That was her tell, but she couldn't help it. She just had to double-check that she still had pocket rockets, a pair of aces, the best hole cards in hold 'em. When another ace fell on the flop—the community cards in the center of the table—she knew she had to go all in. She chugged her drink, another one of her tells, and then pushed all her chips into the center. "All in."

The roustabouts weren't so jovial now. One of them threw their cards into the discard pile with such force the cards flew off the table.

Only Shania had the guts—or the cards—to call. With painted pink nails, she counted Jessica's chips and then pushed the equivalent from her much larger stack into the center. Jessica was head-to-head with the real estate mogul. This would make her or break her. If she lost, she was out. Her mind was racing too fast to calculate the odds. Judging by the flop, Shania could have a straight flush. In that case, even if the river card was another ace, Jessica was toast. Too late now. The chips were played. Anyway, this was her best bet. As her mother would say, "Pocket rockets, time to socket and pick some pockets."

A knock on the door interrupted her concentration. Had Lolita ordered room service? Usually as an intermission, she served dinner or snacks. And usually, Jessica was first in line. At this moment, food was the last thing on her mind. Everyone else stared at the door. Jessica stared at the three cards in the center of the table.

Jack flipped another spade, the king, on the turn card. If Shania was holding the queen and ten, she didn't just have any straight flush—she had a royal flush, the best possible poker hand.

"Too bad you don't have any more chips," Shania said. "I'm itchin' to raise you."

Jessica hoped that was just table talk. Shania's tell was batting her eyelashes. But her eyes were perfectly still.

The knocking resumed. Louder this time.

"So sorry," Lolita said. "Keep playing. I'll see who it is." Like everyone else, she had been watching the final contest.

When Jack flipped the river card, the last community card, Jessica let out a whoop. She couldn't help it. *Another ace.* She had four aces. Which wouldn't matter, of course, if Shania had a royal flush.

"Look what the cat dragged in," Lolita said.

Jessica knew that resentful tone. She twisted around in her chair to see who was at the door. *Holy crap! What's he doing here?* The poker game and the humongous pot she hoped to win were pushed from her thoughts. "Nick." She broke out in a sweat. Her stomach flipped, and she feared she would barf.

"Dulce." Nick rushed to her side, a black velvet box under his arm.

The box was too big for the rumored jade engagement ring found in his pocket at the Parker Hotel. *Does he have something bigger for me?* Something to say he was sorry for letting her think he was dead? For his affair with the marshal? *Where is she anyway?* Why had the sexy marshal let Nick out of her sight?

"Can we talk?" he asked, breathless. He looked like

he hadn't slept in days. Purple bags under his eyes. His hair just slightly oily. His designer jacket rumpled. Even with that desperate sheen, he was still darned attractive.

Jessica stood up. She stared into his deep blue eyes, wondering if she could forgive him. But really, what was there to forgive? It wasn't like they were engaged or anything. She rolled her eyes. How many times had she had that same back-and-forth with herself in the last few days? One second, she thought he was a cheater. The next, she realized he couldn't cheat if they weren't together. That's what happened when her heart said one thing and logic said another.

"Sit down and play," Jack barked. "You're winning."

"Let me finish this hand." Jessica dropped back into her chair.

"You've finished," Shania said, starting to scrape the chips out of the center of the table. "Once you leave the table, you're done." She gave Jessica the look a horse trainer gave a gelding before getting out the whip.

"But . . . but . . ." Jessica stuttered. "I didn't leave. I'm right here."

"Nope." Shania continued gathering up the huge pot. "You left the table. Game over. You forfeit." Her eyelashes were fluttering a mile a minute.

"Show your cards." Jessica reached across the table. "You're bluffing."

"Rules of the game, hon." Shania buried her hole cards in the discard pile. "If you can't run with the big dogs, get off the porch."

Jessica looked to Jack. He just shrugged. She looked to Lolita with a question in her eyes. Something else she'd have to forgive Nick for . . . making her lose her entire stake in a game she'd just won.

Lolita slinked up to the table, holding a bottle of prosecco and two champagne glasses. She stood between Jessica and the mogul. "When someone comes back from the dead, we make an exception to the rules." She set a glass on the table in front of Shania. "How about you two fine ladies split the pot?" *Always the diplomat.*

"But I won." Jessica's cheeks were burning. She knew she was just stalling. Given the jumble of feelings twisting around her heart, she couldn't bear looking at Nick, let alone talking to him.

"That way, you both come out ahead." Lolita set a glass on the table in front of Jessica and gave her a stern look.

"She forfeited," Shania complained. "So, the—"

Lolita interrupted. "As we say in Russia . . ." She filled both glasses with prosecco. "Compromise is the art of cutting a cake in half so both parties think they've got the biggest piece."

"Why settle for half a cake"—Shania was separating the chips into neat stacks—"when you're owed the whole thing?"

"Who cares about this stupid game? There are more important things than money." *Like Nick.* "It's only money." Jessica glanced up at her friend. "Your money."

She pushed the chair away from the table, grabbed her glass of champagne, and then stood face-to-face with the ghost of her happiness. "Why are you here? Aren't you supposed to be hidden away in witness protection?"

"Dulce," he said softly, his eyes moist.

"They told me you were dead." Tears welled in her eyes too. "I thought you were dead." She wanted to hit him, to pound her fists into his chest. And she wanted to throw her arms around him and kiss him.

"I'm sorry." He glanced around the room. "Is there someplace we can talk?"

The only privacy offered by the warehouse of a suite was the bathroom. Jessica closed the lid and sat on the toilet. Nick knelt beside her, the black box still tucked under one arm.

"Dulce . . ." He touched her knee. "I never thought I'd see you again."

"Is that why you were kissing the marshal?"

"What?" Nick stood up. "No." He ran his fingers through his hair. "I mean, yes . . . I guess so."

"Detective Cormier told me they found you unconscious in the Parker Hotel . . . with an engagement ring . . ." She couldn't finish. She chewed on the jagged end of a fingernail. She was dying to know, but it didn't seem right to ask.

"The ring." He patted his jacket pocket. "That ring was for you."

"So there really is a ring?" Sounding nonchalant was not an option.

"There was . . ." He paced the length of the bath-room. "I thought I'd never see you again—"

"So you gave it to her." Her face fell.

"No." He gave her a sheepish smile. "I flushed it down the toilet."

She stared at him. *He flushed an engagement ring down the toilet? Is he nuts?* "Was it like a Cracker Jack ring or something?"

"It was a diamond-encrusted jade ring." He hung his head.

"You flushed a diamond ring down the toilet!?"

He nodded and blushed.

"Jack's right," she said with a laugh. *Rich people are weird.*

"About what?"

"Nothing." She shook her head. "So how did you shake the marshal? I'm surprised she let you come see me."

"She didn't." He made another pass up and down the bathroom. "She's . . . she's . . ." His cheeks turned an ashen color. "She's in Tennessee."

"What?"

"Long story." He stopped pacing. Holding the black velvet box in both hands, he gazed down at her. "I need you to take this to the Center." He knelt next to her again and looked her straight in the eyes. "Put it in the safe until I get back."

"But—" Her lip was trembling.

"Don't tell anyone about it." He gently put a finger to

her lip. "It will be okay, Dulce. You'll see."

"What is it?" she asked weakly.

He opened the case.

"Holy crap!" She reached out and touched the smooth stones and the cold metal. "Is that the missing Romanov tiara?" She'd read about it in a catalogue of the missing Romanov jewels—a catalogue on Nick's computer back at the Center—when she'd thought he was dead. "Where'd you get it?"

"My father."

"Your dead father?"

Nick grimaced.

"Sorry." She fingered the tiara. "Where did *he* get it?" She tried to remember what she'd read about it. "Wait. Isn't this one of the jewels hidden by that nun? Sister Marfa in Tobolsk, wasn't it? She brought food to the Romanovs before they were executed, and they left some of their jewels with her."

Nick picked up the velvet case and examined the tiara. "I think you're right. It's not the Vladimir tiara."

"No." She laughed. "The Queen of England owns the Vladimir tiara. Her grandmother bought it, broken and partially widowed, off Duchess Vladimir."

He narrowed his brows. "Widowed?"

"That's what they call the tiara when the pearl or emerald pendants are removed." She waved her hand like the queen. "When it's a simple diamond tiara."

He smiled. "You never cease to amaze me."

He pulled her close and kissed her. She kissed him back, an urgent, desperate kiss.

A crackling sound ripped through the suite. "Was that a gunshot?" she asked, her face close to his. Was she breathless from the kiss or the thunderous noise?

Nick pulled her onto the floor.

What the— Her heart was pounding like a jackhammer. And not just because Nick was lying on top of her.

25

Before Nick could stop her, Dulce jammed her hand in his jacket pocket and grabbed his P32 pocket pistol. He'd retrieved it from under the mattress at the marshal's cabin before coming to the hotel . . . just in case. It must have pressed against her side when they'd kissed. She really was something. Then, so was the hot marshal. How had his life become so complicated?

Dulce scrambled to her feet, opened the bathroom door, and disappeared into the melee in the other room. As usual, she ran headlong into danger.

Nick wanted to follow her. To protect her. He clutched the velvet box. *The tiara.* What if the shots fired in the other room was one of Teeth's goons come to take the Romanov jewels? He glanced around the bathroom for a place to hide the box.

"Where's Schilling?" A familiar voice boomed from

the other side of the bathroom door. "Teeth wants that crown."

Merde. Danny Quarrels had found him.

CRAPULENCE. Her hand pressing against the gun in her pocket, Jessica stepped into the living room. A couple of the roustabouts cowered under one of the tables. Another looked like a spring-loaded jack-in-the-box ready to pounce. Jack sat as still as a statue at the other table, a deck of cards in one hand and a bottle of vodka in the other. Shania Ripton had an odd look on her face, almost amused. The only person moving was Lolita. She murmured in Russian while crossing the room, slowly approaching Danny Quarrels. He was shouting and waving a gun around.

"Where is he?" Danny Quarrels yelled again, pointing his gun at Jessica.

He'd already shot a hole in the wall above the microwave. What was to stop him from shooting her too?

Her heart was pounding, and her breath was shallow. Holding the tiny pistol behind her back, she took another step into the room. She needed to distract him long enough to whip out Nick's gun and wing the big brute if she could.

Wayne Ford was trying to talk him down. "Look, Mr. Quarrels, if it's money you want—"

Quarrels laughed. "You mean Teeth's money, don't you?"

Ford went red in the face. "I don't know what you mean."

"I think you do." Quarrels swung around and waved the gun in Ford's face. "You took enough of it in exchange for snitching out Nick Schilling. From what I heard, you've been selling information about witnesses to the highest bidder."

"Why, you—" Ford stood up so fast, his chair fell over backwards. "I should—"

The thug lunged at Ford. With the butt of his gun, Quarrels whacked Ford across the face.

This might be her chance. Slowly, she drew the gun out from behind her back. Quarrels swung back around again. She pulled the trigger. *Crapulence.* That only made him angry.

With a growl like a grizzly, Quarrels charged her and knocked the gun out of her hand before she had a chance to fire again. A red stain spread across the arm of Quarrel's shirt. He swatted at it like it was nothing more than a bothersome insect.

Now that he was closer, she could smell alcohol on him. He was drunk.

The ranch owner was slouched over the table, unconscious, bleeding like a stuck pig. The roustabouts and roughnecks, once invincible and boisterous, now looked like kids during an active shooter drill, hiding under the table. Lolita, her muscles tensed like a cat ready to pounce, stood next to Jack, who was drinking straight from a bottle of vodka.

Only Shania Ripton remained unflappable. She sat counting her chips as if waiting for Jack to deal the next hand.

The door to the bathroom creaked behind her. Jessica turned her head. *No. No. No.* "Don't come out."

Nick took a step into the room. She rushed over and tried to push him back inside. "He'll shoot you."

Nick gently pushed past her. "Don't hurt anyone." He held up the black velvet case. "I'll go with you."

"Good." Quarrels smiled. "That's more like it." He pointed the gun at Nick. "No one move." The words were slurred, and he was staggering. He must be really drunk. Drunk and unhinged. Drunk and dangerous.

Jessica gasped. "Don't shoot."

"Let's go, Schilling. Teeth is gonna—"

A loud noise at the entrance stopped him mid-sentence. Someone was kicking in the door.

The door flew open. "Freeze. Everyone—hands in the air." Marshal Colt appeared in the doorway like a movie cowboy: gun drawn, legs apart, steely eyes drilling into the room.

She pointed her gun at the thug's head. "I'll shoot you."

"Okay. Okay." Quarrels lowered his weapon. "Calm down."

The marshal moved closer to Quarrels. "Hands in the air."

"I just want the crown." He flashed a sheepish smile. "Cooperate and I ain't gonna hurt nobody."

"Drop your gun," the marshal said in a tone that meant business. "You're not killing another one of my witnesses."

"I didn't kill no witnesses." Quarrels glanced around the room with a confused look on his face. "Someone else beat me to Boris the Butcher, or I might have offed him." He scoffed. "You can have Nick, but I get the crown."

Must be the liquor talking. He doesn't seem very worried about the gun pointed at his head. Jessica glance down at the pocket pistol on the floor.

"Teeth don't want him hurt." Quarrels raised his gun and pointed it at Nick. "Says he's like a nephew. My orders are to get that crown, and that's what I'm gonna do." He waved his weapon like a flag at a parade.

"This is your last warning," the marshal said, taking a step closer. "Put the gun down or I'm going to shoot you."

Quarrels grabbed Jessica and held her body tight to his torso. She trembled. He put his gun to her head. *Dang.* He reeked of booze.

"Don't shoot," Nick said, holding up the case. "Here. You can have it." He held it out to Quarrels. "Let her go. Please," he pleaded. "I'll go with you. Just let her go."

Quarrels pushed Jessica away and then snatched the box out of Nick's hands.

Jessica ran to Jack's side. It was instinctive. Like the

north and south poles of a magnet. Like two halves of the same forgiving soul. She put her hand on his shoulder. And he put his hand on top of hers.

"I'll be going now," Quarrels said, shaking the black box.

"Not so fast," the marshal said, standing in the threshold.

"Hey, where's the crown?" Quarrels flipped the case open. Empty. It was empty. He threw it on the floor. "Hand them over." He glared at Nick.

What had Nick done with the Romanov tiara? Jessica glanced down at the tiny gun. It was only a couple of feet away. Could she dive for it without getting shot herself?

"Where is it?" Quarrels was red in the face and spitting as he talked. "Teeth told me not to come back without it." He pointed his gun at Nick.

"What?" Nick's eyes went wide. "It's not there?" He rushed to pick up the case from the floor. "I swear—last time I opened the case, it was there." He examined the box and ran his fingers over the silk lining as if he might find the tiara hidden under the liner. "Someone must have taken it." He glanced up at the marshal, who stood frozen, feet apart, holding her gun in front of her with both hands.

With a grunt, Quarrels lunged at Nick. With one hand, he pushed Nick against the wall and, with the other, raised his gun.

Crack. The shot nearly deafened her. Jessica felt the air move as the bullet whizzed by her ear. *What the . . . ?*

Quarrels' eyes got big as poker chips. His mouth fell open. He let out a groan. And then he crumpled to the floor in a heap at Nick's feet.

All heads turned toward Shania Ripton. Her poker face unreadable, the real estate mogul was holding a .44 Magnum. *Holy crap!* Shania had just shot the mobster in the back. "Eat shit and die." She laid her gun on the table.

Jessica put her foot on the peashooter, dragged it closer, and then bent to pick it up. She dropped it into her jacket pocket. It wasn't the first time she'd pocketed Nick's gun.

Marshal Colt, still pointing her weapon, turned on Shania. "Why'd you shoot him?"

"I had to," Shania said, a slight tremor in her voice.

"Why'd you shoot the others?" the marshal asked. "Or should I say 'execute'?"

"What others?" Jessica asked. *Oh my God.* She realized where she'd seen Shania before.

LEXI WATCHED while Shania shuffled the deck. Damn. Shania had just shot a man like it was all part of the game.

"I didn't used to be an only child." Shania continued shuffling cards. "My brother was killed when I was in high school," she said without looking up, "and my sister might as well have been." Her hands were steady, but her voice wasn't. "Poor lamb's never been the same since. Falls to pieces if anyone touches her." Shania glanced up and stared at the marshal. "She can't stand to be hugged, not even by me." She spit out the words. "She's been in a mental institution until last month." Her voice broke off.

"Are you Angelina or Annabella?" Lexi asked, lowering her gun.

"It's her!" Nick's girlfriend said, turning to her buddy Clyde. "That's the woman we saw in the SUV in the suburbs. The day that guy was shot in his underwear." The girlfriend and Nick were holding hands. "I knew I'd seen her before."

And the woman delivering groceries to Jimmy's? Lexi had to keep this woman talking to figure out where the WITSEC leak was. "What do my witnesses have to do with your siblings?" Lexi sat down at the table next to Shania. "You all went to Prospect Heights High School. Is that when it happened?" She quietly reached over and slid Shania's .44 Magnum across the table until it was close enough that she could put her elbow over it.

Shania's lip trembled, but she didn't say anything.

Lexi glanced over her shoulder at Nick. "Is he dead?"

Nick knelt next to Quarrels and put his finger to his neck. He nodded.

"Poor *tupitsa* will join the other ghosts haunting this

hotel." Dressed in black leather, Lolita stood with the confidence of a championship boxer but looked like a supermodel.

Who's she? And what's a tupitsa? Lexi planned to find out—after she sewed up the case. She should have busted them all last time she was here. At least the twerp who knocked her unconscious was behind bars. Lexi couldn't let herself get distracted. She turned back to the shooter. "Was Danny Quarrels responsible for your sister's . . ." She couldn't say the word.

Shania's brows narrowed. "They all were. I hope they all go to hell where they belong."

Without taking her eyes off the shooter, Lexi unsnapped the phone from her holster and tapped it awake. "I need backup at the Prairie Hotel." She turned to the peanut gallery and mouthed, "What room number?"

"Room 422," the dominatrix said.

"Room 422," Lexi repeated into her phone. "And get an ambulance over here." She clipped the phone back onto her belt. "Who are they? Who killed your brother and—and—assaulted your sister?"

The shooter stared off into space. She looked a million miles away.

"Annabella," Lexi said on a hunch. She reached over and touched the other woman's shoulder. "Annabella Carina."

The shooter stirred and came back to earth. Her

head in her hands, her tears fell onto the stack of poker chips. "Angelina is my sister."

"Annabella," Lexi repeated. She'd made an educated guess based on her research. She'd discovered that right after high school, Annabella Carina Fontaine had become a real estate agent and brought her younger sister into her business. The sister dropped out of school, and they worked together as Fontaine Real Estate on Long Island for two months. Then the agency had closed down after the younger sister fell ill and was hospitalized in a psychiatric ward on suicide watch. After that, there were no more records on Angelina Christina for years. It was as if she'd disappeared from the face of the earth.

"It's just Bella." The shooter raised her head. "After what they did, they all deserved to die." She glared at Lexi. "They all deserved to eat shit and die." As she said it, she glanced over at the roustabouts, who were speechless, glued to their chairs. "I had to show my sister she was safe. You understand?"

"The horse crap," Lexi said. *That's what it was in their mouths.* "A unique touch."

"Horse manure?" the girlfriend asked from the sidelines.

"The victims all had horse shit in their mouths." Lexi had to admit there were a few men she wouldn't mind giving the same treatment.

"So the *victims* were all murderers and rapists?" the girlfriend asked. "Sounds like they were perpetrators."

"They deserved to die," Shania said indignantly. She dried her cheeks on a hanky and sniffed. From then on, there were no more tears. "Or at least go to prison for life." Her voice was strong and forceful. "Instead, the government sets them up in witness protection and pampers them." She pounded her fist into the table. "You call that punishment?"

"Their testimony would have put away even worse criminals," Lexi said, only half-believing it.

"What's worse than killing an innocent boy and gang-raping a teenage girl?"

She had a point. Lexi didn't know what to say. "Well, Tiny Quarrels wasn't in WITSEC." She pointed at the crumpled body on the floor. "And neither was Boris Solonik. Did you kill him too? Or did Tiny get to him first?"

"My brother was an honors student. He was on the chess team and the debate team and wanted to become a congressman to do some good in the world. Instead, at sixteen, they killed him. He was just trying to protect me and my sister. Your precious witnesses—they killed my baby brother." Her jaw tightened, and she flicked a poker chip across the table. "And they raped my baby sister. Eventually, she tried to kill herself and was sent to a mental institution."

"That's terrible," the girlfriend said.

"Here. Drink this, *milaya*." The dominatrix handed the shooter a small glass. "Brandy."

The shooter downed the alcohol. "When she got out

of the hospital, I knew what I had to do to show her she was safe."

Lexi could use a drink herself. She never touched the stuff. Times like these, she wished she did. Bella Fontaine was right. She and her family were the true victims, not those murdering rapist mobsters. "Your sister, Angelina, was out at the Cutthroat Ranch last week. Her name was on the guest list."

"I flew her out to see for herself." Shania bowed her head. "I knew she'd have no peace until those murdering rapists were dead."

"Would you like a drink, marshal?" the dominatrix asked.

"I'll have another whiskey," one of the roughnecks piped up.

"And I'd take another brewsky," said his friend.

"Why don't y'all write your names and numbers on this pad and then make yourselves scarce." Lexi pulled her notebook out of her back pocket and slid it across the table. "Names, numbers, addresses. And then go home." She gave the roustabouts a stern look.

The room fell silent as the oilmen dutifully wrote down their information and then filed out of the hotel room. Once they were gone, Lexi's shoulders relaxed. She glanced up at the dominatrix. "I'd take a pop if you have any. Diet Mountain Dew?" It was worth a try.

"Coming up." A few seconds later, the dominatrix delivered a cold can of Mountain Dew. It wasn't diet but close enough.

"Thanks." The click of the tab followed by the distinctive fizzing steeled her nerves and gave her the courage to go on. She took a sip. "Shania. Bella. When did these things happen to your brother and sister?"

"Sixteen years ago, back in high school. The devils that did it were Boris Solonik , Jimmy Giordano, and Bobby Moretti, while their drunken buddy Danny Quarrels egged them on. Angelina was only fourteen. Fourteen. Just a child." She ran her hand across her forehead. "By seventeen, she was addicted to heroin. I tried to clean her up and take her into my business. But she was still traumatized. She couldn't get over it. Five years ago, she tried to kill herself and ended up in the hospital. When she got out last month, I decided I'd do whatever it took to bring justice to our . . . her rapists. Just imagine what it was like for a fourteen year old . . ." Her voice trailed off.

Lexi didn't want to imagine what it was like. She'd had enough close calls when she was in the military. Harassment, catcalls. Being pinned against the wall, groped, threatened into performing sex acts to keep her job—but gang rape of a little girl? Her stomach turned. If they weren't dead already, Lexi would volunteer to kill those bastards herself.

"I don't have to imagine," the shooter continued. "I was there. Danny Quarrels held me down to watch until it was my turn."

"So I was never a target," Nick said, still leaning up against the wall.

"Lucky boy," Lexi said. *Spoiled little rich kid. Always thinking only of himself.*

"All Danny wanted from me was the Romanov tiara." Nick glanced at her.

"Well, he got more than he bargained for, didn't he?" Lexi twisted around in her chair. "Speaking of which—hand it over. It's evidence."

Nick held up the empty case. "Like I told Tiny, it's not here." He ran his fingers through his hair. "You were the last one who had it. I boarded the plane thinking it was in the case and only now thought to open it. I don't know what happened—"

"Yeah. Right." Lexi narrowed her brows. No way she believed him. But she had bigger fish to fry, as her daddy would say. "We'll deal with that later."

Wayne Ford groaned.

"What happened to him?" Lexi asked.

"Tiny pistol-whipped him," Nick said. "Apparently, Mr. Ford has been on Victor Marsiano's payroll for quite some time now."

"He and Mr. Quarrels worked together," the girl-friend said. "So it was kind of like a fight between coworkers."

Wayne groaned again.

Wayne is on Teeth's payroll? Holy shit. That means—

"He's the mole," Lexi said under her breath. Dammit. If she hadn't been distracted by her relationship with Nick, she would have seen it. Now it all made sense. *Of course. An ex-marshal.* She'd always wondered how he could afford that fancy ranch on a marshal's pension. He must have tipped off Teeth about Nick. Maybe he'd tipped off Shania too. How else did she find all those guys? "Shania, did you pay Wayne Ford for information on those witnesses?"

Shania stared at her hands.

"Did Wayne Ford tell you where to find Boris Solonik , Jimmy Giordano, and Bobby Moretti?" Lexi asked more forcefully.

Shania nodded. "He was just trying to help me and Angelina."

Wayne Ford. Ex-marshal gone bad. What a stain on the service. Geezus. That's how he got the money to pay off the ranch. It wasn't a rich uncle; it was selling out witnesses. What a flipping Pop-Tart.

A knock on the door signaled the arrival of backup. *Finally.*

Lexi had called Drake from Tennessee to report Nick missing. But somehow, her colleagues hadn't caught up to him. As usual, it was up to her.

"Noah, can you take him to headquarters?" Lexi pointed at Nick and then turned to face her colleague. "And keep him there until I get back. Then I'll move him."

"Will do, Lex." Noah had his Glock in his hand.

Lexi stood up and moved closer until she was standing face-to-face with Nick. "You're coming back to WITSEC. Either that or prison."

"You sure you've got this under control?" Noah asked.

"Yeah." Lexi nodded. "Can you call the coroner?"

"Yup." Noah holstered his gun.

"And an ambulance for Mr. Ford." Lexi gestured toward Wayne, who was sitting holding his head, blood running down his face. "Put a guard on him. He's our mole."

"Really?" Noah laughed. "No way."

"Yes way." Lexi frowned. "Maybe Ford and Schilling here can share a cell."

"Cell?" the girlfriend asked. "Prison? What?"

Nick blushed and gave a weak smile. "It's all a mistake."

The dominatrix and Clyde scoffed in unison.

"I told you so," the dominatrix said, winking at her friend.

"WITSEC is your best chance." Lexi took his arm and led him to Noah. "Otherwise, you can die inside or maybe on the outside before you're convicted. Your choice."

"WITSEC," Nick said in a resigned tone. He turned back to his girlfriend.

Ex-girlfriend?

"I'll come back to the Center as soon as I can."

Lexi bit her tongue. *He's kidding himself.* The danger to his life wouldn't go away after he testified. And before he testified, Teeth could send another hitman. After he testified, Teeth's guys would kill him to send a message to other stool pigeons.

Nick waved goodbye. "Hold down the fort, Dulce. And until then, remember: enemy has been stopped."

"What?" the girlfriend asked.

"Enemy has been stopped," he repeated. He pulled away from Noah and crossed the room. He wrapped his arms around her and whispered something into her hair.

"Be good." The girlfriend pulled out of the embrace. "And if you can't be good, be careful."

Nick smiled. His smile disappeared when he turned to Lexi. "I'm sorry. It's my fault you got shot."

"Flesh wound." Lexi put one hand to her waist. "All part of the job."

"I was hoping—"

"I'll see you at headquarters." She looked at her colleague. "Noah, can you get him out of here?"

"Sure thing, Lex." Noah took Nick by the elbow.

On the way out the door, Nick turned back. "Remember. *Enemy has been stopped*."

"Enemy has been stopped," the girlfriend whispered.

"What in Sam Hill does he mean?" *Shit*. A twinge in Lexi's side made her press her hand against her waist. It may be a flesh wound, but it was her flesh.

"No clue," the girlfriend said. "Maybe Danny Quarrels?"

The dominatrix slid into a chair at the table and

started piling poker chips into color-coded stacks. "I guess this means the pot is yours, my Montana friend." She smiled up at the girlfriend. "You can make that trip to Italy after all."

"Take it," Shania said. "See if I care."

" I can't go to Italy," the girlfriend said. "The Center—"

"My dad can run the Center," her friend interrupted. "It would do you good to get away."

"Maybe you gals can discuss your vacation plans later." Lexi unclipped the handcuffs from her belt. She reached out to the shooter. "Sorry. Protocol." She snapped the cuffs around Shania/Bella's narrow wrists. "I'm taking you in." She recited the Miranda rights and then coaxed the shooter to stand up.

"Given the circumstances, maybe the judge will be sympathetic," the girlfriend said.

Boy, was she naïve. Given she'd murdered four men in cold blood and forced three of them to eat horse manure, Lexi doubted any judge would be sympathetic.

"Given the circumstances," the dominatrix said, "I think you should let her go. She was just avenging her brother and sister. There's honor in that."

"It may be honorable," Lexi said, escorting her prisoner toward the door, "but it's also murder."

"Come on!" The girlfriend stomped her cowboy boot. "Her freaking sister was gang-raped, and so was —" She stopped and blew at her bangs. "Come on. Let her go," she whined. "The poor woman deserves a break."

"I can't do that." Lexi tugged at the cuffs, coaxing her prisoner to move. After a couple of steps, Lexi stopped. "Of course, if Bella escapes . . . or if one of you hits me on the head . . ." She winked. "Nothing I can do about that."

26

It had been almost seven months since Jessica last saw Nick in Wyoming. *Weird.* She didn't really miss *him* but the way he made her feel about herself. She missed seeing herself through his eyes. Maybe she could learn to see herself like he did.

He'd promised to come back. And she believed him. As impossible as it seemed, she believed him. It wasn't that she didn't care whether or not he came back. It was more like she'd resigned herself to a life without him.

She thought about him every single time she walked through the galleries, which was pretty much every day. She thought about that kiss—the one in the hotel bathroom just before the shooting started. Strange. She hadn't really felt anything. Sure, she'd kissed him back. But the sensation hadn't moved past her lips. It was like she was acting. Like the scene called for a kiss, and she'd delivered, but her heart wasn't in it.

Today, the galleries were full of elementary school kids on a field trip. Jessica zigzagged through the chatterboxes in their pint-sized navy blue slacks and skirts. Usually, the galleries were quiet. Most people treated the museum like a library and talked in hushed voices. But not these little hoodlums. They ran and shouted. As long as they didn't touch the paintings.

Nick would have been so happy. The Center was introducing young people to art.

As she walked from the Kandinsky gallery to the Soviet art gallery, the guard gave her a pleading look. She shrugged. What could they do? The kids were having fun.

Two boys were play fighting in front of an Usipenko oil painting of a tank and soldiers. She hated the war paintings. Obviously, these boys didn't. She approached the boys. Not to tell them to stop horsing around. But to tell them about the history of the painting.

"This was painted in 1941, the year Germany invaded the Soviet Union." She pointed to the painting. "See that tank?"

"Tank. Tank. Toilet tank." One of the boys ran circles around the other, taunting. "Toilet tank."

"You're the toilet tank," the other boy shouted as he kicked his friend in the shin.

The two little tyrants tussled until both were wailing.

"Boys. Please." Jessica didn't know what to do.

Should she pull them apart? Was she allowed to touch them?

Luckily, she was saved by one of their teachers. He dragged the boys over to a bench for a time-out. Jessica put her hands together in a gesture of thanks. He must have the patience of Job. How in the world did anyone teach those little monsters anything?

She stood in front of the Usipenko, trying to see it through the eyes of a nine-year-old boy. *Toilet tank.* She smiled to herself. *Toilet tank.* She thought of Nick. *Who would flush an expensive ring down the toilet?* Nick, that's who.

He really was going to propose that night at the Parker House. That's what she'd wanted to know. Now she could close the lid on that chapter . . . at least until Nick came back. *Tank. Tank. Toilet tank.*

Holy crap! She leaned closer to the plaque next to the painting. *Of course.* "Enemy has been stopped." That was the name of the painting. *Enemy has been stopped. That's what Nick said at the poker game.*

That night in the Prairie Hotel, after the marshal left with Shania aka Annabella, Jessica had searched for the Romanov tiara. She'd never found it. She knew it had to be somewhere in that bathroom. But where?

Now she knew. *Enemy has been stopped.* A painting of tanks and soldiers. *Toilet tank.* That's it. That's where he hid the tiara.

She had to get back out to Wyoming and check the tank of that toilet.

WITH ALL THE grace of a goose, Lexi waddled into the kitchen. She opened her refrigerator. Glancing at the can of Diet Dew that had been tormenting her for the last two months, she grabbed the gallon jug of organic vitamin-fortified lemonade. July twenty-eighth couldn't come soon enough. She poured a tall glass of lemonade. Maybe a snack? Something to munch on with the drink? She went back to the fridge and took out the bowl of leftover lamb stew. She puffed as she carried the glass and the plate back into the living room.

Her hands full, she glanced around for a place to put her food. She settled on the couch. She carefully balanced the glass and the plate on the cushion, then went to fetch a TV tray from across the room. Unfolding the tray, she stared at the sofa. That's where it happened. Maybe she should wrap it in plastic or something, enshrine it. A holy place. She gathered up her snack and slid the glass and plate onto the TV tray.

Dropping into the nubby La-Z-Boy, she closed her eyes. *Where is he now?* She pulled the lever on the side of the chair. *Ahhh.* It felt good to elevate her swollen feet.

She hadn't seen Nick since he was transferred to California and another marshal's turf. The less she knew, the better. Still, sometimes she was tempted to find him. To tell him.

No. She had to have faith. *Everything happens for a*

reason. If it's meant to be, it will be. And if it's not meant to be? She'd gotten by on her own up until now. She could get by on her own from now on too. *But I won't be on my own.* The thought filled her with fear and trembling. And tears of joy. The awesome power of life.

There was a knock on the door. *Who could that be?* Like a bug on its back, she struggled to get out of the chair.

She opened the door and was met by the cool spring sunshine. *Lordy, what's she doing here?* The Chicago girlfriend. "What in the Sam Hill are you doing here?"

The girlfriend's eyes widened as she stared at Lexi's belly. "You're—"

"Yup."

The girlfriend got a terrified look on her face. "Is it—"

"Why are you here?" Lexi interrupted again. She didn't want to talk about Nick. Or his daughter brewing in her belly. Bad enough she didn't know when she'd see him again. Now she had the jealous girlfriend on her front stoop.

"I was in the neighborhood." The girlfriend blew at her shaggy bangs. "I just thought I'd stop by and see—"

"If you could lead the mob to another witness?" Lexi couldn't help herself. Hormones mixed with truth made her even more blunt than usual.

"I've quit looking for Nick." The girlfriend moved from foot to foot, holding a small Dairy Queen bag in front of her. She was still wearing those goofy red cowboy boots with some antique dress and tiny sweater. She looked like a hayseed come out of the backwoods—or given her hair, a cave—for the monthly barn dance. "That was a mistake. I realize that now. I almost got him killed."

"Yes, you did." Had the girlfriend really quit hunting for Nick? Had she wised up or just moved on? It was obvious that her friend Clyde had a thing for her. Maybe the girlfriend had reciprocated. Lexi hoped so. Less complicated that way. In case Nick did come back.

"It's my fault he got kidnapped."

"True."

"And you got hit on the head."

"Maybe. But your *friend* Vanya is out on parole, doing a good two years of community service for that one."

"And it's my fault Mr. Quarrels is dead." The girlfriend stared down at her red cowboy boots.

"I wouldn't go that far. Shania Ripton pulled the trigger." Lexi shifted her considerable weight. "Just because you were there doesn't make it your fault." Her therapist's words echoed in her head. *Just because you were there doesn't make it your fault.*

"Are you okay?" the girlfriend asked. "You look flushed."

Lexi didn't answer. "If you're not looking for Nick, who *are* you looking for?"

"You."

"Why me?"

"To thank you." She put the bag behind her back.

Lexi arched her brows. "What for?"

"For being such a badass." When the girlfriend smiled, there was a glint in her gunmetal-blue eyes. "I know what it's like to swim upstream in a sea of men."

Caught off guard, Lexi stammered, "Is that right?"

"Yeah. And you're quite something, you know that?"

Lexi couldn't help but smile. "It's Jessica, right?"

The girlfriend nodded. "And you're Marshal Colt."

"Call me Lexi." She glanced back at her hovel to see just how much of a mess it was. "Would you like to come in?"

"Nah. I've got to catch my plane." She tucked the bag under her arm. "Thanks anyway . . . Lexi."

"Are you still working at Nick's precious Center?" She rubbed at her aching back.

"Only for another few months." Jessica screwed up her lips. "Then I'm taking a sabbatical and traveling."

"Yeah. I'll be taking a *sabbatical* in a few months myself." She patted her belly.

"Do you think he's working for Teeth?" Jessica blurted out.

Lexi eyed the girlfriend. "What do you think?" She put her hand on her hip.

"I hope not."

"Me too." Lexi changed the subject. "Where are you traveling to?" She'd seen a lot of the world but mostly from aircraft carriers.

"I'm going to a special school in Italy to learn about art fraud." She shuffled her red boots.

"Art fraud." Lexi leaned into the doorframe. "Maybe someday you'll work for the Federal Marshals Service."

Jessica shook her head and laughed. "I'll leave the marshaling to you." She glanced down at the belly again. "Unless you're going to quit when the—"

"Nope," Lexi interrupted. "I'll never quit. The service is my life."

"Right on." Jessica twisted around and looked at her car as if someone was waiting for her. "I'd better go. Good luck with the—"

"Thanks for stopping by." Lexi watched as the girl-friend—*hopefully ex-girlfriend*—climbed into a red Kia.

Jessica waved and then took off.

Wow. Lexi never thought she'd see that hot mess again. For Nick's sake, it was just as well the girlfriend would be off the continent instead of leading mobsters to federal witnesses.

Badass. She smiled to herself. *More like fatass.* She laid her hand on top of her belly. Hard to believe a new person was brewing in there. Famished, Lexi went back inside to her lamb stew and lemonade.

Jessica's whirlwind trip had been eye-opening. Weird. She was more surprised than jealous. Maybe Nick would have to settle down after all. A federal marshal of all people. Not a society girl or an artist or even another art history professor. But a glorified policewoman. Who would have thunk it.

A Nietzsche quote popped into her head. *One must learn to be a sponge to be loved by hearts that overflow.* She'd have to remember that one the next time Jack mentioned Nietzsche. *Strange.* Thinking about Jack made her heart lighter. Thinking about Nick made it heavy.

She glanced at her phone. *Yikes.* She'd better get a move on. She was going to be late to meet Lolita at Blind Faith for their regular Monday lunch. *Geez.* She had a lot of news. *Wait until Lolita hears the marshal is preggers.*

She tugged on jeans and stuffed her feet into her cowboy boots. She didn't mean to oversleep, but her flight had been so delayed she hadn't gotten home until after midnight. Stumbling around her crap, which was strewn across the floor as usual, she once again vowed to tidy up the place when she got home. Her efficiency apartment was cozy in the way a rat's nest was cozy.

Should she bring the Romanov tiara to lunch? What if she dropped it or lost it or it was stolen? She pulled the priceless jewel out of the paper bag and sat on the edge of her tiny kitchen table—not that she actually had a kitchen—staring at it. The whole Romanov family was executed. And this tiara once sat on one of their pretty heads. One of those three beautiful daughters led like lambs to the slaughter.

Now the priceless Romanov tiara was stuffed into a Dairy Queen bag.

She'd intended to turn it over to the marshal. But when she saw that big belly, she just couldn't do it. She knew she should have. Then again, Nick risked his life to get it to her for the Center. And the Center is where it belonged. Either that or back in Russia on display in some museum in Moscow. After all, it wasn't part of Chicago history. It was part of Russian history, a bloody past full of sacrifice. Did the royals really have to be executed? Couldn't they just have been deposed?

She slid the tiara back into the bag and hid it behind a half-eaten pint of Ben & Jerry's in the tiny freezer compartment of her miniature fridge. Had the tiara graced the lovely head of Grand Duchess Olga Nikolaevna, the eldest daughter of the tsar, who had been murdered when she was just a few years younger than Jessica's age? The diamonds and jewels sewn into her clothes, repelling the bullets and denying her an instant death?

Jessica shuddered.

Crapulence. She was going to be late if she didn't get a move on. She grabbed her wallet, slammed the door to her apartment, and trotted down the hallway to the stairs. Taking them two at a time, she felt like a hoofer in an old musical. Barely noticing the daffodils and crocuses blooming in patches around the front lawn or the cardinal building a nest in an elm tree, she high-tailed it to the curb, where her Uber was waiting.

Twenty-seven minutes later, she was sitting at the counter in the café, waiting for Lolita. For a change, she'd gotten there first and happily nodded when Sally asked if she wanted her usual chai latte.

Lolita whooshed into the café like a spring breeze, turning heads as she went. In her black leather and pink faux fur, she stood out in the lunchtime crowd. She sidled up to the counter, gave Jessica a double-cheeked air-kissing, and then slid onto a barstool. "*Ciao, bella.*"

"You're speaking Italian now?" *Who knows? Maybe Lolita is fluent in Italian.* When it came to Lolita, nothing would surprise her.

"You've got to practice for your big trip." Lolita reached over and tucked a lock of hair behind Jessica's ear.

"I can't believe I'm actually going." Unless you counted the Canadian side of Glacier National Park, Jessica had never been out of the country, let alone off the continent. Heck. Until she arrived at Northwestern for grad school six years ago, she'd never flown on an airplane, eaten Thai food, or stared up at a skyscraper.

"Believe it, my Montana friend." Lolita smiled at Sally, who had just delivered a double espresso and a jar of sugar. "By this time next month, you'll be at ARCA in Amelia, Umbria."

ARCA. Association for Research into Crimes against Art. She couldn't wait. Between Dmitry's "forgeries," Bratva's Kandinsky theft, and Nick's hot jewels, she'd already gone through the school of hard knocks and was lucky to be alive.

"Who knows?" Jessica lifted her cup. "Maybe I'll become an art cop."

"The wrong side of the law." Lolita flashed a sly smile.

"Speaking of the wrong side of the law." Jessica winked. "How's Detective Cormier?"

"He's fine . . . damn fine." *Was Lolita blushing?* "Won't he be surprised if you become a cop."

What was Lolita's relationship with the Detective? Was she still working undercover? Or was she really working with Bratva? Jessica knew it wouldn't do any good to ask. "Nah. I've been too bad to start being good now." She shrugged.

Lolita was pretty cozy with Detective Cormier but claimed it had nothing to do with business. *Yeah, right.* Vanya was out on parole and back to tending bar at Pavlov's Banquet, along with working with the refugees at the Center and doing his other community service. Jessica didn't even want to know who he was really working for.

"How was your whirlwind trip to Wyoming?" Lolita asked, raising her eyebrows.

"How did you know about that?"

"I have my ways."

"I'm sure you do." Jessica sipped her tea.

Sally delivered a steaming plate of Kamoosh. The usual.

Jessica smiled. The sticky smell of melted cheese made her mouth water. It was good to be home.

"I saw that marshal. Marshal Colt."

"And how is the good marshal?"

"She's pregnant."

"Reproducing justice, eh?" Lolita said thoughtfully. "Good for her. A federal marshal and a mom. Who says women can't have it all?"

"I think the baby might be Nick's." Jessica stared down at her hands.

Lolita laughed. "I told you he was a player."

"Is that why you don't like him?"

"Believe me. That's just the beginning." Lolita stirred her espresso with the tiny spoon.

Jessica narrowed her brows. "What do you mean?"

"Let's not talk about Nick. Too boring." Her friend swiveled her stool around to face Jessica. "Let's talk about Italy and your upcoming adventures in Europe."

"I'm nervous. I've never been abroad. What if I fall on my face?"

"I'm sure you'll hit the ground running, my Montana friend." Lolita dabbed her lipstick with a napkin.

"Only thanks to you." Jessica pinched the corner of a chip. She stretched the cheese until it broke away from the mountain of nachos. "Otherwise, I'd hit the ground headfirst."

"You may not be graceful . . ." Lolita sipped her

espresso. "But like a cat, you always do manage to land on your feet."

Jessica laughed. "Let's just hope that like a cat, I also have nine lives."

THE END

ABOUT THE AUTHOR

Kelly Oliver is the award-winning and Amazon Best-selling author of three mystery series, including *The Jessica James Mysteries*, *The Pet Detective Mysteries*, and *The Fiona Figg Mysteries*. When she's not writing novels, Kelly is a Distinguished Professor of Philosophy at Vanderbilt University in Nashville, where she lives with her husband and three demanding felines.

To learn more about Kelly and her books, go to www.kellyoliverbooks.com.

If you liked the Jessica James Mystery series, please leave a review on Amazon or Goodreads. Those reviews mean a lot to indie authors like me!! Thanks.